Critical acclaim

'This is a fine, heartfelt no... controlled, unshowy, observan...

'[*Seeds of Doubt*] deals with loss, the self and its inscrutability, and, as an ever-present seam running through, the darker deeds that society sanctions . . . brilliantly rendered . . . James Ryan has chosen a wide setting to tackle this theme, which continues to surface appallingly all around us, and he writes masterfully' RTE Guide

'Deconstructing his idyll as skilfully as he creates it, Ryan exposes the grief and loss lying beneath the family fabric with great poignancy' *Image*

'Dark, powerful' *Independent on Sunday*

'*Seeds of Doubt* has the emotionally implosive effect and economy of style of Ryan's earlier work, but there is an added expansiveness, both in terms of language and thematic resonance' John Kenny, *Times Literary Supplement*

'His controlled, careful writing builds up a picture of surface lives, where the pain of the past lies simmering beneath. He captures accurately the emotions that drive the women on, painting with clear brushstrokes the deadness in their lives, as the world of childhood is soured and spoiled . . . There is no doubt that Ryan is an accomplished writer' *Sunday Tribune*

'Brilliantly structured . . . engrossing . . . The dialogue is superb . . . brilliant at getting the interweaving, interwoven stories of the five sisters and their lives . . . There wasn't a dud note, I felt, in the entire book' Niall MacMonagle, RTE

'A delicate, sensitively written novel . . . riveting and absorbing' *Books Ireland*

'Moving and poignant' *Irish Tatler*

'It is a very fine line between the sensitive and the trite in fiction but Ryan maintains the equilibrium' *Sunday Business Post*

James Ryan grew up in County Laois, Ireland, and graduated from Trinity College, Dublin, in 1975. He now lives in Dublin with his wife, a journalist, and their two children.

By James Ryan

Home from England
Dismantling Mr Doyle
Seeds of Doubt

SEEDS OF DOUBT

JAMES RYAN

PHŒNIX

A PHOENIX PAPERBACK

First published in Great Britain in 2001
by Weidenfeld & Nicolson
A Phoenix House Book
This paperback edition published in 2001
by Phoenix,
an imprint of Orion Books Ltd,
Orion House, 5 Upper St Martin's Lane,
London WC2H 9EA

A CIP catalogue record for this book
is available from the British Library.

ISBN 0 75381 290 8

Printed and bound in Great Britain by
Clays Ltd, St Ives plc

The three mystic monkeys, Kikazaru who listens to no evil, Iwzaru who speaks no evil and Mizaru who sees no evil, are attendants of Koshin, the Shinto God of the Roads. At shrines dedicated to this deity, old dolls are offered in memory of the departed.

Kikazaru

I could sing once. Like a bird.

Everyone said so. They said it in school, in the shops, outside the church.

'Nora Macken, you have the voice of a linnet.' That's what they said. 'The voice of a linnet.'

Those words made me feel light, made me float high into the vaulted ceiling of the church, billowed up with pride.

Down below, far, far down, my father, my mother, my aunt, their heads held high. Beside them, one, two, three, four, my sisters all on their tiptoes, rising up with me as I scaled the peaks of the 'Ave Maria'. And there at the very pinnacle of that, my hymn, they would all gather, poised for my descent. That's what I did best, shimmy down.

I could sing all right. No doubt about it. I still can, but not in the same way. I sing for myself now. Sing whatever I like, whenever I like.

And my sisters, they have long since sallied out into the world. All except Flossie, who stands eternally in the doorway of Templeard, hushing the collies, dabbing her hair with the palm of her hand, forever about to step forward, reticent and welcoming.

This is how it is when I arrive on Christmas Eve. Flossie, leaning out of the partly opened front door as I pull up, her questions about my journey flung across the gravel sweep in such quick succession that my answers, loud and all as they are, go unheard.

As we troop in, bags and hold-alls held high above the lapping collies, I look about, this way and that, tracing the vaguely surgical smell to the geraniums on the window ledge. There is a trickle of relief running through the joy I feel in seeing them there, just as they always are, stalky, almost leafless, tangling with the wisps of lemony winter light shooting through the top of the porch window.

I could dawdle indefinitely on these, the opening notes of my arrival, wonder at the way they merge with all my other arrivals down through the years, ousting the in-between times until all that remains is one long, protracted arrival. A seamless fusion of movement and talk culled from countless homecomings to Templeard.

'Leave the bags here. We'll bring them up later.' Flossie takes charge, ushers me on.

Soon we will be drinking tea, leaving the bustle and jostle of unloading behind, settling into talk.

'Tea,' I begin.

Flossie smiles in anticipation of what I'm about to say.

'It's never the same anywhere else. Never as good as here.'

I raise my cup to my lips and through the thinning, liquoricy vapour see the rest of our conversation unfolding before me. It is a familiar path. We move along it briskly, me citing the next landmark.

'It's the water. The water in London is full of chlorine. That's what gives the tea a sort of . . .' And before I have said 'chemical taste', Flossie's face is all angles, full of puzzlement, so poised to say, 'Imagine that – the chlorine,' that I want to grasp her by the hand and race forward, gallop headlong through this set piece conversation, until we arrive at a place we have never been before.

In a brief, thinly ciphered memory, snatched from a long

4

lost sequence, we run down the slope in Duggan's field in our matching buttercup dresses, faster and faster until we tumble forward, rolling dizzily to the edge of the furze thicket. I dally with that memory a while, watching as the possibilities it initially held out fall away.

'Imagine that, the chlorine.'

I search her face, certain we have already passed that point in our conversation. But all I see is its high colour, ruddy and wind blown, now fired by the heat of the kitchen, smiling expectantly.

'Imagine that, the chlorine,' she reminds me.

'It's the one thing I've never got used to, not in all my years in London. You can taste it in the tea, no matter how strong it's made.'

'Terrible, not being able to make a proper cup of tea.' Her voice is full of conviction. The dogs look up, their ears taut.

'And it's getting worse. They're putting more in than ever now.'

'A hot drop?'

She lifts the tea pot and presses the lid down as she pours. We both know it's time to move forward.

'All well in Lambeth?'

I smile, recalling how that was always my father's, Daddo's, first question when I arrived home, 'All well in Lambeth?' Flossie pronounces *Lambeth* precisely as he did, two separate words, intoned to sound like a nearby townsland.

'All well,' I reply, though there isn't an 'all'. Like Flossie, I live alone.

I continue to think about Daddo's fulsome '*all well in Lambeth*', and the way it created the impression, sometimes even in my own mind, that I was the keeper of a prosperous household, the mother of a teeming family in a neighbouring parish. That was the only world he understood. It was the one in which we, the Mackens of Templeard, lived surrounded by others like us, Campions of Crossmokler, Quinns of Friar's Island, Crottys of The Glebe and Laceys of Derrinalty Cross.

One thing for sure, our lives had not taken the course they were expected to take, though as Daddo got older he came to believe they had. It was an illusion Flossie allowed to go unchecked down through his ailing years; one which he looked to her to bolster so much that in an oblique sort of way she came to cherish it herself.

I arrived back a few days before he died. January 1975, three years ago next month. I went directly up to his room, stole across and sat on the edge of his unruffled bed, swallowing the panic I felt in finding him so shrunken. His hands, waxy white, were locked together, identical in colour and texture to the two unlit candles on the windowsill. His eyes were closed. I thought he was asleep and was startled when after about ten minutes he spoke.

'Now, Nora, you have your own to look after, you're here long enough with me. Come back later, when you have the time to spare.' His voice was clear as a whistle, so clear and self assured that I just agreed and left quietly, planning to return in an hour or so. When I came back he did not recognize me.

Late on that first night, the night I arrived, I heard him call out, heard the clip-clop of Flossie's shoes on the landing, heard him call out again, louder. Then her voice, rising and falling, its routine tone reassuring in itself. I got up and tiptoed across to the open door, unsure if I ought to go in or not.

'That child has me awake all night,' I heard him say to Flossie, his voice rasping in torment. 'Will you for the love of God, tell Nora. Tell her to whist it up.'

'I will. I will. I will,' Flossie answered, matter-of-fact, no effort to disguise her impatience. But then on her way out she

6

stopped. 'Listen. Shhh . . . Listen. Can't you hear? It's stopped.' I did not wait to hear what she said next. All I wanted to do was make sure I was back in my room, the door closed behind me before she came out.

For the rest of that night, I battled against sleep, bolting upright whenever it encroached, terrified that in passing from the waking world into the world of sleep I too might hear a child cry.

I used to think it was a great kindness on Flossie's part to indulge Daddo like that. In a way I still do. But I do not want to go down that road of illusion myself, not now; not now when I know how difficult it is to find a route back.

I'm searching for a way to remind Flossie that we both live alone, that we did not become women at the helm of big households, when I hear myself defensively staking out my own territory.

'I'm going to decorate the flat in the New Year.'

'The whole place?'

'Yes, the whole place,' I reply, wishing as I speak that the words were not so sharp edged, clipped to remind her that we are talking about two rooms. Two rooms I love. Still two rooms none the less. But I need not be concerned, sharp edges and clipped endings pass Flossie by.

'It's the only way to do it,' she assures me, leaning forward. 'The whole place at once. The only way. After I painted the hall there in September everywhere else looked shabby.'

We both look around the kitchen, Flossie in search of shabbiness, me seeking out the few remaining features which tally with the outdated image I carry of it. As I move from one thing to the next, from the rusting ceiling hooks to the deep-silled window behind the sink and over to the wooden rail at the back of the door, a different room takes shape. It's the busiest place in Christendom, full of clang and clatter. My sisters running from the cooker to the sink. Saucepans held

7

out before them. Calls for the colander, for the flat skimming spoon, for the big sieve. And I'm there in the middle of it all, no different from them then, wholly in the grip of that panic which tightened us all together in those frantic moments before the first call for dinner went out.

By early afternoon everything was back in its place, spic and span. Aunt Cassie, Daddo's sister, saw to that. When she finished she loosened her navy blue cross-over apron and sat near the cooker, hefty arms folded and a globe of dampness spreading out from her midriff. There, surrounded by gleaming pots and well-scoured pans all stacked on the overhead rack, she guarded the order she had created. Her face stern, mildly bothered, her legs apart, firmly planted on the floor.

There are no pots and pans on view now, not a single dish or plate to be seen. Everything from the huge stock saucepan to the salt spoons is stored in a long line of cupboards, hidden away as though part of a way of life which was somehow wrong. And maybe it was. Maybe there was something wrong at the very heart of it.

'Just look, look at that flaking paint.'

I follow the line she draws through the air, anxious to conceal how absent I feel.

'Look, there, over the sink. I may paint it as soon as the Christmas is over.'

Flossie sips her tea, peering inquisitively over the rim of her cup at me.

'What colour are you going to paint it?'

I'm taken by surprise.

'The flat?' She sits forward, places her tea cup carefully on the table and tugs the hemline of her skirt down with both hands.

'Appleyard green.'

'It sounds lovely. Appleyard green.' Flossie repeats the

words. *Apple. Yard. Green.* Her enthusiasm, girlish and sudden, roots me firmly in the here and now.

'We'll take a walk,' I say.

'Just as far as the outer gate,' Flossie replies, 'while there's still light.'

The dogs spring up and in their frantic scramble for the door slither and skid on the polished linoleum.

The world outside is calm, noiseless except for the slow drip of glassy droplets from the briar-rose on to the swell of dead leaves below. High above, steady and enduring, the limes break up the dwindling light, scattering it in patches on the gravel sweep. As we pick our way across the dappled ground Flossie warns me about the pot-holes that lie ahead.

'You must have noticed on your way in. They're worse than they ever were. Much worse. Out past the inner gate.'

I look ahead. The dogs are already haring across the clover field, sleek-maned and wavy in the distance.

'Aren't the Campions supposed to look after that? The avenue? The pot-holes I mean?' My question touches Flossie more directly than anything else I've said since I arrived. She stops in her tracks.

'Not once have those Campions put so much as a shovel of gravel on this avenue, not since Daddo died.'

Once again we are walking in the long shadow cast by Daddo's death, invoking that death to measure the passage of time.

'Don't talk to me about those Campions.' Flossie is indignant, shaping up to continue.

The Campions are cousins, first cousins, whose lives have been threading in and out through our own for generations. Daddo's sister, Aunt Han, was married to Job Campion. In addition, the Campions were what Daddo called *friends*. Steadfast allies. 'People you can count on to the grave,' he'd

9

say, a family woven tighter than any other into that densely textured tapestry that was his world.

Sonny Campion has been renting the farm from Flossie since a year or two before Daddo died. Maybe longer. Every Saturday evening he brings a box of groceries to the house, staple supplies – tea sugar biscuits butter. Leaves it on the table, chats to her for a while. On Sunday morning he and his wife Marian drive her to Mass, squeezed into the back of the car with their children. Then she goes back with them to Crossmokler for dinner. When I'm here I'm included. If I go we take my car, drive behind the Campions in convoy, become part of the steady stream travelling across the headland to the church.

At the Campions' Flossie remains tight lipped, sits stiffly on her chair, unapologetic in her demand for humouring. The only topic certain to draw a response from her is our nephew Patrick, our sister Margaret's son. 'The nephew' as Sonny Campion calls him. He comes up in conversation a great deal. It's part of an ancient game, with the Campions plying Flossie with questions about him. In this roundabout way they acknowledge that he is her heir, the front-runner for Templeard. But by the same token they are staking out their own, lesser, claim, proffering themselves as family too, contenders for the eighteen Irish acres, the wet fields, joining their land but separated from Templeard by the river.

There is something primitive, even fierce in the way Flossie exacts concern and interest from them, something unnervingly contrived in the way she feigns interest in Patrick, now fifteen and more reluctant than ever to come down to Templeard with his parents at Christmas. She lavishes praise on him at the Campions' but hasn't a good word to say about him elsewhere, reminding people every single time his name is mentioned that he chased to its death, years ago, a Rhode Island Red hen, a prize-winner to boot.

Flossie slaps the bolt of the inner gate across, full of purpose. And aware of how fast the light is fading, strides forward, ignoring the smaller pot-holes, resolutely on her way to a very large one a few yards on. She points her foot at it, tentatively dipping the tip of her shoe in, balanced like a swimmer testing the water.

'Look, look at the depth of it. Now tell me what you think of that?' She puts her foot in deeper, waits for me to do the same.

I'm looking into the pot-hole, gauging its depth when I begin to lose my balance. Not quickly, but in that awkward way which allows enough time to take in the places I could end up but not enough time to choose.

Before I know it I'm in the firm grip of Flossie's arms, laughing.

Laughing about the Campions and the pot-holes.

Laughing, because I fell, because Flossie caught me, because she did so while still fathoming the depths of the pot-hole with her foot, partly losing balance herself.

Then just laughing.

Alerted by our voices, the dogs begin to bark, clear and cold in the distance, their shadowy forms glinting in the half light as they tear back towards us. Suddenly they are looping around us, round and round, spinning our stumbling laughter into an unlikely mid-winter pantomime.

Everything I planned to say to Flossie about the future, about the past, the conversations I rehearsed as I drove through those slushy towns on the way here, is now all firmly lined up before me, ready, waiting to be said.

'Things have changed a lot,' I begin.

Flossie steals a sideways glance in my direction, aware, I imagine, that our conversation is about to take a different direction.

'They have, I suppose. But sure aren't things always changing?'

'They are . . .'

Each step we take from then on is taken with exaggerated caution. She approaches the pot-holes as she might a series of mine craters. In a fleeting sliver of memory I catch a glimpse of her, well over forty years ago, ahead of me in the sweltering heat, the skirt of her frock gathered up in one hand, the other thrown out for balance as she picks her way from one rock outcrop to the next, down stream to Fogarty's bridge.

'I think we'll turn back,' she says with concern. 'It's getting dark.' But we continue to troop forward.

When we reach the outer gate, I do not want to turn back. I want to walk out on to the road, further, further. I lift the gate a little, making it easier to slide the bolt across.

'We better not go any further. Not without the leads . . .' her words trail off as she looks over her shoulder. When she cannot locate the dogs, she turns around. Begins to click her tongue.

'Brownie, Brownie. Bess.' Her concern rings out across the clover field. The dogs leap out of the dark, their tails swishing, their sticky tongues lobbing out over their jaws.

'Things are different now, you know that, Flossie, don't you?' Somewhere between us my words seem to sink.

'Of course they are, Nora, Of course they are.'

'I don't want you to think I'm unhappy.'

'Of course you don't, Nora. Of course you don't.'

We are walking briskly, staying clear of the pot-holes by keeping to the edge of the avenue.

'No. I'm not unhappy.'

'Of course you're not, Nora.'

I forget from one visit to the next how Flossie's readiness to agree with everything I say places her outside my reach. It always takes me a while to remember that, to remember how she cordons off her territory with agreement. I think it is a step she intuitively takes, a step all my sisters take, to safeguard the lives they have created for themselves beyond my story.

As the lights of the house draw near, words like *happiness* and *unhappiness* begin to lose their meaning, recoiling like creatures of the wild before those brightening lights. Soon I will have to abandon them altogether, unleash them into the darkness, knowing that they have no place inside the walls of Templeard. Whatever currency they once had, and certainly the house has known its share of both, has been too long usurped by other words, words rooted in the practical world of hard work and order.

I walk past the high corrugated farmyard gate, imagining sounds no longer heard rearing up as though from behind it; the buckety turmoil of the feeding sheds, wailing calves, the early morning rasp of the tractor. Then traipsing into the hall behind Flossie I hear the house's long ago sounds, the slap and scorch of irons, billowing sheets being tugged, flicked and folded and late into the night the soft mumble of the rosary.

Flossie takes off her hat, looks at it, smiles.

'I know how hick it is.'

She puts it back on, pulling the curling rim down over her ears and looking at herself in the hall-stand mirror.

'It's the comfort of it I like.' She touches the edge, a dainty tip. Pulls a comic face.

The impulse to grab her and rush her through all this empty talk returns. Again I want to strike out into new territory, leap clear of the years of fading voices that lie ahead, that road leading further into silence, mapped out by men and women long since dead.

2

During the lost, nameless days between Christmas and the New Year, I wade further and further into the familiar moil of Templeard, gradually abandoning the resolve to speak with which I arrived. Each day the world beyond the outer gate grows more hostile and the house more isolated, reverting to the place it once was, an island at the edge of the world, upholding all that is good and right.

Flossie and I anxiously await the arrival of the others, Margaret, Ber and Girlie, speaking of their homecoming as though they were out on rough seas.

Ber is first to arrive. We watch her drive down the avenue, a starched end of December morning. She is racing the yelping dogs, skirting the pot-holes, waving furiously. Flossie stands in the doorway, her arms folded squarely. I stand behind, looking out over her shoulder.

'And with a hair-do, how can people be expected to know?' Flossie says watching Ber open the inner gate. 'How on earth can they be expected to know she's a nun?'

She speaks as if there is a conversation in train, as if we have reached some sort of agreement about how misleading Ber's appearance is. Flossie often converses in this way, silently holding the earlier part of a conversation with herself, then drawing people in half-way through. Sometimes I get the impression that she spends a lot of her time in silent dialogue, going about the house, the yard, wandering the fields talking to people, to the Campions maybe, to Ber or me, people she is sometimes inclined to regard as a bit of a nuisance when they are actually there to answer for themselves. And, quietly weaving its way through the mix and gather of these thoughts, is the notion that loneliness has its own defences, its own way of rebuffing people who aggravate it by offering occasional, short-term companionship.

'That's been the way since Daddo died,' she continues. 'His funeral, that was the first time our Ber drove a car. They all got cars, every nun in that convent was given a car that year.'

In the leap from Daddo's death to Ber's driving, I lose whatever foothold I imagined I had in the conversation. But even if I had held my ground, I don't think I would have done so for long. For days I had been listening to Flossie's random speculation about the degree to which Ber is or isn't a nun. All along I was hard-pushed to keep pace, not so much because of the arbitrary points at which she expected me to join in, but because I've never been able to see Ber as a nun in the first place. Not fully at any rate. She remains the loud, laughing girl, stomping up and down the stairs here in Templeard, 'the only one besides Flossie', Aunt Cassie used to say, 'with an ounce of obligement in her'.

Flossie is still giving out even as Ber opens the door of her car. 'They want the best of both worlds, those nuns do. Out here, there and everywhere. But when it suits them they're back in the convent at half six, their feet tucked under the table waiting for their high tea to be put in front of them.'

Ber comes and goes all the time now, although for over twenty years she was not allowed to leave the convent at all. We went to see her there, frequently at first, then less so as the years went by. By the time the rules changed, Ber's was only a dimly remembered presence in Templeard, there fading in the static world of family photographs.

I was back on holiday the laden, thundery August afternoon when she arrived back for the first time. She seemed not to see the small group gathered in welcome under the limes, just swept through us and straight into the house. We followed but came to an uneasy standstill when we saw her, weighed down by all that black serge, lurching from the hall-stand to the parlour door and from there to the standing clock, falling greedily on everything, intoxicated by memory.

She has her own room in the house now. At least, the landing room is called Ber's room. Two pinafores, one navy blue, the other grey, hang in the wardrobe and a floral washbag sits, prim, on the chest of drawers.

She marches across the gravel sweep towards us carrying a flat box, a crate of sorts, full of different coloured wool. Some project or other, an activity for the in-between times, mid-afternoon, early evening. That's Ber, intent on staying busy all day every day.

'I thought I'd never get here,' she announces loudly, leaving Flossie and me lost for a response.

She plonks the crate in Flossie's arms, grips me just above the elbows and begins to examine me. First my face, next my hair, then swinging her head rapidly from side to side, my earrings. Her grip on my arms tightens. She looks into my eyes. Makes me feel as though I'm somehow unfathomable. Pitiable maybe, then cherished in a crude sort of way. 'We're all here, safe and sound.' Her voice is suffused with a mixture of wonder and relief. 'Thank God,' she adds triumphantly.

There is still a sense of victory in our arrivals at Templeard. A moment when returning takes on the elation of a battle won, drawing us together as we once were. Proud as peacocks. Inviolable. That's how it is now, the three of us standing there in the hall, words flung rapidly this way and that. Caught by one. Tossed to another. Repeated with awe, doubt, laughter.

Soon Ber will be in the kitchen, her sleeves rolled up, the butter-coloured baking bowl on her hip held fast by her arched arm. And a wooden spoon slapping and stirring to beat the band – the first of a bevy of cakes already well underway. Soon Flossie will be complaining again, taking me aside in the back hall to tell me that every time Ber goes back to the convent she leaves a week's washing up behind. But those first, warm, intertwining moments in the porch will stay with me, a lasting testament to the affection that underscores a lot of Flossie's complaining, not just about Ber but about everyone.

As the days amble by Flossie loses sight of the empty world she lives in much of the time.

'She's more herself,' Ber confides, plying the words with that sense of mission which marks all her asides about Flossie. 'Much more herself with us here,' she adds.

'Mmm . . .' I hum flatly, already distanced by the way Ber clings to the belief that we are all more ourselves when we are with each other. I'm not so sure about that. I want to say so but it seems like such an unfriendly stance, callous in the face of her eagerness.

'Not as quick to find fault with people,' she urges me to agree.

'No. Not half as quick.' I look at her as I speak, seeing in her unlined face the arid course of her life, and once again begin to wonder to what extent her story is entangled in my own.

'It's the company. Takes her out of herself.'

That's certainly the case. Every day there is less talk about the Campions' neglect of the avenue. About the pot-holes.

About Mr Kilcar, owner of the travelling shop, who Flossie says ought to be in gaol. So by the time Sonny Campion shows up, as he always does on New Year's Eve, trailing a brace of pheasant, she is delighted to see him. We all are.

The dogs are at the door barking long before he lifts the knocker, their ears pricking, their snouts buffing the door lip.

'The Campions, New Year's Eve. The pheasants,' Flossie gasps in rapid succession, quick-stepping her way to the hall door.

There is laughter at every turn, a rolling merriment punctured here and there with sighs of relief. Flossie, buoyant and self assured, is pouring whiskey into a tumbler for Sonny Campion. We all sit in the pale yellow light of the parlour, the sweet, medicinal fumes of the whiskey leading the way back through countless New Year's Eves.

Somewhere in there, holding out against the laughter, a thin, almost unrecognizable voice continues to rehearse opening lines for a conversation I now realize is not going to take place. Templeard has its own language, a language woven for a group, one that is ill suited to charting individual journeys.

Margaret's homecoming on New Year's Day, uncertain for days beforehand, has us all on edge. Throughout the afternoon there are forays to the porch, stop-start movements which make the dogs restless, calls for hush as heads tilt mechanically, angled to track the progress of a distant car.

Her eventual arrival, alone in the late afternoon, marks the end of almost a week of phone calls. There is a definite pattern to these calls, built up over the last couple of years, but we do not say so. We do not risk the complacency which might set in were we to tell each other that a similar series of calls, a similar reluctance to come, preceded her visit last year and the year before.

Margaret and her husband Pat and their son Patrick had always come for the whole of Christmas, arriving in a great flurry on Christmas Eve and staying until the New Year.

Then three years ago, the Christmas after Daddo died, Margaret rang at the last minute and announced a change of plan. They had decided to postpone their visit to Templeard until the spring. The weather. The roads. Patrick.

There was an immediate sense of betrayal. We, particularly Ber, viewed their decision to stay in Dublin as a defection, a hostile move.

'Was it *might not come* or *probably wouldn't come* or *definitely wouldn't come*?' Ber asked Flossie, her voice growing more and more puzzled as she spoke. 'I mean what way was it said? Was it something Margaret just said on the spur of the moment? Or did it sound like she had given it a lot of thought?'

Flossie's attempts to provide answers to these questions were quickly scotched by further questions, with Ber stomping ahead determined to prove that the call had been far from conclusive. Before long she had talked Flossie into ringing Margaret back, had her primed to coax Margaret into changing her mind.

That return call did not alter things. In a half-hearted way Margaret said she and Pat would discuss their plan to stay put, but didn't think they would change their minds. And on it went, their absence casting an air of gloom over Templeard that Christmas, a heavy pallor that grew heavier as the days wore on, filling even the shortest lulls in our conversation with a kind of melancholy.

The odd thing is, I thought I could walk out at will from beneath that gloom. But when, after the whole business of Margaret's coming and Margaret's not coming had been endlessly talked about, I tried to do just that, tried to walk away, I was unable. Hopelessly drawn in, I was almost as fearful as the others, as put out as they were to see our world thinning out, Templeard losing yet another voice.

We then came up with the idea of inviting them for the New Year. But when Flossie rang to put the new plan to them, Pat explained that Patrick, then fifteen, had arrangements. He would have to stay there with him, 'keep an eye on him', he told Flossie, adding that Margaret was free to go to Templeard alone. It was a freedom that we supposed she would eagerly grasp but that was not the case. She had to be persuaded, cajoled over days, humoured into coming.

And that's the way it has continued, only this year it is Ber, not Flossie, who is doing all the cajoling. Anyway, Margaret has agreed to come and that, Ber keeps telling us, 'is the main thing'.

We stand in the porch, Ber and myself, dancing hand and foot on Margaret when she arrives in the darkening afternoon of New Year's Day. Flossie looks on, her arms folded implacably.

'You were great to come,' Ber says. 'Great to come.'

I shake hands, smile, ask how Pat and Patrick are. Agree and disagree as she speaks both proudly and disparagingly of them. I wish her a happy New Year, ask her about the journey down, all the time keen to contribute to the din we are creating to keep her arrival buoyant. Ber admires her jacket, her skirt, her shoes. But, for all that, there is apprehension in every one of these gestures, in every word a false note threatening to expose her coming as a pyrrhic victory.

'As lively as ever. Never lost it,' Ber says reassuringly of Margaret as we bunch together at the porch door. 'As lively as ever.'

Margaret has changed in appearance over the years. Besides ageing in the usual ways she has got very stout, large even around the shoulders and arms where she used to be conspicuously thin. This was very apparent in the photographs Ber took of us all last Christmas. Beside Margaret, Flossie and I appear almost frail.

She and Pat are more married than most, each relentlessly attentive to the comfort of the other. There is a lot of checking and counter-checking, treats and surprises, whispering. Their carry-on provided continuous entertainment the first Christmas they came to Templeard as a couple. Girlie, still a teenager at the time, eavesdropped on them at every turn, then waited until we were all together to repeat the endearments they exchanged.

Don't stir, honey bunch, just give me your plate. That sort of thing.

In the parlour in the evenings Girlie would take cushions from whoever was willing to give them up, including Daddo, and offer them to Pat. Unaware that he was being mocked, he allowed himself to be propped up and tucked in like an infant.

They were married for five or six years before Patrick was born and, right up to his arrival, full of newly wed perk. I used to wonder at their intimacy, especially the furtive, conjugal glancing that went on whenever we were all together. It occurred to me they felt constantly compelled to lay claim to each other in a house which, with equal constancy, claimed Margaret as a daughter.

Girlie lives in Tullamore, about an hour's drive away. She breezes in around eight, the collar of her fur coat arched behind her head, a sleek backdrop to a big bounce of curls. When we ask how the girls, her three daughters, are, she raises her eyes upwards. 'Don't ask.'

'And Peter?'

She smiles indulgently and launches into an account of her husband Peter's delight at the return from a specialist company in Scotland of their walnut billiard table, restored, she tells us with mock amazement, 'beyond recognition'.

Here Girlie begins to lose interest in what she is saying. Digging deep into her shoulder bag she fishes out a bottle of wine.

My sisters' voices, at first an orderly train of questions and answers, are soon a racing throng, one as eager as the next to accelerate the pace at which we tear back to Templeard in its heyday. This and that detail is recalled, plucked from the past as though from a single memory. The precise colour of a dress is disputed. Turquoise? Aquamarine? Duck egg? And the first time it was worn – a Macra dance during the Emergency? No. A golf do in Thurles. The invitations that did and didn't come. Kathleen Quinn's wedding. And the favourite, there forever hobbling through the collective memory like an injured bird: Una Lacey's broken engagement.

'A note delivered three days before the wedding,' Margaret leads, no less shocked than she was when she first heard the news over thirty years ago.

'Cold feet. He got cold feet,' Flossie pitches in.

'She took to the bed,' Girlie and Flossie say in unison, laughing as Flossie gives way.

'There for well over a month,' Girlie continues, half chanting the words, leading the way into a Requiem for Una Lacey.

Late into the evening Flossie turns to me. 'Nora, you start, "If I were a blackbird". You sing the best.'

I search for the words in a memory that is no longer my own.

'If I were a blackbird, I'd whistle and sing
And I'd build my nest in the ship that my true love sails in.'

One by one my sisters join in, Flossie first, then Ber, Margaret and, when we all look at her, Girlie. She has her own song, 'When the swallows come back to Capistrano', but she won't sing it until everyone else has sung their song. By that stage there is no talk, only singing. All the old songs, thrown like mooring lines across the half-century since we first began to sing them.

3

Fumes of charred toast drift up through the stairwell, at first faint, then sharp in the morning air as they pocket in the landing. I pause, listening to the muffle of my sisters' voices below, unable to distinguish one from the other. Through the grainy glass of the landing window, I look out across the low-lying fields, always flooded in winter but fully iced over today; a broad silvery plane pocked by outcrops of cottony scutch and tufts of frozen fenreed.

I think about my journey back, wondering if I should leave earlier than I had intended. Before lunch, *the roads*, I half whisper to myself, unwittingly rehearsing the words, just as I used to rehearse the messages I brought from Ammie, my mother, sitting here at the landing window, to Aunt Cassie in the kitchen.

Every day in the early afternoon Ammie left the kitchen, climbed the dozen or so steps to the landing and settled here in the green basket chair. Mostly she read, abandoning Templeard for far-flung places, for the heady climes of romance and courtly intrigue. There she danced and schemed, swirling alone to the great waltzes of the nineteenth century, swept into a world as real to her as it was unreal to Aunt Cassie. She must have heard the racket directly below in the kitchen, been forced by all that clatter to think of Cassie at the sink pounding her way through the wash-up, the tip of her tongue clamped determinedly between her lips.

We did not question the part Aunt Cassie played in our lives. She was Daddo's elder sister and we supposed she was content to live out her life with us in the cantankerous sort of way she did. Only once did I ever hear her describe her position, the afternoon a Department of Agriculture official came to inspect the outhouses.

Daddo had applied on our behalf to set up a small hatchery. It was a scheme introduced nationally after the Emergency to improve poultry stock, with grants provided for the purchase of quality brooders and the like. In the course of reading out the rules and regulations the official kept addressing Cassie, then in her sixties, as Mrs Macken.

After the inspection of the outhouses the four of us, Cassie, the official, Flossie and I, sauntered back across the yard.

'Miss,' Cassie said. Just like that. Out of the blue. The official looked at her blankly. Maybe he did not realize that she had spoken directly to him.

'Miss Macken, not Mrs,' she added hurriedly, her face reddening deeply. But she recouped quickly.

'Came with the place, as they say.' Then, more jocosely, 'Didn't marry.'

'Not yet at any rate,' the official smirked, only to smile piteously when he saw Aunt Cassie's colour deepen again.

I admired the way she said *didn't marry*. It implied choice and there was a certain dignity in that.

We thought these small humiliations laughable. And maybe some of them were. We smothered our laughter with our hands, watching her cycle behind us as we travelled to Mass in the trap, her head bent in effort, one hand holding her hat in place. Later, on outings in the car, driving back to school or wherever, we forced her forward to the edge of the seat knowing she would not complain, not with Daddo and Ammie in front.

Anyway she rarely took issue with us. When she did, it was always in the same vein, 'Wait 'til your own turn comes.' Or 'We'll see what's in store for you.' Feeble and all as we considered these warnings, they still brought our taunting to a rapid halt, not because we grasped what they implied, but because of the rancorous way she hissed them at us.

Lurking with uncertainty among the fragments of our cruelty to Aunt Cassie is the spectre of Daddo and Ammie's complicity. Unwitting complicity, but complicity none the less. They preached kindness but there was often a hollow ring to it, prompting us to look behind the scenes in search of a more credible sentiment. What we absorbed in the course of that search was their unvoiced resentment at having Cassie under their roof, witness to their every move. And because our search was unsupervised we grasped that resentment in its rawest form, as children will, collectively becoming its mouthpiece.

Flossie would never say something like that about herself, never say *didn't marry* or *didn't . . . anything* for that matter. She goes out of her way to evade conversations which could lead to any sort of appraisal of our lives. And more so than ever this Christmas. When I try to speak about the past, as I often do in a bid to leave it behind once and for all, she tells me I am talking as if I am on my deathbed, reminds me that she is only in her mid-fifties. And I look at her, smiling pleasantly in her stubbornness, wondering if she secretly believes that a fuller, more engaging life lies ahead.

Aunt Cassie ended her days staring into the fire, her eyes as bright as moonstones, her knobbly hands clamped to the frayed arms of her basket chair, waiting for death. A whole decade, virtually silent. Very occasionally, maybe once or twice in a year, she laughed loudly, a terrorized hee-haw of a laugh, casting about the kitchen as if in her dark meanderings she had stumbled across something as funny as it was tragic. A great irony maybe, which out of some kind of washed up, residual loyalty to the living she vowed to take with her to the grave.

In her own view of herself Cassie was first and foremost a Macken of Templeard, a sharecropper of sorts in whatever it produced. That was her birthright, the bedrock on which her whole life was built. Although far from beautiful, she frequently boasted of my mother's great beauty. This she seemed to do in good faith, never hankering after it herself because she had a sister-in-law in whose beauty she had a recognized stake.

'Bea Coady,' she used to say, always calling Ammie by her maiden name, 'turned more heads in this parish than the rest of them put together.' And here she might stop whatever she was doing, savouring, we supposed, the pride she felt in Ammie's beauty, secure that she herself had been adequately compensated for her own lack of it.

Attributes were dealt out like playing cards in the under-standing that they would ultimately be pooled for the greater good. Cassie had been singled out as a worker, a strong girl, who followed her calling to become a mainstay in the running of Templeard. She carted buckets around the yard, pulped mangels, heaved the milk churns off the back of the trailer and spun them on their rims into the milking parlour. She cleaned and managed the hen-houses, separating clockers from layers, her arms flying this way and that in the great feathery cackle she created. We called out to her as we left for school, watched while she swung around, her arms full of straw, her cheeks damson red in the raw morning air. All afternoon she toiled in the kitchen, then after supper went to the dairy to churn butter. In this way she left Ammie free to play her part, free, once she had supervised the preparation of dinner, to be the great beauty she was. So when in the afternoons Ammie came up here to the landing and sat reading her romances, dancing her way around the ballrooms of the great palaces of Europe, she did so in the secure knowledge that she danced for us all. Not least Aunt Cassie.

We too were given parts, singled out for the contribution we would make to Templeard. These parts came wrapped in praise, a scarce commodity in itself, so carefully doled out that it never lost its potency, never failed to make even the bitterest of pills seem sweet.

'Flossie. Now there's a girl with a heart and a half. Never let you down. Always willing to lend a hand.'

I cannot say for sure who voiced these words. They were heard as though from on high, echoing throughout the house in a mix of voices, all familiar yet not belonging to anyone in particular. Templeard, relentlessly chanting self-fulfilling prophecies.

'Flossie, always willing to lend a hand.' And so it came to pass, Flossie nursing Ammie, nursing Aunt Cassie, nursing Daddo. The greater part of a life spent ferrying trays up and down the stairs, the collective voice of Templeard forever ringing in her ears, 'a girl with a heart and a half.'

I could sing. And not just parlour songs. I could sing better than the best, a voice worthy of professional training. Twice a week at first and then every day with the renowned Sister Patricia, almost blind by that stage but one-time teacher of Anastasia Delahunty who, at the height of her career, was considered on a par with Margaret Burke Sheridan.

If I listen carefully I can still hear my calling chanted in the collective voice of Templeard.

'With singing like that, you'll have the pick of the country.'

I would go out to the world, not as a professional singer but with a repertoire of songs that would enthral and delight, sing my way to a great marriage – an event once so firmly on my horizon that in some hidden recess, locked away from all the actual facts of my life, I stand resplendent in a sea of white, centrepiece of a glorious June wedding under the limes in Templeard.

I leave Ammie's dance floor and amble downstairs, humming my way through *Meet Me in Saint Louis*, playing a part I might well have gone on to play in a provincial town production. The impulse to twist a bluesy lilt into the frilly chorus takes hold and before long I am humming my own version; a version shot through with jazzy inclines, hesitant and haphazardly broken up, but for all that more in keeping with the part I went on to play.

The kitchen door opens before I reach it. Flossie walks out, purposeful, followed by Girlie cloaked in her coat, nestling into it as she steps into the cold of the hall.

'Here you are, at last.' Flossie is moving towards me, so resolutely that I step backwards.

'Here I am. Didn't think anyone would be leaving this early.' I pause, about to say 'what with the ice', when I see that Girlie's eyes are shut, lids drawn in what appears to be annoyance.

Behind them Ber is pointing at Flossie, mouthing words I can't make out, elbowing Margaret in a gawky school-girlish way. We all bunch together in the narrow space between the banister and the wall.

'Whatever you have to say,' Girlie snaps officiously at Flossie, 'I don't see why you can't say it in the kitchen. It's daft going into a different room. Daft. Daft. Daft. And a bloody ice box at that.' Flossie remains silent, just forges ahead. I coast along behind.

In the parlour, Girlie and Margaret remain standing, set to join forces in protest against the cold when Flossie, one hand reaching for the mantelpiece, blurts out: 'I'm selling Templeard.'

Her words seem to bounce off us, willed directly back to her, becoming unsaid again.

'I said I'm selling the place.'

Ber scrutinizes Flossie, searches for an explanation. I look from one to the other, then hear Margaret clear her throat authoritatively, see her puff herself up to her full size.

'It's not yours to sell.'

'It's mine to do whatever I want with,' Flossie rattles off in a sing-song voice. Rehearsed beforehand no doubt.

Margaret's face tightens.

'I mean, we all know Daddo left it to you, but on the understanding that it would be passed on . . .' In that instant the rest of us manage to catch up with her, glare at her, collectively forbidding her to say *to Patrick, his only grand-son.*

'There was no such understanding. Nothing written.' Flossie is quick to reply.

Ber, Girlie and I nod in agreement, but skid to an abrupt halt when Margaret swings around, confronts us head on, her chin jutting out, lips drawn. 'You're trying to tell me that Daddo would want to see Templeard sold, want to see it passing into the hands of someone without a drop of Macken blood in their veins?'

'It might not be what he would have wanted . . .' I begin. Steady. Reasonable. 'But it's . . .'

'Who are you to talk?' Margaret's anger bolts out of control, 'Who are you to talk? ' And here she stops, aware no doubt, that she need go no further. I feel myself recoil in the face of her words, determined above all else to steer clear of the guilt which – in the blink of an eye – would have me agree that I should have no say in this whole business. I have long since lost the right to participate on an equal footing with my sisters, even in ordinary, everyday chit-chat, had it wrenched from me in a series of events which have stalked unnamed around Templeard for forty years.

Girlie smiles. Shrugs. Laughs, shrugs again, tears spilling

through her laughter. 'You'd think it was the end of the world, for God's sake.' Nobody speaks. Her voice is shaky, she looks for agreement but nobody agrees.

Margaret stomps out, pulls the door behind her with such force that it swings open again. She picks up the telephone receiver and we sit in silence as if instructed to remain quiet while she makes a call.

There in the wintery stillness of the parlour, almost tangible between Ber, Flossie and myself, is the absence of children. Difficult to imagine anything we could say now that would not somehow lead to that absence, prompting us in different ways to confront our incompleteness. We remain silent.

'Yes,' Margaret begins, which I assume is a response to a question from Pat. Something like: *What's up?*

'No. Worse . . . Worse . . . Yes.'

Margaret manages to conduct the call without saying the actual words *sale* or *sell*, a show of complicity between her and Pat which unnerves Flossie.

I listen so intently that I do not notice the arrival of other thoughts, do not hear the anarchic cheering until it is pounding in my ears. Suddenly I am racing ahead, chasing the notion of a world without Templeard at its centre. But it remains out of my reach eluding me at every turn. I slow down, content to wait until later when I am alone, free to seize it with both hands.

I smile at Flossie, but she pays no heed, too preoccupied by the names Margaret is listing, neighbours from whom Pat might borrow a car.

'No. Too late. They'll all be gone by then.' Margaret catapults her words down the line.

'Yes,' she says firmly. 'I'll wait at the outer gate. Twelve. The roads are like glass.'

Each detail of Pat's projected arrival causes Flossie to

flinch. He may as well be standing there in his big, blue, tightly-belted anorak telling her to forget the whole thing. I can hear his voice, with all its nasal resonance.

'Personally speaking . . .' 'In my opinion . . .' 'The way I see it . . .' I begin to wonder if Flossie will stand her ground. Smile at her again, but again she pays no heed, bracing herself for Margaret's return.

'Daddo said it to Pat,' Margaret begins before she gets to the parlour door. 'Said it to him here in this very room,' she stomps in, 'the Christmas after Patrick was born, how it was a relief for him to know for sure that whatever else happened the place wouldn't be falling into the hands of strangers.'

Ber nods cautiously, by the look of it offering herself as an intermediary. Flossie thinks otherwise.

'You have the convent, haven't you?'

'Templeard will always be my home.' Her voice is feathery light, her eyes pious.

'Well, if it was always your home, where were you when the people in it needed minding? When Ammie was dying. And Daddo? And Cassie?' This comes so fast that I immediately suppose it too has been rehearsed, a part of one of those discussions Flossie conducts on her own in the fields. Suddenly all her talk about Ber and the convent over the previous few days takes on a different shape.

'I'm going.' Girlie leaps to her feet. 'I hate this kind of thing. Hate it.'

She disappears inside her coat and heads towards the door, picking her steps carefully as if the floor was strewn with rubble. I follow, trying as I do to catch Flossie's attention.

'I'll see her to the car,' I whisper. 'Say goodbye.'

'I'm selling, that's all I know,' Flossie blurts out, her mouth clamping defensively, all her courage now used up.

'You don't have to be here when he comes. You're not accountable to Pat Dempsey. Or to anyone else for that matter.' I am holding Flossie's forearms, astonished to be speaking those words and at the same time trying, against the odds, to will the bewildered look from her face. For a moment I think I will not be able to keep it up, imagining Margaret approaching from behind, her padded shoulders swinging from side to side, set to intervene.

'Come on. Come back with me for a few days, a week or two,' I say. 'Let everyone get used to the idea.'

Flossie blinks. Allows herself to be led out.

'You can't go. Pat is already on his way down,' Margaret's voice trails away behind us only to pick up again. 'The least he deserves is the good manners of a hearing.' Then, just as we move out of range, 'You haven't heard the end of this.'

We knew full well we hadn't, but we also knew that Templeard would be sold. Knew it as a certainty. Some things once stated force an immediate review of all that has gone before, and so no longer appear sudden or arbitrary. That's how it is as we stand in the porch, Flossie, Girlie and I, with so much falling into place around us that we stand in silence, mesmerized like children in falling snow. Aunt Cassie's voice is there somewhere cheering us on, Ammie's too, together holding out the possibility that Templeard, as well as doling out destinies like playing cards, may well have an intuition registering wrongs.

[4]

Outside the world unfurls in the late morning thaw. The frosted ivy loosens its grip on the tree trunks and, high above, boughs and branches lurch out to catch the insipid January sunlight. There is a rustling in the undergrowth, a winter bird scampering through the leafmeal, alarmed by our arrival on to the gravel sweep. The impulse to throw my arms up in triumph is there but kept in check. I am reluctant to turn around and look at the house, afraid that the optimism I feel in entering a future without it will somehow become apparent. I steal a glimpse, a side-eyed glance, to gauge its mood and find an emptiness which I would never have thought possible.

Of all the fates I ever envisaged for Templeard, selling was the least likely. We had always looked on selling as the last resort before the poor-house, a failure so profound that the word itself remained unspoken. It was isolated with other unspoken words, harbingers of disaster too terrible to mention – diphtheria, bankruptcy, tuberculosis, scarlet fever. Selling flew directly in the face of all our principles, made a mockery of our self-reliance, our solvency. It relegated us to the level of people who had been forced off the land. Daddo occasionally mentioned one such family, the Mosses, 'poor unfortunates' he would say in a hushed voice, as if they had died tragically. 'Borrowing was the death of them.'

Everything we were was bound up in being the Mackens of Templeard. The memory of the buying of the place in 1887 waited to be evoked whenever there was a moment to take stock, an occasion: Girlie's wedding, Cassie's funeral, Patrick's christening.

'We were leaseholders,' . . . Daddo would find an opportunity to say, '. . . leaseholders going back to the earliest of times. Then our chance came . . .' Here his voice took on an apocalyptic tone, his stance a princely magnificence, 'the year I was born, the chance to buy outright. The whole place, one hundred and sixty-nine acres and a two-storey slated house.' He always paused there, maybe for an ancestral cheer. '. . . my father, God rest him, a young man at the time, his hair black as a raven's wing, went grey overnight.'

I marvelled at this, wondered if the change could have been witnessed like a changing cloudscape. I conjured up an image of my grandfather, pacing the low ceilinged house they then lived in, demented by the momentous decision facing him. Would he buy? Would he break faith with a long line of cautious forebears and borrow money? The full purchase price, to be paid back over forty-nine years.

I was always Daddo's keenest listener, quick to correct him if he left out some detail or other. In that way I played my part, ensuring the great leap, leaseholders to proprietors, took pride of place in the annals of Templeard. But even if that fateful event had never been recalled, I think its sway over our lives would have been every bit as powerful, kept alive by the deep-seated anxiety about holding on to the place which Daddo had inherited. He was plagued by the fear that we might somehow lose it, that it might be reclaimed by some greater authority. When that did become a possibility, a very real possibility to our way of thinking, in the summer of 1934, he was quick to take a stance. So was Aunt Cassie.

A small torch-lit procession, marching from Derrinalty Cross to the town, had filed past the outer gate earlier that year, men with burning sods of turf tied to sticks held high in the air, shouting a slogan we could not make out. They passed again at the beginning of the summer, this time their cries louder but no clearer.

'Hooligans,' Daddo called them, 'the lowest of the low, ignorant no-goods out to bring ruin to decent people, to the whole country if they're let.' We knew them or at least knew them to see. A lot of them lived down the maze of boreens at the other side of the river. Small farmers most of them, men with wives who walked to the town, their shoes in their hands until they reached the outskirts.

All summer there was talk of compulsory purchase, of communists, of annuities. *Our Crowd*, as Daddo called them, Cumann na nGaedheal, were in a state of high alert. Men drove down the avenue at times no one ever called, great clouds of dust billowing behind them as they swerved up in front of the house. Usually they just hollered news of a meeting from an open window and tore away again, but occasionally they got out and leaned against the side of their cars, arms folded waiting for Daddo. When he came he took up the same position, his head nodding gravely as conversation got under way.

Whenever they stayed to talk like that, Aunt Cassie would rush in from the yard and put the kettle on, then send me out to say there was 'tea made and sweet cake cut'. I think she would have given anything for an opportunity to join in their talk. She was an ardent supporter of O'Duffy, party leader at the time, and had written to tell him how much she admired him. The signed reply she got was one of a number of effects we found after her death in a willow-patterned tin she kept beside her bed. The others included a prize bond certificate, a newspaper cutting about my performance at a Feis Ceoil, a small box designed for sending wedding cake by post and a silver thimble.

The men who came to talk to Daddo invariably declined the offer of tea and cake. Their refusals, reported by me to Aunt Cassie in an *I told you so* voice prompted no more than a firm, tight-lipped nod from her, disappointment on one hand, acceptance of her place on the other. But for all that, her loyalty to those men and the politicians they served did not waver once during that whole period. I don't think I ever saw her as eager, as fiery as she was on those summer evenings, seeing Daddo off to the meetings. It was as if she herself was marching into battle, taking her place alongside the other Blueshirts, Albert Quinn of Friars Island, Sonny Campion's father Job, Pat Joe Crotty of The Glebe, Moss Lacey of Derrinalty Cross, all convinced that their holdings were about to be seized any day.

'Taken by statute order,' I heard Daddo warn her, waving a clothes brush in her direction as he prepared to leave for one of those meetings. 'Taken and given to spailpín fánachs. The likes of Rud McCormack, the laziest man in Christendom.'

She stood there, proudly holding his polished shoes, furiously nodding agreement, her bobbing head reflected in the celestial shine she had worked up on them.

'Don't you think so, Nora?' Girlie's voice summons me to the here and now, a journey I do not complete quickly enough to save her repeating the call.

'Don't you think so, Nora? Don't you think selling is the best thing Flossie has ever done in her whole life?'

Flossie stands there, her head tilted to one side, waiting for me to pass judgement.

'The best,' I say, aware that these are Girlie's words, keen to find my own, but Flossie speaks before I'm ready.

'What about the dogs? If I'm going to be leaving them for a few days?'

37

Girlie and I wait, aware from the faltering way Flossie put the question that it is addressed to herself.

'I'll put them in the wash house and ring the Campions. That's what I'll do. And they'll come and collect them later.' Flossie is suddenly pleased with herself, pleased to be negotiating her way through familiar territory.

We wave to Girlie when she gets out of her car to close the outer gate behind her, then amble back into the house.

Ber steals out of the parlour and into the hall, her index finger on her lips bidding us to be quiet, tiptoeing towards us as if there were a sleeping child inside.

'I think I'll be able to get Margaret to come round,' she whispers. 'I mean, you'll have to consider a settlement for Pat, for Patrick – if you sell.'

'I know the settlement I'll give that Pat Dempsey. A bill. Who told him he could take the fishing rods after Daddo died?'

Flossie has found her voice again. Well and truly. I steer her in the direction of the stairs, urge her to get her things.

'Do you think she'll see sense about selling?' Ber whispers when she is out of sight, pleading with me to say yes.

'Maybe it's for the best.'

She bows her head, a gesture of submission so familiar that it happens without thought. When it comes down to it, Ber, despite all her bossiness, is quick to acquiesce. I would like to believe that this will not always be the case. But looking at her now it is difficult to imagine how she might unlearn a lifetime's habit of obedience.

Flossie appears on the landing with a suitcase, one of a set Ammie bought for us in Todds of Limerick when we were going away to school. Uncommonly smart then but something of an oddity now.

'Stay here as long as you want,' she says to Ber, making her way downstairs. 'You know about the locking up.' Flossie's

38

voice is strained by her efforts to fend the heavy suitcase to one side with her knee. She rests it on a step and begins to rattle off a series of instructions about the back door, the front door, the inner gate, the outer gate. Ber pays little attention.

'Maybe you'll see things differently after a few days away.'

'I will not. Why would I? I'm not going to live out my days minding this place for a young lad who'd have it up for sale before I was properly buried.'

'But you're not just minding it for Patrick, Flossie, you're minding it for us all. And that's what Patrick would be doing too, minding it for all the Mackens to come.'

Flossie walks past, indignant.

'She's minding it for us all, isn't she, Nora? We're all . . .' Ber looks to me for agreement but I just stand there. She goes to the parlour door, turns the knob as quietly as possible and slips inside.

I drive slowly towards the outer gate, Flossie beside me, her handbag on her knees, held with both hands.

'As soon as we are on the road a bit we'll stop for a cup of tea.' I pause, glance at Flossie who is looking straight ahead, 'We have plenty of time.'

Minutes pass. Slow, concentrated driving, the road ahead looming like an apparition in the reflected sunlight.

'I'd sooner something a bit stronger. Not tea. The thought of that Pat Dempsey.' Flossie settles herself into the passenger seat, leaves her bag down by her feet.

'What are you going to do when you sell? Where are you going to live?'

'I'm buying a house in the town.'

'The town?' I smile at those words, *the town* . . . People like us, people of consequence, landless in the town. Thoughts I ought to have left behind years ago but which somehow have stayed with me.

We stop at a motel, a flat bunker of a building with a sort of concrete sail rising from the roof. The slap of flagpole ropes fills the forlorn car park. A bus full of sleepy people pulls up near the entrance, its doors hissing open, though nobody seems to want to move. Flossie heads for the bar and to my surprise orders a Jameson. 'A double,' she tacks on, when the bartender begins to pour. 'And a gin and tonic.' She nods sternly in my direction, defying me to order anything different.

In that moment I lose sight of her as the Flossie I have always known, seeing instead a confident woman going about things in a worldly way. I keep looking at her, expecting her to become the Flossie I know again; predictable in her every move, taking me aside in the pantry, the back hall, on the landing with her long list of complaints about the others.

'A house in the town?' I wait for her to reply, imagining that the sound of her voice will restore her to her familiar self.

'Yes. A house in the town.' She sips her whiskey, even less recognizable now than she was a few minutes earlier. 'A house in the town.'

I trail behind, slowly adjusting to the notion of Flossie with a life plan decidedly at odds with the one she was dealt. She fills her glass up with water until the whiskey loses all its colour. Drinks most of it in one go. 'Yes, a house in the town and a man in my bed before the year is out.'

In a memory, graphic as can be, Flossie edges her way out along a fallen willow, a slippery bridge down near Campion's sheep dip. Beneath, the torrential brown water is whorling around the splayed branches. She beckons me to follow, come on Nora, her voice giving way to my own in the carpety clam of the motel bar.

'Marriage? You're getting married?' I draw breath, wondering how I managed to stage such a smooth response.

'Don't be daft, Nora. Why would anyone of my age get married?'

'Is there someone. I mean is there a man . . .' I falter, picking my steps carefully past the word *boyfriend*.

'There might be. But even if there wasn't, I'll tell you they won't be long coming. Widowers, that class of man.'

I examine Flossie, try to see her as others here in the motel bar might, her dark eyes full of hope, youthful, her high colour, an elegance about her if she wasn't wearing a cardigan she'd knitted herself. She thinks I'm assessing her chances. Which I suppose I am, without intending to.

'I'll be a woman of means living in a house in the town. A nice house.'

'I'm not doubting it, Flossie.'

She isn't convinced.

'Nora, there are thousands. You should hear them . . .' She gets very animated, loses her way. 'Every day on the radio. Ordinary too. Like you and me. Only last week there was a woman who goes to Australia for the winter, every year. Sixty-three years of age. She's from over near Roscrea and she has an affair waiting for her there when she goes. In Australia. She said it on the radio.'

I wish Flossie would keep her voice down, but she's on a crusade, full sure I need to be convinced that we are free to lead lives of our own choosing. I can't believe that it is her and not me who has steered our conversation to this point, Flossie reassuring me that our destinies are not written in stone.

'I think . . .' Pause for a split second.

'That's your trouble, Nora. You think too much about everything.'

Once again the foundation on which I have built my life begins to tremble. I hold my breath, think of my flat, the hospital where I work, the choir, night classes, friends, sensing once again its fragility, knowing that it could be toppled as quickly as a house of cards.

'You're right to do what you want, Flossie.'

She smiles, suspiciously at first but then gratefully.

'And you're right about me thinking too much about things. Come on, we'll go.'

We are spun out through the revolving doors, both bracing ourselves against the cold as we quick step our way to the car. Within minutes of setting out, Flossie begins to doze off, telling me as she does that the Campions are good sorts, sure to have the dogs over at Crossmokler already. I look across at her, consider for a moment or two how impossible it would be to tell her that I do not want to think too much about things. That I am, in fact, stranded, endlessly skirting the same things which long ago forced me to take a path I would not otherwise have taken. I summon my own story, look at it in the light of her announcement to sell. Before long I am spinning around, catching it in snatches but at the same time aware that it is taking on a more coherent form than ever before, shaping itself around the demise of Templeard.

5

Bringing Flossie back with me seemed like a good move on the day. But almost as soon as we arrived in London I began to question the wisdom of that decision, wondering if Flossie wouldn't have been better off staying in Templeard. That way the whole thing might have come to a head quickly and not dragged on as it did all week, with Ber ringing two or three times a day, keeping Flossie posted on Margaret's every thought.

Shortly after we left Templeard, Margaret and Pat went into Fahy the auctioneers and, full of authority, according to Ber who went with them, told him the place was no longer on the market. Fahy contacted Regan and Pyle, Flossie's solicitors, who promptly rang Flossie here. Templeard, she assured them, was very definitely up for sale, adding that if Fahy had any more truck with Margaret or Pat she would find another auctioneer. The outcome was the arrival in Templeard, later that afternoon, of Fahy's van – full of For Sale signs.

'They've put them everywhere,' Ber reported. 'Tied them to the outer gate, nailed them to the chestnut trees down by Fogarty's bridge. There are three at Derrinalty Cross and more than you could count on the road between Crossmokler and Friar's Island.'

'Good,' Flossie said. But there was, despite her best efforts, an unmistakable hesitancy in her voice.

'Good,' she said again, trying to recoup, but it sounded even thinner. In the same breath she asked Ber if the Campions had collected the dogs, but was too flustered to wait for the answer. By the end of the call she was in a panic, demanding details about the For Sale signs, their size, colour, height, in between giving garbled instructions about feeding the hens.

And this foundering was, no doubt, presented by Ber to Pat and Margaret as evidence of a change of heart.

Despite her determination to sell, the vision of For Sale signs all over the countryside touched Flossie more deeply than anything else. She wondered if the place could be sold with-out them. She considered the consequences of asking Fahy to take them down, revealing the disloyalty she felt to neighbours and friends in flaunting the sale so flagrantly. There was, I knew full well, something shameful about those signs. I felt it as I listened to Flossie question Ber about them, felt it more keenly than I would have ever thought possible. They advertised our failure to keep a life going, told the world of our intention to drop the Macken baton. But for all that, Flossie did not, for one instant, waver in her decision to sell.

Confronted by her steadfastness and aware that there were no legal grounds on which they could prevent the sale, Pat and Margaret changed tack. Margaret wrote, describing to Flossie the shock she got on first hearing the news, explaining that she had lost the run of herself and said things she now regretted. She wished Flossie good luck with the sale and then over several pages of small, neat handwriting proceeded to list all the reasons why it would be in Flossie's best interest, in everyone's best interest, for her to go and live permanently with them in Dublin once Templeard was sold.

I imagined that the calm way in which Flossie related details of that proposal to me, periodically scanning the letter for Margaret's exact words, was a build-up to a great burst of indignation. She would, I kept thinking, stop suddenly, purse her lips tightly then launch in with one of her stock responses. 'The nerve . . .'

That was more or less the direction in which I was heading myself as I listened, embarrassed at first by Margaret's efforts to impress on Flossie how fond Pat was of her and then sickened by the way she went on about blood being thicker than water and the necessity for families to stick together.

'It's worth considering, well worth considering,' Flossie said, her eyes softening as she drifted into what I supposed was one of those silent dialogues.

'Flossie?' I half whispered, all set to point out the folly of the plan when I saw just how far she had retreated into her own world.

'Well worth considering,' she nodded, folding the letter in a slow deliberate way, pressing each crease firmly and slipping it into its envelope with a finality intended to bring the matter to a close.

'Flossie?'

'I'm off tomorrow, back to Templeard.'

'Flossie?'

'Back to God knows what, but there you are.'

'Flossie, surely you're not thinking of Pat and Margaret's, I mean, of living with them after it's sold?'

'I am. And I'm not. Either way I'm writing to say yes before I leave here. Better safe than sorry.'

'What do you mean?'

'I mean everything might be different after the auction.'

'What about the house in the town?'

'That too.'

It then began to dawn on me that she was only accepting Margaret's invitation to humour her and Pat, keep on their right side until the auction was over. She watched me piece her scheme together, visibly alarmed that I was about to evaluate it. And certainly I would have liked to, liked to tell her how clever I thought it was, and necessary too, but she leapt up and in an instant was over at the desk rooting noisily for a pen, shaking the drawer, nervously refusing the complicity I was offering.

Flossie's bid for distance struck me very forcibly then, sustained as it was by hardened anger, so integral a part of her now that it is rarely visible in itself. Suddenly I'm on thin ice, aware that rising fast beneath, set to break through, is the thought that she has good reason to be angry. But I'm well practised at fleeing from that and from the many other thoughts which rise from the same queasy swirl of memories. So before it can surface fully I have manoeuvred myself back to where I was. There, watching Flossie preparing to write to Margaret, relentless in her determination to negotiate her way alone, the distance between us in sharp relief to the closeness of our early years.

A memory from primary school shoots across the decades: Flossie and I going from room to room showing the gold medal we won at a feis to the different classes. It is no larger than a small coin but we both keep a grip on it throughout, neither trying to increase her stake. We are asked to sing and as we do our voices cross, sometimes fusing in such a way that neither of us can tell for sure which belongs to whom.

Flossie would not acknowledge that the situation to which she was returning was relatively calm. She preferred to present her departure as a convenience for me, drawing attention to the size of the flat, making sure right to the end, that the distance between us did not diminish.

She spent much of the evening before she left telling me about the troubled lives of people as recounted on the radio show to which she listens every morning. She was particularly fascinated by a woman whose daughter had married a Muslim and gone to live in the Middle East. Regular reports of the hardship endured by this girl were, it seems, broadcast – with listeners ringing in with advice. While Flossie had never actually been on air, she had rung the programme so frequently that she was known by name to several of the researchers. And that's what she is looking forward to most about returning, listening and responding to that radio programme. A strange turn of events to say the least. It is as if Templeard has been outwitted and the house long since deaf to so much that went on within its walls, is now full every morning with voices, women of all ages recounting their lot. In an idle, disjointed way I drift off with the notion that those voices – muffled down through the decades for what was thought to be the greater good – had in a mysterious way been accumulating out there somewhere and were now returning to flood the house through the airwaves.

I used to wonder how she could enter so fully into the lives of people she had never met and disclose, which no doubt she has, details of her own situation to faceless young researchers. But that holds little wonder for me now. Those faceless young researchers are eager to listen and that in itself is a triumph in a world where so many people have kept their hands firmly clamped to their ears.

From time to time I have tried to imagine what it would be like to speak about the determining events of my life. Just dawdled at the edge for a moment or two, long enough to remind myself of how impossible it would be. My story, if it can be called a story, hasn't got a beginning, at least not one I can pin down. It just fills the centre of my world and, even after all these years, is as alive and dangerous as a swarm of bees. My impulse has always been to steer clear, to tiptoe around it. And whenever it encroaches into the tight space where I conduct my day-to-day life, I brace myself for combat, willing its raw, unruly scenes back into the darkness.

The morning Flossie announced her plan to sell, I could just about contain the sense of impending liberation I felt. Templeard, the stronghold of all the beliefs and rules, conceits and illusions which shaped our lives would, I firmly believed, no longer hold sway over me, over any of us. But its reign had not come to a close. Its power to impose its rules remained, and in particular its power to impose the most injurious of those rules, silence.

At first, I thought this was because the finality of its demise had not sunk in. So, in the weeks following Flossie's return, I trudged over the facts of the sale again and again, never at any point considering that the real difficulty lay in my own reluctance to grasp them. I was, despite myself, a prisoner of memory, clinging to the old order.

I had whiled away decades imagining a life not dominated by the events of my middle teens. Then, with Daddo's death that imaginary world began to crumble. It was as if his death brought an end to hope, the hope that one day I would, despite what had happened, lay claim to the whole-some, fulfilling life mapped out for me. Daddo had pride of place in that life, there as in a family photograph, centre of a great swell of smiling people, children, grandchildren.

In the years after his death I went on trying to recreate that triumphant image, but with less and less success. I watched it give way to other images, each as lifeless as the warm, spreading family scene had been fanciful. Grey, rainy images of Flossie, Ber and myself, looking out at the empty road ahead but still smiling for the camera.

I was not in the least consoled by the steady, officious voice announcing my arrival at the facts of my situation. My late arrival – at that. There, moving rapidly through my forties at the time, unable to return to the dreams which had kept me looking forward.

Every time I went back to Templeard, I arrived as I did last Christmas, hoping to break the silence, hoping to piece the events of my life, our lives together with my sisters. I wanted to talk about their toll on us all and, I suppose, arrive at a point where they would see, beyond a shadow of doubt, that what happened wasn't my fault. But I always failed to break the silence, defeated both by my own inability to look at what had happened and by the skill with which my sisters kept their distance. That was always our way, the way of Templeard, everybody's way.

Throughout the spring Flossie kept me posted on how the sale was progressing. A date at the end of June had been set for the auction and if the reserve price was reached, as Fahy told her it would be, she wanted us all to return for a few days to sort out the contents. She intended taking nothing from the house with her. 'Not a button,' she said. 'Only the clothes I'm standing in on the day.' When I mentioned this or that heirloom, the hall clock, Ammie's sewing table, the silver candle sticks, she was ready with a firm 'No.'

'Whoever wants can take them,' she said, 'only nothing is going with Ber to that convent.'

I looked forward to Flossie's calls. Her self-absorption ensured that we discussed only her concerns, and that, during those dismal months, came as a welcome diversion from my own. How was it – I repeatedly asked myself – that forty years on, I had hit a level of hopelessness as profound as any to which I had plummeted in the past. It made all that talk about time being a healer seem like gibberish.

With that hopelessness came fatigue, making even the smallest tasks appear too great. I had to reserve every last whit of energy just to get through my working day. I valued my job more than ever, grasped the frosty hand of English kindness, bartering cheeriness in the hospital corridors at every turn.

By the end of April, my world was so diminished that at times it seemed unfamiliar. There were respites, glorious

49

moments when, with the record player turned right up, I kept pace with Joan Sutherland, high in the chilling climbs of *Madame Butterfly*. Times when Jeanette MacDonald stepped aside, allowing me to take my rightful place beside Nelson Eddy and soar into the skies with him. I loved those wild excursions, heady flights to loss without ever having to consider what it was I had lost.

Then some time early in the summer a change took place. It happened imperceptibly, which makes me think that change has its own momentum, likes to surprise. I fix on an evening on my way home from work, not because it marks the precise beginning of that change but because it is one of a number of times when I was unaccountably overwhelmed by a sense of possibility.

There was a downpour, sudden as can be. Not a single warning droplet, but sheets of torrential rain, belting violently against everything in sight. All around me people were wincing and crouching, struggling with umbrellas or just putting on brave faces and soldiering on. It ended as abruptly as it had started, ousted by sunshine before its force was fully spent. I continued on, soaked to the bone, unable to hold out against a kind of recklessness, a mood Aunt Cassie would undoubtedly have described as divil-may-care. Before long I was – for whatever reason – smiling to myself, happy in a vague sort of way.

Happy, of all things, blithely swept along, each step effortless, carrying me what felt like a great distance forward. And all the time I continued to smile, giddy in the steamy sunshine, striding confidently through the sodden throngs. That it turned out to be short lived mattered little, mattered hardly at all. It was possible. And that's what I carried away with me, certain I would return to wherever it was that sense of possibility had taken shape.

When I did, I was again taken by surprise. I drifted out of

sleep one morning with an altogether different set of thoughts to those which regularly stalk my waking moments. Ebullient, racing thoughts, their source an image of myself aged about thirteen or fourteen with my sisters, all of us swinging from our knees in the paddock in Templeard. In the uncharted space between sleep and waking I felt drawn towards that upside-down self, there almost within reach, laughing. For a moment or two, an eternity in that half sleep, I felt I was moving nearer, about to merge into it, when inexplicably frightened by what was happening I chose to wake.

Several times throughout the morning that image loomed up before me, each time leaving a mix of hope and fear in its wake. Soon I began to summon it at will, my fear giving way to a growing sense that a long-forgotten self had turned up asking to be reclaimed.

6

All through the summer that image of the five of us swinging upside down from the paddock jump served as a fixed point in the past towards which I worked my way back, untangling my story as I went along. I heard our laughter, heard it ring out in the late evening, at times scarcely able to believe that I was getting an opportunity to reshape that past, to harness it to serve a future of my own making.

It seems that memory creates its own order, serving whatever future is most persistently, most passionately imagined. And it can remain slavishly servile to that future, long after it has become impossible to realize. That, as far as I can see, is about the sum of it. Only when there was absolutely nothing of my old future to play for, Templeard sold, its key players – Daddo, Aunt Cassie, Ammie – long since dead, was I able to approach the events of my middle teens with any degree of calm.

Still, I approach with caution. Decades of botched attempts to pretend that perilous stretch was a route I had not taken, have left it buckled and twisted. I examine each piece as it presents itself, reconciled to the fact that not all or nearly all of this, my own story, is in my possession.

A light tap on the frosted glass of the classroom door fills the room. There are twenty, perhaps twenty-five of us, sewing. It's April 1939. I'm fifteen, a fourth-year pupil in

Our Lady of the Psalms. The Psalms as everyone called it, a small boarding school on the outskirts of Limerick. A hissy whisper fizzles across the room like a burning fuse wire. Arms rise, draw thread upwards then swoop down to harpoon yards of tightly held calico. Sister Frances is kind. Her room, the sewing-room, is the cosiest in the school. Her needle work is legendary. Samples of it, in the form of gold-braided vestments, hang on the wall at the front. Sister Frances goes to the door, her habit swishing hurriedly past my desk. All eyes follow her but no one looks up until the door closes behind her.

I can see her silhouette through the frosted glass, like a grey cardboard cut out. I try to remember what she looked like but only that silhouette remains, and maybe something of her warmth.

Suddenly she is bending over my desk. Confidential.

'Nora. Leave your work. Mother Rosario wishes to see you.'

I move slowly, trying to stay a pace or two behind Mother Rosario as she walks around the convent garden. Beneath our feet the gravel crunches like broken glass, filling the enclosed space with a harsh sound. Great tangles of forsythia hang from the top of the high walls, shedding yellow petals whose fall I follow intently. Mother Rosario says the word 'arrangements'. Says it for the first time though it feels as if I have been trailing behind her in that cloistered garden for centuries, hearing her whisper it over and over again. For a moment or two the scene takes on a static quality. I stand and stare at myself, at how marooned, how small and out of scale I appear, trailing behind a nun armoured from head to toe in black serge. Then all at once the scene comes to life again, animated by falling petals and some fierce desire on my part to scale those walls. Up and over, away for ever.

'Arrangements.'

Mother Rosario turns in my direction. I nod gratefully, terrified that she is going to anchor the conversation in words I have not dared say to myself. I fall further behind, hearing only the odd fragment, fixing on one in particular, *in everyone's best interest*. I repeat that fragment to myself, *in everyone's best interest*, repeat it again and again until it becomes a loud jumble of meaningless sounds blocking out all other sounds.

If Mother Rosario had been angry, if she had been her haughty, correcting self then I might have been able to participate, answer her in the yes-Mother-Rosario, no-Mother-Rosario way I always did. But she was quiet, calm.

'Nora. You must never speak of this.'

I imagine her moving along that narrow gravel path, sailing away like a great ocean liner, leaving me trundling behind with 'arrangements – in everyone's best interest'. But I know there must have been more to it than that. She must have outlined a plan, a procedure, which has somehow disappeared into the bottomless terror I felt.

I had reached the seventh month of the pregnancy, doggedly holding on to a version of myself as someone to whom it could not have happened, to whom it had not happened. And I returned to the sewing room reunited with that self, not wholly, but enough to shrug nonchalantly, whisper 'choir'. And that was sufficient. I was frequently called out of class by Mother Rosario. Under her direction I had been singing solo at Mass since the end of my first year at The Psalms. 'Soul of my Saviour' unaccompanied from start to finish. Many times, in the course of that year, she had spoken of the honour I had brought to the school the previous September, selected from all the other schools in the dioceses, to sing at Bishop Mulhall's consecration. Before long I am back there, back in the cathedral again, high up in the gallery filling the great vaulted roof with *Kyrie Eleison*, icicle sharp, humming it to myself now, still moved by its power to ferry me past Mother Rosario, out over the wall, way beyond the facts. I have to remind myself that there is no need to flee, not now. I slow down, hover for a moment or two before deciding to tackle the unanswered questions gathering beneath.

Some of these questions are unanswered simply because they have never been asked, at least not by me or within my hearing. Others will always remain unanswered because those who might have answered them are dead. Mother Rosario died some twenty years ago. Aunt Cassie sent me the short tribute to her life's work which appeared in the *Tipperary Star*. I read it as I might a poison pen letter, tore it up immediately, unnerved. I wanted to believe that Mother Rosario was acting independently, that she had just observed my being pregnant, that it was 'a matter about which I must not speak', a matter about which she had not spoken and would not speak, something that could be dealt with and then forgotten. I did not want to believe in her complicity.

I could not, not for one second, tolerate the possibility that other people knew. Scotched the notion instantly and hammered it full force on the head any time it re-emerged. This required rigid policing of my own thoughts, constant surveillance to ensure those thoughts would not betray me and conjure up the terrifying spectre of behind-the-scenes collusion. It's a habit of mind I ought to have abandoned years ago, but on the contrary, I have perfected it, become a master of self-censorship and it now stands as the greatest obstacle to the unearthing of my story.

It would be easy to lose sight of the purpose that self-censorship once served, to forget that it was a habit of mind which saved me from despair. People knowing was my worst fear. It was akin to death, more frightening than death in a lot of ways, a life sentence to the outer reaches, at best pitied.

I wanted to believe that when it ended, when whatever was going to happen had happened, I could tiptoe back into my world, continue where I left off. My sights were firmly fixed on the end of the pregnancy which, strange to say, I did not, in an actual sense, equate with the birth of a child until Mother Rosario first spoke of 'arrangements'. Up to that point it was all happening within the confines of my own world, a place from where unwanted thoughts could be banished at will.

Kyrie Eleison rings in my ears, all the torment of those dark days absorbed into its shrill, endlessly extended pleas. Suddenly, the wild hope that the baby would be born dead approaches like a meteorite. I draw breath, preparing for an onslaught from legions of banished memories.

None appear.

I wait, reluctant to believe that I can wander safely among the events of those grim months. Mother Rosario, from whom I have run, full speed on every sighting for the last forty years, appears imperious, a figure of towering strength. I take stock, sufficiently distant now to see her courage, to note that, regardless of her motives, she was taking a daring course. Unwed pregnant girls disappeared, never to be heard from again. Many went to England. Those who remained were led into a fortress-like building in the town where they laundered the clothes of their betters. More than a few of them went quietly insane in the steamy ironing rooms. I saw some of them once, mindlessly gawking from the basement window, sullen, defeated souls lifting dripping clothes with wooden tongs from vats of boiling water. Mine was to be a different fate and I thank Mother Rosario for that.

I linger with those demented women a while only to be confronted by an altogether unfamiliar memory. Mother Rosario stands in the convent parlour, her head bowed, listening to the archdeacon who stands at some distance from her. His face is angular, full of resolution. I am trying to work out how I come to be in possession of this memory when it dawns on me that I was there with them, sitting rigidly beside the parlour window, swerving dangerously from one desperate thought to the next. Half-delirious with fear, I dally with an impulse to push my hands through the large gleaming pane. With all my might I will myself to die, imagining as I do that I hear Daddo's voice, hear him storming across the hall towards the parlour.

'Nora. Come on. Quick with you, into the car.'

Light-headed with relief I stand up, walk towards the parlour door.

Neither Mother Rosario nor the archdeacon moves. The weight of the world masses in my head, slips slowly down through me and lodges in my feet. I look down, expect to see them swelling.

'Nora, what's keeping you.' It's Daddo's voice again, but far away, disappearing fast.

My feet, now so heavy, are anchored firmly to the ground. I cannot budge them. I hear a car door slam, then feel my knees buckle.

'Nora,' Mother Rosario says gently, leaning over me, the small space between us darkening as her veil falls to both sides of my face. I examine her, unsure of how she came to be there. I close my eyes when I realize I'm lying on the parlour floor.

'You've . . . you'll be all right, Nora.' Her voice is liquidy, kindness fusing the words together, but her face is rigid with alarm.

The cushion under my head has a sulphury smell that saps every last ounce of my concentration. I turn a little, watch the wavering contours of the petrol-green brocade merge queasily into each other then decoagolate like sour milk. Through the blinding shine of the parlour I see the archdeacon looking out the window, twisting his immaculately clean hands behind his back.

'Water. You need a drink. I'll be back shortly.' Mother Rosario straightens to her full height, disappears into the changing light.

The archdeacon is still looking out the window, raising his heels off the parquet floor, swaying forwards and backwards rhythmically. I hope with every fibre of my returning strength that he will not look around. Among my floating thoughts is the absurd idea that he does not know I have fainted and am lying on the parlour floor, that he must be protected from finding me splayed out in this unseemly way. In that same instant, I feel a turning, heaving movement inside. I clutch my swollen stomach, try to contain the movement, gasping as the baby turns. All my attention is still focused on the arch-deacon, willing him not to look around. Then the baby's movements ease, slowing to an occasional fluttery jab. Some-where in the distance I hear a door close, the first of a series of distinctly everyday sounds.

'Nora, your head, lift your head.' Mother Rosario edges her hand in under my neck. 'A bit more.'

I sip the water she is dribbling into my mouth, allow her to help me up and lead me back to where I was sitting before I heard, before I imagined I heard, Daddo's voice.

As soon as I am seated, the archdeacon swings around, lips drawn closely together, a sense of purpose about him. He clears his throat as if he is about to speak but then just tilts his head in the direction of the door, indicating his intention to leave. Mother Rosario nods her understanding so vigorously that the large crucifix pinned to the outer layer of her habit bounces back and forth on her bosom. He approaches, heels clacking across the parquet floor, hand outstretched. I fail to see that he wants to shake hands with me, have to be prompted by Mother Rosario, nudged – and even then am so slow off the mark that she lifts my hand to meet his. I drift back to the edge of consciousness again, idling on the slithery carbolic feel of his skin, his thin, watery smile.

I pause now to consider him, intrigued by how still he remains. I look into his face, close up, like I might into that of a notorious criminal in a waxwork museum. I expect to find malice, cruelty, something along those lines. But all I see is the tight, steadfast expression of a man whose greatest crime will always be silence.

That encounter in the parlour, excavated in one unbroken piece, tumbles forward like a great boulder, bringing with it an avalanche of other scenes, other facts.

Before he leaves the parlour; the archdeacon raises his eyebrows a fraction, and Mother Rosario follows him out. They stand outside the open door, their elongated shadows overlapping incongruously on the parlour floor. Now and then the archdeacon's flustered whispers break sharply into recognizable words . . . 'at stake', 'essential'. In an offhand way, I set about filling in the gaps between these stray words but give up before long.

When Mother Rosario returns she kneels down beside me, places her elbows on the arm-rest of my chair and joins her hands in silent prayer. I look at her tightly shut eyes, her quivering lips, ashamed to be considered in need of such pleading prayer.

She eventually crosses herself, speaking the finishing words aloud, '. . . the Father, the Son and the Holy Ghost.'

There is an instant, passed before I can fully register it, when I think I will be able to hold back the great deluge of tears welling in the back of my throat. I think of Templeard, of Ammie reading aloud on the landing. I hear her lower her voice at a sad turn in the story, holding my breath as I raise my hands to cover the tears scorching down my cheeks.

Mother Rosario stands up, her habit falling into place like a rising sail.

I must stop here. Catch her as she is, in full flight across the parlour to the window with her hands clamped firmly to both sides of her head. I want to shout down through the years at her, order her to speak, certain now that she knew enough to tell me I was not responsible for what had happened. And that, little as it seems now, would have been a formidable ally in the long battle I went on to wage against the legacy of it all.

She stands looking out of the window, her hands still pressed to her ears, loosening slowly and falling to her sides. She seems far away, cut off by the fence of white sunlight which divides the room.

'Nora,' she speaks without turning around. 'You have acute anaemia.'

I'm not sure if I ought to respond or not.

Hear her say the words again. 'Acute anaemia.'

The words come spinning towards me. Acute anaemia. I seize them as a drowning person would a life belt. Hang on tenaciously. I do not know what acute anaemia is. All I know is I am very pleased to have it, very pleased to enter an illusory world where for the time being my pregnancy fades into the background, teetering on the verge of becoming a misdiagnosis.

'The infirmary, straight away.' Mother Rosario is her familiar self again, her voice full of authority, words clipped and released mechanically.

I could, I suppose, let her have her say now, allow her to tell me she was every bit as frightened as I was. But I sense danger in that type of generosity, see it as a step toward a kind of fatalism which in itself breeds silence. The hard, insoluble fact remains, there was something very wrong at the heart of it all.

7

There are five wrought-iron beds in the infirmary; all empty. A slate grey bedspread and a slack, caseless pillow on each gives the place a penitential look. In the corner there is a life-size statue of the Blessed Virgin, carried, Sister Alphonse the cleaning nun tells me, from the side altar in the chapel during the influenza epidemic in 1918. Four girls died in one night during that epidemic, eleven in all before the then Mother Prioress ordered the statue to be brought up. And not one after. Sister Alphonse tells the story every day, chants the names of the dead girls as she polishes. Describes each of them in such minute detail that they become familiar, stealing back late into the night to keep me company. Welcome, and envied.

I don't know how long I spent in the infirmary. The final six weeks at least. And nearly a week after the birth. The days merge into each other, become one long, vacant day. Sister Alphonse cleaning, cleaning, cleaning. Meals brought and left by a thick-set girl about my own age, who stares at me from beneath heavy, black brows. The chapel bell rings out so often that its burly pounding lingers in the room all day. Mother Rosario comes and goes, monitoring my acute anaemia. Every morning she leaves a bowl of disintegrating prunes by my bedside and peers into it whenever she returns during the day.

Flossie, one year ahead of me and Margaret, two behind, come on Saturday afternoons, escorted up to the infirmary by Mother Rosario. She stays with us, rearranging the May altar on the high table in front of the statue. The linen cloth is changed and the moist, freshly cut flowers she brings bundled in newspaper are placed, one by one, in a brass vase. Daffodils, lilac, bluebells, lily-of-the-valley, a lavish tribute to purity, a constant reminder of all that I have lost.

Flossie and Margaret sit at the edge of my bed, talking of this and that, each topic trickling to a close before it gets properly under way.

The summer. Holidays. Would I be better?

'Please God,' Mother Rosario says, smiling at them.

Flossie swings around, looks directly at her, taken aback by the warmth in her voice, then turns towards me, registers her suspicion, her face bunched into a quizzical grimace. I shrug my shoulders, stave off the deceit I feel in keeping so much from her. Once or twice I catch her looking at me, curious in a vacant sort of way. Would she, I wonder now, have asked more questions if Mother Rosario had not been there – how would I have answered? I would never have confided in Flossie, not under any circumstances. She was a mainstay in the life to which I was determined to return. I longed, all day, every day, to be safely back there with her, with everyone, just as before.

They brought Ammie's letters with them on those Saturday visits. One each week . . . 'Dear Flossie, Nora and Margaret . . .' Everyday news from Templeard, related with that dreamy detachment which marked much of Ammie's commentary on what went on around her in the house. But when it came to describing the changing skies or the grazing cattle or whatever she observed from the landing window, she could draw us back instantly, root us so firmly in Templeard that while we read, heads bunched tightly together, we lost all sense of being elsewhere.

Flossie and Margaret left Ammie's letters with me in the infirmary and I pored over them, soaked up her delight in the arrival of summer. I followed the first butterfly, whose flight path she meticulously charted in her long, dramatically slanted hand. Chased after it through the apple trees, over the orchard stile and down the slope to the low fields, breathless without ever moving a single limb. She told me she had had anaemia when she was my age, had often fainted in Mass. The holidays, fresh air, sunshine, would cure it. In the mean time I was to take a tablespoon, every day, of the rose-hip syrup she sent wrapped in layers and layers of old newspaper.

I do not know for certain when she became aware of what was going on.

'Your parents are good people, Nora.' Parting words from Mother Rosario on the day I was due to leave the infirmary. 'They understand the importance of keeping this matter . . .'

I nod, slowly at first, then rapidly, hoping she will abandon her search for a more concrete way of telling me they know.

Somewhere at the back of my mind I have the idea that it was Mother Rosario who told them, a scene – the three of them in the convent parlour together – from which I fled in terror the instant it crossed my horizon. Looking at it carefully now, it seems very unlikely that it ever took place, inconceivable that Daddo could have been so silenced by a woman, however authoritative and commanding, however well the hallmarks of her gender were concealed. It makes much more sense to suppose that it was the archdeacon who told him, citing an even higher authority in making his case for absolute silence. Then Daddo would have told Ammie. How the archdeacon came to know it in the first place is a matter for conjecture but conjecture within the bounds of a few stark facts which point to a plausible source.

Daddo said nothing, nothing at all, when he came to bring us home for the holidays. He just drove along through the dappled light cast by the thickening hedge rows, his window wide open. Margaret is in the front. I'm in the back with Flossie, listening to him whistle 'The Gypsy Rover', his hair tousled and furrowed by the steady June breeze. I wait, imagining that every time he stops to draw breath he is going to say something, acknowledge in some cloaked, indirect way that he knows how far I have travelled from the life to which I am returning. But nothing, not even a furtive glance in my direction, so much his usual, good-humoured self that I re-enter that life, steal back as I had unceasingly hoped and prayed I would.

Daddo and I struck up a life-long bargain that afternoon, cordoned off the conception, birth and fate of the child, marking it out as territory we would never enter together. And we kept our bargain, kept it to our cost, venturing into that forbidden territory only once, seven or eight years later, and even then, so briefly that we were able to retreat without acknowledging we had actually been there.

I encourage Daddo to speak now, all these years later, look to him to account for the stance he took.

Nothing I could have done, Nora. Not a thing. Nothing anyone could have done. If it had been a layman, any layman, I would have known what to do. But a man of the cloth, a man who had already repented and been forgiven, gone to make amends in the service of God on the mission fields of Africa. It was in everyone's best interest, the way it was done.

But I have to be careful with the words I attribute to him. Spurred on by the affection, the love I still feel for him. I know I am inclined to cast him as the most reluctant of players, forced against his every impulse to maintain silence. The scene is now set to reappraise his part but I do not have the will to begin. And maybe that's for the best. There is a truth in my love for Daddo, forged long before we ever entered that corrosive bargain to leave so much unsaid. I do not want that truth diminished, however much it might help to unravel the sequence of events that summer. But despite my resolve he strides directly into my line of vision, stands there talking to the archdeacon on the gravel sweep in front of Templeard. And I watch while that imagined scene spins out further and further to include the other players, all gathering under the limes, then fleeing in different directions, their hands over their ears. Somewhere in the distance a voice is calling them back, a voice I trace to a now familiar image, myself aged thirteen or fourteen, swinging with my sisters from the paddock jump. Then, in what seems like the same sequence – my voice still calling them back – I catch a glimpse of myself fleeing from the paddock with my sisters, my hands clamped firmly over my ears, just like them.

During the weeks following my arrival home from the Psalms there was talk of war, of distant places, Czechoslovakia and the like. Aunt Cassie had a great deal to say about it all. She had theories about Hitler and Mussolini. Stalin too. And given the opportunity she would hold forth, predicting the course and outcome of a war that at the time seemed unimaginable. We encouraged her, not because we were interested in what she had to say but because of the way she pronounced some of the names. Stalin became *Stallion* and Hitler, *Hiteler*, an awkward jamming of *Heil* and Hitler. Mussolini became Mousellini. The fun was in drawing Daddo in, catching his eye when she mispronounced these names, making him smirk against his will.

In that and countless other ways I re-entered life in Templeard. It was a hot summer, the hay was cut and saved early. We, Flossie, Margaret and myself, spent hours down in the cool of the dairy, making sandwiches, thick slices of crusty batch-bread from the town, caked with butter and clapped together with a slap of ham between. We filled billy-cans with milky tea and stood back while Cassie, never convinced that we had put in enough sugar, scooped up a handful from the bowl and, fired by some clearly held notion of herself as an expert in men's taste, tipped it into the can nearest to her.

Laden with baskets and boxes we trooped across the fields to where the men were working. Once we had alerted Daddo to our arrival, we put the boxes and baskets in a shaded place and set out for home again. The journey back could take the whole afternoon. We sauntered slowly, often stopping at Fogarty's bridge or at the great chestnut tree down by Campion's march. Each of us had her own 'horse' on that tree, a low limb on to which we climbed, edging our way out until we came to a point where we could rock the branch, make it rise and fall like a galloping horse.

Margaret continually begged Flossie and me to play a game called IF. Make up a story, beginning with IF, each adding a bit in turn. IF . . . it started to rain and never, ever stopped . . . IF everybody who had ever lived came back from the dead . . . Sometimes we agreed to play, sabotaging the story cruelly when we got bored, as we rapidly did with most of the other games Margaret wanted to play. Flossie and I went in for composing letters. Letters of complaint to Cadbury's or Rowntree's, describing our disappointment with some bar or other we had supposedly bought. Letters of enquiry to shipping companies asking for information about cruises, describing the accommodation and service we hoped would be on offer. Letters we rarely if ever sent but which had us falling about the place in paroxysms of laughter.

If, in the course of that summer, I was troubled by what I had been through then I have no memory of it. I'm inclined to think, though it is not possible, that I had brought nothing of the experience home with me. Templeard had its own pace, its own way of denying the outside world. Even now, with the outer and inner gates flung open, and new owners, a young solicitor and his wife due to take possession in the autumn, I see that there was an outrageous cost to the life it fostered, one that was borne largely by those it considered it was protecting.

If I could see beyond the illusory happiness of that summer, I know I would find Ammie in her green basket chair on the landing, her book resting on her lap. Hers was a gradual voyage into vagueness, coupled with a reluctance to come downstairs which hardened over the years into a phobia. She had to be lifted down for Girlie's wedding. Lifted like an invalid, Daddo on one side, Ber on the other, Ammie holding her hat and smiling beatifically. 'Miles away,' Flossie said fondly, reassuring those of us anxiously watching at the bottom of the stairs. Ammie was in her mid-sixties at the time, as frail and brittle as a woman thirty years older. Nobody searched for the source of her decline in the many euphemisms used to describe it. Silence was not seen to have a cost, so her growing helplessness was viewed with a sort of distant pity, its source a mystery. Concern and wonder were voiced all right, but there was never a suggestion that it was a fate she might have been spared. And all the time my story, like poisonous gas, seeped undetected through the house, changing the course of the lives within it.

If I sift through those first few weeks at home in the summer before the outbreak of war, I will find evidence of behind-the-scenes talk, kept to an absolute minimum no doubt, but there none the less. Even the memory of a short church ceremony arranged for me after Mass one Sunday remains indistinct, relegated to the shadows by the trivial events preceding and following it. As I venture into those shadows now, I see something of the ingenuity of memory. It is as though it has fixed on an inconsequential slice of Sunday morning life in Templeard, recorded its every hue, breadcrumbs on the breakfast table, a mild, chemical smell, Silvo fumes, rising from the hot teapot, Girlie, then about four, pushing her plate away – these and other memories are stored meticulously to divert attention from what followed.

It was the last Sunday in July. Daddo decided, seemingly on a whim, that instead of going to Mass in our own parish we would go to Aughacorthy, a small church five or six miles away. 'We'll stop on the way back,' he promises, 'pick fraochans on Pollard's hill.' He is rounding up the scattered breadcrumbs with the side of his thumb, massing them into a little pile near the breadboard.

Ammie does not appear at all that morning, her absence glossed over so smoothly that it raises no questions. Aunt Cassie takes her place in the coveted front seat of the car where, garrulous with excitement, she talks about everything, the fine weather, the likely effect of war on the price of eggs, the Treaty ports, doubling back rapidly to amend what she has said whenever Daddo is anyway reluctant to agree with her. And she shifts about all the time, lifting herself a little to straighten her coat, raising her arm to shield her eyes against the sunlight, changing the angle of her pearly hat-pin. Daddo asks me to move the basket and the colander behind me, says they are blocking the rear-view mirror.

Straight away we are scrambling up Pollard's hill, bursting with after-Mass energy. Flossie has the colander, I have the basket. The fraochan bushes lie ahead, the sun-spangled hill alive with criss-crossing voices.

'Look, here. Much more here.' Flossie is breathless, unable to decide whether to continue picking where she is or join Margaret who, lips pursed and head down, has already half filled the jam-jar she is clutching.

I am reluctant to leave that scene now, to go back down Pollard's hill and into the dimly lit church where less than a half an hour beforehand I had stood with Cassie.

Ammie was churched following the birth of Girlie. It was around the time we got the Ford, our first car. We sat in it outside waiting for her.

Someone, Margaret I think, asked why she was delayed. 'She's getting churched,' Cassie announced with hearty acceptance, and might have gone on to say more if Daddo had not cleared his throat. That was the first time I ever heard the ceremony named, though I had often seen women sidle up to the altar after Mass and wait there until the priest came back out of the sacristy, dressed in a different outfit and holding a candle.

I cannot picture myself clearly in Aughacorthy church that Sunday morning, but as Mass draws to a close – *in nomine patris, et filii et spiritu sancti* – can feel Cassie's grip on my arm tightening. The others stand up, are ushered out by Daddo, Flossie casting a backward glance at us which stays with me.

And all the time, while the church empties, Cassie keeps a tight grip on my arm. Her head is bowed as if in fervent prayer, her eyes, straining upwards, are fixed firmly on the sacristy door. When the priest, gaunt and slightly stooped, appears her grip loosens a little, loosening further as he approaches the altar rail. Cassie nudges me and I stand up, walk towards him, quickening my pace when I see him beckoning me forward, his long white index fingers curling slowly. I want to turn, race down the aisle and out the door but whatever self-possession I have just drains away. I kneel down in front of him.

As he prays over me I focus on the intricate lace-work of his surplice, follow the latticed pattern obsessively, desperate to fix on anything other than what is going on. Now and then his words break through, 'Go out of this woman thou unclean spirit.' Words I trample across, racing frantically to wherever my thoughts will take me. To the sewing-room in the Psalms,

69

to the vestments on display there. Gold and green. I try to think of the other colours, bowing lower as the priest's hand comes to rest on my head.

'You are free now.' He pauses, clears his throat.

'You are free to partake of the sacraments now.'

I want to stand up but he keeps his hand on my head, pressing down with what feels like the weight of the whole world. And the sensation of weight remains, bearing down heavily long after he lifts his hand.

When eventually I stand up and turn to leave, I see that Cassie is no longer there.

The churchyard, bleached by white sunlight, is almost unrecognizable. Looks like an overexposed photograph of itself as I emerge, eyes squinching, from the murky interior.

'It's a scorcher,' someone says. Agreement ripples through the loose, shifting group gathered in front of the church. I peer into the blinding light, searching for the others. Hear their voices in the distance, over by the rickety shop at the far side of the road. They are eating ice cream. Flossie is holding the one they bought for me.

'It's melting. Quick.'

I take it, hurriedly licking the sides as we pile into the car.

Soon we are scrambling up Pollard's hill, bursting with after-Mass energy. Flossie has the colander, I have the basket. The fraochan bushes lie ahead, the sun-spangled hill alive with criss-crossing voices.

[8]

A letter arrives from Margaret at the beginning of August, accompanied by a typed list itemizing the furniture and household goods Flossie has given away. In brackets after each item is the name of the person to whom it has been given or, in a few cases, a question mark. A number are added to the end in Margaret's own hand, scripted to appear the same as the typeface. She wants me to sign a letter, to be sent collectively to anyone who has been given anything by Flossie, explaining that the goods and furniture in question are family possessions. I scan the list, see Marion Campion's name crop up in brackets several times, check to see what she has been given. The weather barometer, the hallstand, the breadbin. Margaret tells me Pat is furious, tells me neither of them can understand it, particularly as they have been so generous as to invite Flossie to go and live with them in the autumn.

I reply by return of post, explain as amicably as possible that whether we like it or not Flossie's right to do as she wishes with the contents of Templeard is absolute. It occurs to me to point out how hard earned that right was, to go through the years of work involved in looking after Ammie, Cassie and Daddo. But any kind of reasoning infuriates Margaret, she regards it as an aggressive tactic, often retaliating with wild, abrasive accusations.

She rings the evening my letter arrives.

'There's so much going on.' She sounds exasperated. 'Can't tell whether I'm coming or going.'

I try to think of a reply, any reply, but only manage to say, 'Oh?'

She waits, expectant.

'Flossie . . .' I begin.

Margaret cuts in straight away. 'She's having a breakdown if you ask me. Pat says it too.'

'A breakdown?'

'The way she's doling everything out.'

'They're only bits and pieces, Margaret. She just wants to thank people.'

'What do you mean? It's not only bits and pieces. I mean, would you call three spoon-back dining chairs bits and pieces? That's what she gave to that laughing fool with the van.'

'Who?'

'That travelling-shop fool, Kilcar.'

'Well she must have good reason . . .'

'It's all right for you to say that. You don't have a use for them. And no one to pass them on to.'

Margaret breaks the silence which follows. 'Well?'

'I'll try and talk to her about it. If she rings.'

'The sooner the better. Before you come, otherwise she'll have everything given away.'

I want the call to end. Suddenly I speak. A rush of words, outpacing the impulse to hold them back.

'Margaret, Flossie has given her whole life to the place. You and Pat have no business telling her what to do.'

Margaret shouts Pat's name, tells him to come quickly, then goes in search of him. Foolishly I hang on, fending off the feeling that I'm not entitled to speak in this way.

'He can't come at present.' Her voice is tight and officious. 'But I can assure you, he will have something to say about this. Something very . . .' And, unable to think of very what, she hangs up.

I wait for her – for them – to call back. Wait for over an hour, mostly dreading it but in a peculiar way half looking forward to it, somehow ready for the fray. When it becomes clear that they are not going to, I decide to celebrate. Two capfuls, Gordon's, a third for good measure. Ice and lemon. Before long I'm imagining situations where I might use my new-found mettle to similar effect. I conjure up an encounter with Pat. Bombard him with home truths. Leave him gaping as I'm whisked away by Mario Lanza to accompany him in *Cavalleria Rusticana*. And there I remain, a defiant Santuzza singing my heart out until exhausted I call it a day.

In the wake of that conversation with Margaret there was the first inkling of a wholesale change, a change I did not grasp fully until I arrived back in Templeard for the 'sorting'. All along I had hoped that by telling my sisters about those weeks in The Psalms' infirmary, telling them about what had gone before and what followed, I might open the way back to the closeness, the unquestioning trust we had in each other and in our world before it all happened. But the nearer the 'sorting' got the more difficult it became to focus on that hope. Each event from those dark days, once pinned down and confronted, not only lost its power to terrorize but straight away began to recede. It became a memory among other memories, holding no promise of change. I came to see that it was not possible to undo what had been done, but there was the future to play for.

Sensing I was on course to make something of that future offered its own version of hope, an unfamiliar one, but one I came to rely on more and more as I took possession of what had happened.

The facts of the conception and birth are far from tame. They shoot off at random, link up with other, sometimes unconnected facts. It is as if the collective wish not to hear them still has the power to thwart every effort I make to line them up.

Bishop Mulhall was consecrated in September 1938.

I repeat that to myself, not once but several times, each time trying to haul it back from the position it instantly assumes as the gateway to memories of his fabulous consecration ceremony, a magnificent event crowding out everything else that happened on that day. I have no choice but to let it unfold on its own terms, hoping I can steal into the margins. There, in the squalor of all that went unheard, my own story begins.

Bishop Mulhall was consecrated in September 1938.

The Mass was concelebrated by archdeacons, deacons, monsignors. Nine in all, moving in unison with the principal celebrant, Bishop Carmody. His great sequinned robe makes him appear conspicuously bulky, a herd leader setting a slow, solemn pace. The pews on both sides of the nave are overflowing with priests, a spread of starched white surplices, the like of which people said had never been seen before in the cathedral.

Standing in the front row of the choir, high up in the gallery, I watch that great armada assembling, see the dignitaries line up in the pews beneath, separated from the priests by one completely empty pew. These are men whose names I have often heard bandied about by Daddo and Aunt Cassie in the kitchen at home. P. J. McNamee. Alphie Condron. Big Jim Costigan. The organist, Mrs Mellor, craning as far out as is permissible over the parapet, turns and whispers a name to us every few seconds, too excited to notice Mother Rosario's unease at the stir she is creating. Flossie and Margaret are standing directly behind me in the second row, covertly urging me to look for Daddo, Ammie and Cassie, who we know are coming.

In between bouts of panic brought on by the thought that I am to sing solo, I try to locate them, but I dare not lean over the parapet. There is an understanding that we ought not be visible to the congregation below. Ours should be celestial voices, an ethereal response to the earth-bound avowals of the celebrant below.

And so it is. We enter the *Credo* as Bishop Carmody's faltering voice gives way at the end of the opening line *Credo in unum deum*. Take it to ourselves and fill the whole cathedral with it, soar above the congregation until there is nothing in the world except our voices.

My solo comes early on. *Kyrie Eleison*, spun into the heavens, then eased down slowly to meet the rest of the choir who join in at the lowest point. Mother Rosario stands in front of me, her hands gathering the sounds, her expression proud in a fierce kind of way. This is her finest moment. It is also mine. Everything the Psalms stands for is on show and even at that early stage in the Mass we know we are surpassing ourselves.

And on we proceed, wholly enraptured by our performance, *Sanctus*, *Agnus Dei*, words whose sounds extend far beyond whatever literal meaning they had for us, transporting us to the point of hallucination.

Out in the churchyard afterwards there is a sense of suppressed excitement. People mingle quietly, hushed by the magnificence of the ceremony. I stand with the rest of the choir, whispering as if I were still inside the church. The September sunshine casts long shadows, the congregation unfurls in slow motion. Sounds have an unexpected resonance, distinct like those on a winter's morning when a thaw sets in.

'Well. There's no doubting who can sing around these parts.'

It's Daddo, suddenly in front of us, handsome in his belted Crombie, his hair sleeked back. Ammie, a pace behind him, is smiling, as is Cassie, a pace or two behind her. Ammie's pillbox hat is the height of fashion. I make a beeline for her, anxious to show those who do not already know that she is my mother and not Cassie with her flat, brown beret.

Daddo and Mother Rosario approach each other. She is flustered, blushing a little.

'Sister Rosario.' He pauses, corrects himself. 'Mother Rosario.'

'Mr Macken.' She bows very slightly in Cassie's direction as she shakes hands with him.

'The girls have been asked to the Bishop's palace,' she announces. 'Invited for refreshments. The choir.' She raises her chin a little. Daddo appears startled, a jest to show how impressed he is.

'That singing came from her mother's side,' Cassie elbows her way in between them. 'The Mackens could sing all right,' she continues, 'but not like that, nor anything near it. And the good looks, they're from her mother's side too.' Cassie makes room for Ammie. The four of them look at me. I feel as if I am going to levitate with pride.

The bishop's palace, though not at all as grand as I imagined, has an air of sanctity about it. Even the leaves clustering to the left of the front door seem different from other leaves. Precious, just by virtue of where they have gathered. Decades of constant cleaning have eroded every surface in the hall to a similar texture. There is a smell of cough lozenges or some kind of medical ointment.

We tiptoe across the parquet floor, gripping each other's arms as if we were on ice.

Behind us in the porch, Mother Rosario is conferring with the nun who let us in.

'Straight ahead, and down the stairs,' Mother Rosario commands in an urgent whisper, ushering those at the back of the group forward.

There is a long trestle table set in a room connected to the enormous basement kitchen by a door with a grill at face level. It is difficult to know what use this room might have in the normal run of events. There is a smell of apples which I trace to the windfalls laid out on the deep sills of the two barred windows.

We stand behind our chairs in silence. 'A priest,' Mother Rosario tells us, 'is on his way to say grace.' To the right of each place-setting is a small, brown bottle of orange. The windows steam up rapidly and the smell of apples gives way to that of broth. Then a head appears around the door, surveys us sternly.

No one moves. It is as if we have been caught, fifteen stowaways deep down in the hull.

He crosses himself as he enters, bowing a little in Mother Rosario's direction. I do everything in my power to resist identifying the spilling sound I hear on the floor nearby. The hope that the priest will quickly begin to say grace is evident in every face, the whole choir as anxious as I am to flee from the fact that Denise Cotter, a friend of Margaret's, is urinating. There is no question of acknowledging what is happening. No question of anyone asking where the toilets are, not then or at any stage in the course of the two hours we spend in that basement room.

Directly overhead the priests are having lunch. The ordinary curates, thirty or so. In a separate room to the front of the palace, also having lunch, though on a much grander scale, is the newly consecrated bishop with the archdeacons, deacons and the like. Periodically the sharp creak of a floorboard shoots through the muted din above, reducing our furtive chatter to a whisper. Towards the end of the meal, the door leading into the hall opens again and there is instant silence. A priest with a flushed face inspects us one by one, nods when he gets to Mother Rosario.

'A moment,' he says across the silence.

Mother Rosario carefully replaces her chair and walks towards the door, her departure modulated to appear as if the decision to leave was made independently of the priest's request. Fumes of cigarette smoke suffused with a tawny, alcohol smell waft in through the open door. Laughter too, hearty in itself but thin and distant in the vast emptiness of the palace halls.

When she comes back, Mother Rosario's lips are pursed judiciously, her most pleasant expression.

'Nora, you have been requested to sing.' She points upwards.

'And Flossie,' I say without thinking, unable to imagine singing in a social way without her.

'There was no mention of Florence, just you.' Mother Rosario casts her eyes downwards.

All at once several voices ask me what I will sing.

'It can't be a hymn. That's not what they want.' Someone says, 'An Irish song.'

Unaware that the priest is waiting outside I join in, mention this and that song. 'Beir mé ó, oró bhean'. 'Sliabh na mBan'. The priest's face appears in the doorway, even more flushed than before now that he is smiling. I jump up, tell the others to wish me luck as I leave.

As I approach this stretch of my story, I am disarmed by how accessible it has suddenly become. There is something suspicious in the crisp, sanitized way events present themselves. I remain on guard, unprepared to let go the notion that this may be a ploy by memory to induce me to skip over what subsequently happened and have me sneak into the back of the chapel in The Psalms at seven that evening, late for devotions. Nauseous with distress, but first and foremost late for devotions.

The flushed-faced priest tells me I have the voice of an angel as we climb the stairs. 'The voice of an angel,' he repeats, extending the words to keep pace with his slow, heavy steps on the wooden stairs. The smell of cigarette smoke gets stronger, the voices louder. He tells me to wait outside the room, points to a highly polished settle, where I can sit down.

Periodically, one or other of the priests comes out of the room, disappears down the hall. Returns a few minutes later. Some smile, others look at me curiously. One comes out mumbling to himself and, on spotting me observing him, holds his index finger to his head, twists it and laughs. I begin to wonder if the priest who brought me up has forgotten about me, more and more convinced, as time passes, that he has.

After about an hour, Mother Rosario appears. Listens impatiently while I explain what has happened. Tells me Mr O'Connor, the school driver, has arrived to bring the first group back to The Psalms. Three runs, it takes, five on each one. Just then the flushed-faced priest comes out, raises his hand dramatically and slaps the side of his head with the flat of his palm. A light-hearted attempt at self-censure to which Mother Rosario does not respond.

'*Mea culpa*,' he exclaims, shutting his eyes tightly.

Mother Rosario outlines to him the arrangement made with Mr O'Connor. Points out, in a terse formal voice that Mr O'Connor is waiting outside. A second priest joins the group at that juncture, a man Mother Rosario seems to know. She reiterates our position, speaking solely to him, agreeing in a hesitant sort of way when he suggests that I could return to the Psalms on the last run, an hour or so later.

I never saw Mr O'Connor that afternoon. When he came back to collect the last group I had only just been summoned in to sing. He was told, I don't know by whom, that I would be dropped back to the Psalms in an hour or so.

The man driving the car, Father Whelan, whom I have only

met once since, has coursed violently through my waking and sleeping thoughts for longer than I care to consider. In some ways I know him better than anyone else, know him as an intrepid tormentor, someone I have tried and failed to corral, a man around whom I have, in one way or another, built my adult life. Turned it into a fortress against his incursions, occasionally aware that in trying to protect myself against him I have sealed myself off from the rest of the world as well. But now that I am giving him free rein, effectively for the first time, he seems confused and pathetic. Not that I feel sorry for him, not one bit. I only believe in forgiveness to a point.

The covers on the front seat of the car Father Whelan borrowed to drive me back to The Psalms are old. Light green, fading to grey except at the edges. The ashtray, clogged with cigarette butts, is fully extended. Directly above is a St Christopher medallion, magnetically attached to the dashboard. There is a hurley on the back seat and a folded travelling rug, Foxford – similar to the one we have in the Ford.

Father Whelan is humming 'Dún an Óir', the song which got more encore calls than any of the others I sang that afternoon. He was standing at the back of the dining-room, listening in a melancholy sort of way, his eyes fixed on the floor, arms folded squarely. His freckled face and shock of wild, sandy, reddish hair made him conspicuous among the sallow faces and groomed grey heads around him.

He is driving fast, a carelessness about him which I have never seen in a priest before.

'I'll tell you . . .' his face pains with certainty, '. . . there was something in the way you sang that.'

I shrug my shoulders.

He looks directly at me, smiles fiercely.

'I suppose you wouldn't sing it again.'

'Now? Here?'

He does not reply, says nothing at all for about five

minutes. I begin to wonder if my response was in some way wrong. Insolent, too curt maybe. By the time we get to Newmarket I have decided it was. Definitely. And I want to make amends, so when he says 'We'll take the Sixmilebridge road,' I say yes, straight away.

The yellow light softening everything in sight, trees, hedgerows, roof lines, gives way to a hard white light as the great breadth of the lough comes into view.

'It'll be a while before I see the likes of that again.' He tips his head to the left, to the steely white water flicking through the black hedgerows.

I want to reply but I don't know what he means.

'Six weeks from tomorrow, I'm off,' he volunteers, looking straight ahead, his face full of intent. 'Liam Whelan is going on the missions,' each word more charged with disbelief than the one before.

'The missions,' I repeat after him, pleased to get a foothold. He seems startled. It strikes me he has forgotten I am in the car.

'What would you know about it?' He looks over at me, seems to be gauging the impact of his words. Laughs.

I feel responsible for whatever is going on, try to think of something to say. I even consider singing 'Dún an Óir', thinking that my reluctance to do so in the first place has made him angry. We are not far from The Psalms, no more than fifteen minutes or so. I wonder if it is too soon to thank him for driving me back, decide it's not and am about to speak when I see his lips curl into a leer.

'What would you or any other woman know about it?'

Vaguely straddling my attempt to work out what he means is an urge to get out of the car.

'Thanks for taking the trouble to bring . . .' I begin, as we drive through Sixmilebridge, losing sight of what I am about to say when, instead of heading for Cratloe, we go straight on.

'Thanks for . . .' I begin again, feeling the words pass dryly through my lips.

'No trouble at all. Not a bit of it. Why would it be?'

I haven't the courage to ask why we are no longer going in the direction of The Psalms.

The silence tightens, becomes more and more taut as we tear along the narrow road, suddenly snapping as we cross the high, humped bridge just before Clonlara.

'There's a place up here a bit.' He is sitting forward, peering in such an intent way that his eyes, nose and mouth bunch together. 'Not too far up this stretch. A view of the river. Take the sight out of your eyes. We'd often cycle out here. Young fellas, out to get the bulrushes.' He glances over at me, then in a burst of dry laughter, adds, 'Not as long ago as you'd think.'

I'm wondering if I should say something about devotions, point out that I'll be late if I'm not back in The Psalms before half seven.

'We can't be far off now. Can we?' In a series of quick upward spiralling head movements, he surveys the road ahead, impatiently reiterating the question, 'Can we?' I feel I ought to know the answer.

Minutes later we take a right on to a narrow lane. A line of moss and grass runs down the centre, gradually broadening until there is nothing of the lane except two deep furrows. I search for a source of my unease, look at Father Whelan, see only his priestly attire, then look back through the overhanging hedge rows, sapling ash, hawthorn and elder closing in as the lane recedes into thick vegetation.

He begins to hum 'Dún an Óir'. I feel suddenly cold.

And here I come to a standstill, no longer able to keep events in sequence. Those few moments with the car chugging to a halt have already begun to break up, spliced through with all that is about to happen. I pause before beginning to pluck the cardinal details from the riot of thoughts in which they are embedded, proceeding as carefully as a surgeon picking shrapnel from flesh.

There is a clearing to the right. Father Whelan spreads the travelling rug on the ground in front of the car. I look on, feeling I ought to help but at the same time unable to lift a limb.

'Well, seeing as we have come this far we may as well sit down and enjoy it for a bit.'

A now familiar voice shouts 'Run.' As loud as I have ever heard it any time down through the years. 'Run, Nora.' And away I race through the undergrowth, quick as a fleeing doe, over the rickety fence and down through the clearing. 'Faster, faster.' I cheer myself on, savouring the sense of triumph I feel before I look back at what is unfolding, vowing as I do that this is the last time I will allow myself the illusion of escape.

'What's up with you? Sit down.' His hand grips my wrist, not tightly, at least not straight away. Not until I topple down beside him and am trying to get up, which I can't.

And I don't feel entitled to go on trying.

He starts to stroke my arm, continuing to hold my wrist tightly. His grin, taut and questioning, is bordering on rage. And still, not until my head is firmly clamped between his hands do I sense serious danger, a danger that immediately turns to panic as he pushes his tongue against my teeth. I want to spit, rid myself of the stout sludge with which he is coating my mouth. But I do nothing, nothing at all, either then or at any other point in the course of what follows.

Pinned beneath him, I try to stay at the periphery of the frenzied thoughts coursing through my head, grasping at those which lead furthest away from what is happening. I search for the name of the knotty stitch on his pullover, a fleeting moment of escape to the sewing-room. But very quickly there is only the terror of suffocating, shot through with queasy despair as his hand ferrets through the tight space between us. All at once I'm in the grip of wild, searing pain as he saws his way into me. And I gulp breath, bracing myself against the blunt scalpel of his finger nail, holding out for a fraction of a second only to find the pain has intensified, doubled in that scant respite stolen from it. Then, violently pounded into the earth, I feel the fulcrum of pain shift to my head, tightening until I think my eyes are being pressed out through their sockets.

Half dazed, I move through the aftermath of what I do not know how to name. I look about, feeling as if I have been abandoned by my former, familiar self, imagining that the person I was is lingering in the woodland nearby, observing me pick myself up.

I drift over. The rank smell of ragwort mingled with the whiff of woodland mushrooms is startlingly pungent. A small animal scurries through the undergrowth. I stare at the wafery bark peel of the silver birch directly in front of me, plagued by the need to go in search of the self I imagined I saw a minute or two before.

I wade into the undergrowth, lifting the dead weight of my foot to crush the tangling briars, suddenly overtaken by an all-compelling need to wash.

The car engine sounds out, a reveille in the wilderness followed by the quick, flapping wing beat of a roused pigeon.

Father Whelan, lurched over the steering wheel, looks straight ahead as I get into the car. He does not speak, not then or at any point on the way back to The Psalms. His movements are brusque and elaborate, every transaction, changing gear, lighting a cigarette, performed with aggressive exactitude. Now and then he steals a glance in my direction, each time routing the hope that we will crash, that he will be killed.

As I step out of the car back at The Psalms I begin to wish I had sung when he asked. Somewhere in my thoughts, roaming about like a bewildered child is an inclination to say sorry. But I cannot reach my voice.

He clears his throat, mutters something, drowning it out with a quick succession of engine revs.

Whatever power or will I might ever have had to say something then had been long since usurped. It was as though the greater part of my life had been spent in preparation for silence, not only through that ordeal, but for ever afterwards. And, all the way back I go now, blundering angrily through the world which guaranteed that silence, back through the small towns, Newmarket, Sixmilebridge, Clonlara, to the cathedral, to The Psalms, to Templeard. Places where everyone had their hands tightly clamped on their ears.

The church is dark and safe. Evening devotions are underway, clouds of incense smoke engulf the altar and waft down over the pews. When the final hymn ends the church empties. Most of the nuns and a few of the seniors remain behind to pray privately. I stay too, kneel down and cover my face with my hands, feeling its contours, unable to believe that it is not in some way mutilated.

In the course of the next hour or so the others gradually leave. Mother Rosario looks briefly in my direction as she sails down the dark nave, bows so slightly that I do not respond, fearing it might not be a bow at all. To my left is a large copper-brown radiator. I press the back of my hand against it, momentarily distracted from the thudding pain in the pit of my stomach by the tangy coldness of its ridges. And I follow the intricate, swirling lines scored into the metal, concentrating as though my life depended on keeping my mind fixed on those lines. Fixed on anything in the world except what had happened.

Last to leave, I go straight to the dormitory, timing my arrival as near as I can to lights out at nine-thirty.

Late that night, obsessed to near madness by a need to immerse myself in water, I steal over to the infirmary bathroom, the most remote in the school. I do not even consider the consequences of being caught. And there in the pitch darkness I run the bath, believing the self-revulsion I feel can somehow be washed away.

I soon come to see that it cannot, that it is destined to endure long after the bruising disappears, its deep roots feeding on the belief that what happened was of my own doing. Something to do with singing solo, with pride, with having a tip about myself. And whatever possibility there was of thinking otherwise in the years to follow, was dealt a mortal blow by the arrival of Father Whelan at The Psalms some three weeks later.

It was mid-morning. All the nuns, except Sister Alphonse, the cleaning nun, were teaching. She called me from class, told me I had a visitor, pleased in a simple sort of way to be the bearer of the news. I assumed it was Daddo, dropping in something, apples from Templeard, a brack from Cassie, as he occasionally did on his way to the mart in Limerick. I began to panic at the thought of meeting him, terrified that he would somehow see what I dared not look at myself.

Sister Alphonse leads the way to the parlour, her heaving limp slowing the pace at which we move. She wants to talk about Bishop Mulhall's consecration ceremony, about my singing, already a legend in The Psalms. But I do not join in. I cannot. Every last ounce of my concentration is focused on shutting out the events of that day.

She opens the parlour door and shifting her weight on to one leg, moves to the side, bidding me walk in. Father Whelan is standing directly in front of me, his voice booming out like that of a music-hall impresario.

'The girl with the golden voice.'

No trace of anything except goodwill in his wide, fulsome smile. He holds out a book, encourages me to walk forward and take it. I look back at Sister Alphonse, she is smiling too, a shy, self-effacing smile. I approach, inexplicably released from the paralysing fear which struck me when I first saw him.

'*Songs of our Forefathers*,' he hands me the book. 'And who better to sing them, than yourself.'

I willingly enter the charade, each step leading further away from what happened. Further and further until it is fully out of sight.

'Thanks,' I say, wide-eyed with interest in the book. Sister Alphonse sidles up and, in admiration, brushes the cloth-textured cover with the tips of her fingers.

'You'll have time for a cup of tea,' she announces, turning to leave before he has an opportunity to reply.

The instant the door closes, he strides to the far end of the room, then swings around mechanically, all the bonhomie disappeared from his expression.

'Nora, what you and me did was wrong. And no question about it.' He begins to move forward.

My head bows.

'You know that, don't you?' he adds in a kindly voice.

I nod.

He begins to say something about God's love, which almost immediately trickles into incoherence. Stands there, poised, an actor who has forgotten his lines, 'Anyway, I want to tell you I've confessed and got forgiveness.' He turns, goes back to the other end of the room.

In the pause that follows I grasp the first line of thought which offers escape; the car on the way back to The Psalms. Crossing the bridge at Clonlara. I lean over, grab the steering wheel, twist it until we are heading for certain death, straight into the water.

'The way it is now, what I've come for is to give you the chance.'

I am unable to lift my head, let alone speak.

'To confess. The chance to confess, in case you wouldn't want to . . . I mean, confess it to someone else.'

I will Sister Alphonse to return, keep imagining I hear her shuffling towards the door.

'Unless, of course you have already . . .' His voice is light with delicacy, inflected until it seems to evaporate.

I shake my head. Violently.

'In that case, if you . . .' He takes a confessional stole from his pocket, drapes it around his neck. 'No need for . . . just to say that you repent.'

The car, tumbling towards the water, hits the glazed surface with a ferocious splash. He is slumped over the steering wheel, blood dripping from his down-turned face. We glide through the muddy water, come to rest gently among the wafting reed roots. I watch the water-level rise in the car, wishing it would happen faster, wishing it would all end.

'Sorry will do.' He hesitates. 'Do fine.'

I nod, and when he does not speak, I nod again, several times.

He begins to recite the familiar Latin chant of forgiveness, Te absolvo . . .' reaching Amen in a hurried, slapdash sort of way.

I do not feel forgiven. I feel accused.

His face pains in a way that has remained all too memorable.

'I'm sorry. Sorry for the way it went.' He pauses. 'I'll have you know a vocation isn't all plain sailing, Nora. Not a bit of it.'

I hear the clatter of crockery, anticipate Sister's Alphonse's arrival with deep, physical relief.

'Now and then a fellow gets doubts. Goes through a spell of doubt. But God is good.'

He searches my face for agreement. I want to agree, but I'm unable to speak. I fix on the word *doubt* in an effort to work out what he has just said, sensing that it was offered as an explanation which I was obliged to accept.

Just then Sister Alphonse backs into the room, turns and puts the tray down on the sideboard.

I watch him drink tea and eat biscuits, bewildered by how at ease he is, how friendly.

Sister Alphonse holds a plate of pink wafer biscuits in front of me. She seems to be standing there for an eternity, a moment which will not move forward. And here things begin to fragment, resisting all attempts I make to piece them together. I do not recall hearing Mother Rosario approach or seeing her enter. She is just in the room, cool and detached. Father Whelan is talking about going to the missions, about the great task ahead of him. Sister Alphonse is standing demurely by the door, overly intent on showing she knows her place.

I scrutinize the scene, searching for evidence to explain why I think Mother Rosario has the measure of Father Whelan, why I feel so certain that, at the very least, she suspects some sort of impropriety in his visiting me mid-morning. But I cannot find anything, except perhaps her austere silence as he talks animatedly, almost euphorically about what he is going to do in Africa.

'Nora. It's time you returned to class.' These are the first words I remember her speaking, words I dally with awhile, still puzzled by the part she played, catching a glimpse – and not for the first time – of the wiliness of memory, its independence, the liberties it takes, the devious way it hangs on to truths too disturbing to confront head on. A performance I might easily applaud, except that memory is an incompetent judge, too ready to obey the often thwarted dictates of the world at large, destroying the very life it purports to protect.

Somewhere buried in the debris of it all is the birth of a child. I try to move closer, to say the words *I gave birth*, take full possession of the facts, but I cannot. I never saw the baby. I know nothing about it, not even its gender. It has appeared in countless different guises down through the years, a grasping, tiny-handed girl battling her way into my consciousness in the early hours, an infant trailing unseen behind me on the High Street, a dark-eyed young girl staring accusingly at me from the pages of a magazine. It can be a boy scaling the walls I have built to exclude him, a child who has never grown, curious about me in a ghostly sort of way. But mostly it takes no form at all. It's just an absence, not an absent child, more a chasm stretching between me and other people, a great gulf created by the habit of secrecy and silence.

It seems peculiar now that the birth itself, the delivery of that faceless child, should be so small a part of my story, an event reduced almost to insignificance by what went before and came after. I cannot remember being afraid, which in itself leads me to question my recollection of it. Nor can I remember any monitoring of the labour which, however short, must have preceded it. But then maybe giving birth is, as is sometimes claimed, self-obliviating, leaving only the vaguest traces of what is involved. I fix on that notion awhile, sure that I had begun to drift into such a state of mind when the two nuns, who subsequently delivered the baby, arrived. I catch a glimpse of one of them, a moment that has spun out beyond the orbit of oblivion, a nun I have never seen before, small, dressed in white, wheeling two tall cylinders into the infirmary, each with a mouth mask dangling from the brass dispensing tap at the top. The cylinders are a dull, copper colour, just like the radiators in the church and, for some unfathomable reason, I am pleased with the similarity. In what seems to be part of the same thread of memory, she enters the room again, this time holding a black scarf. She looks about, locates the only chair in the room and pulls it over to the statue of the Virgin. From what feels like a great distance away I watch her get up on the chair to blindfold the Virgin.

I recall few actual facts beyond that. There is just a burning, yellow confluence of light towards which I strain, craning forward for the mask one of them is holding inches from my face. The quasi-hallucinatory world I enter is both familiar and unfamiliar. At its very centre, like a seam of gold running through rock, is the kindness of those two nuns. Illusory or otherwise, the way they abandoned their piety stays with me. Powerful figures, strangely physical, forcibly absorbing the birth until I cannot distinguish the strains of my own voice from theirs. Then they are gone. Suddenly. Gone without trace, disappeared into the nether world as mysteriously as they had emerged from it.

In a new light, a tinselly June morning, sunshine spangling the edges of the infirmary curtains, I wake to the sound of Mother Rosario approaching with a tray. Tea, floury brown bread. A silence about the place that seems like a prelude to an important announcement.

But not a word. She leaves quietly, straightening the bedspread beside me on her way out. Thoughts of death and dying, of tumbling towards the water, fill all the vacant moments. And, in between, a sense of having being plundered, disgorged. The birth, only hours past, already receding into the dimly lit world of partly remembered nightmares.

I tiptoe away from the scene, follow the others into that arid world of silence, Mother Rosario, Daddo, Aunt Cassie, Ammie, the archdeacon, every bit as certain as they were that it is the only way forward.

It was years before I began to see that it was not a way

forward at all. Nothing seeps into the past from that arid world of silence. It is a sealed tomb where everything remains intact. But now, with that seal broken the events of those dark days crumble like artefacts in such a tomb, taking their proper place in the distant past. And so in the course of a single summer, I have become a spectator, a tourist – forty years on – at the site of a great battle. A quiet landscape now, but one which, in the blink of an eye, can become a vast, muck-sodden tract strewn with wasted lives.

[10]

I know the towns on the road from Roslare Harbour to Templeard like the back of my hand. It's a route I have travelled three or four times a year for over thirty years, its landmarks, church steeples, bridges, pubs, forming a back-drop to the same old thoughts, each a reminder of how unchanged my lot had been since the last journey home. But driving back now, for the sorting, as Flossie calls it, my head full of new thoughts, much of the route seems unfamiliar. There are whole stretches I seem unable to recall. Testimony perhaps to how preoccupied I was on all those previous journeys, driving along rehearsing what I was going to say when I got to Templeard, always believing that things were just about to change. I never worked out the details, just kept skipping to what I hoped would be the end result; a coming together with my sisters built on their understanding and forgiveness.

No question of looking for anyone's forgiveness now.

I suppose I wanted my sisters to see what I could not see myself, to acknowledge how deeply divisive it had all been. But now that I have managed to sink new foundations as it were, I don't want to go over it all with them. At least not for the time being. An irony, maybe, but I don't want their pity. It would just open up a new chasm.

I mull over that for a while, trying to devise ways of telling

94

my story without evoking pity. Soon I am drifting carelessly around the past, with whole tracts opening up. Years a new voice is loudly declaring safe to traverse.

I returned to The Psalms at the end of the summer holidays in 1939, three months after the baby was born, already adept at negotiating my way along the path on which I have stayed until recently. Mother Rosario was a formidable ally. Not one word, not a glance acknowledging what had taken place. It was business as usual at The Psalms, a world I re-entered with unrelenting zeal. Member of the Children of Mary that autumn, a prefect the following year, main stay of the school choir, a whole winter spent in the cold music room perfecting a version of the *Ave Maria* that would be nostalgically recalled by every nun in the convent when Girlie went there almost a decade later.

I wept on and off for days when the time came to leave The Psalms in June 1941. Just burst into tears, unable to hold back regardless of where I was or who I was with. I could not understand it myself, let alone explain it to anyone else. But I know now that somewhere, well out of reach in my waking hours, was the notion that the baby was still in the building. An absurd notion, one of a number of similarly absurd notions floating about in the dark hours, all possible answers to the questions I did not dare address.

Strange to say, one of the challenges of taking possession of it all, is the baby's age. A person in their late thirties, their life's course well in train. Whenever this strikes me now it comes as a shock. Of the many appearances the baby has assumed over the years, never once has it moved beyond childhood and only rarely beyond infancy. That is where it has always remained, banished on every sighting, not permitted to grow and take its place in the world as it surely must have done.

I cast around as I drive through these quiet towns, find

myself measuring the lot of those in their late thirties or thereabouts, trying to imagine what might have become of that child. But no image forms, nothing at all. Perhaps this is because I do not want to pursue that grown child, fearful that some day I might find myself faced with the task of disclosing the grim circumstances of their birth, or more disturbing, the sordidness and violence of their conception.

I had no plans when I left The Psalms in the summer of 1941. None beyond returning home to Templeard. The War, the Emergency as it was always called, was in full swing and the days weren't long enough to keep up with all that had to be done around the place. The statutory tillage scheme introduced by the government that year entailed growing crops never before grown at Templeard. And Daddo, a cattleman through and through, was unreservedly critical of it. He said it would be the downfall of Templeard, of Ireland. He said we would be better off in the hands of the Germans, every bit as enraged as he had been by the policy of withholding the annuities, which a few years previously sparked off the economic war and led to a total collapse in cattle prices. Daddo held de Valera personally responsible for everything that went wrong in Templeard during those years, all the hardship, all the setbacks. It was as if he, and he alone stood between us and the prosperous, county life which was our birthright. I recall him pointing to blood in the upper yard drain, the blood of calves that had been killed because they were worthless, telling Flossie and me that the only thing stopping him from wishing it was de Valera's blood was the fifth commandment.

I took over some of Cassie's jobs the summer I finished school, the poultry work, the churning, while she took on other jobs not normally hers. Chief among these was going for the messages, shopping. The Ford was out of action because of petrol rationing, and the travelling shop for the same reason. So cycling to town for the messages became part of Cassie's routine, often taking up the greater part of her day. Very occasionally Daddo brought her in the trap. Red-letter days for her. There, sitting opposite him, even prouder in hard times, the Mackens of Templeard, people of consequence speeding across the countryside, face to the wind, invincible. I loved Aunt Cassie, but without liking her very much, if that's possible.

The all-hands-on-deck spirit with which people embraced the Emergency gradually gave way to a kind of despondency which did not lift even when the war ended. I was all the time expecting something to happen. A hope which I think first began to ebb during the savagely cold winter of 1947. We were snow bound in Templeard for what seemed like months on end. Even the Tuesday night card games at Campions, no more than fifteen minutes' walk away, were called off as often as not.

I suppose what I was waiting for was the road to marriage to open up, waiting for someone to turn up at one of those Macra dances we went to or the golf club dos in Thurles. Anywhere really. And there were a few dalliances, as Ammie called them on those rare occasions she strayed out of the refuge of her silent musing and into the if-and-maybe talk Flossie and I spun out in the course of an evening. Those so-called dalliances, half understandings with eligibles, smouldered for a while, fizzling out before they ever took off properly. And how could it have been otherwise? I was, despite myself, holding back, always afraid that the secret I harboured would become visible at close quarters. Taking stock now I am inclined to think there is, in fact, no such thing as an absolute secret. Even those that never pass their keepers' lips are divulged in the way they mould those keepers' lives.

Anyway there was, if I had wanted to look, evidence that my story, at least a version of it, was in circulation.

Whispered speculatively perhaps. Denied, I like to think, by people who knew me, but nevertheless there. Relished, no doubt, in that it gave an opportunity to those who looked for it, to nod knowingly, to speak of how the mighty had fallen.

During the 1947 winter I frequently thought about leaving Templeard and going to England. Two girls I knew, and with whom I had kept in contact, had already qualified as nurses there. But as the summer with its long, busy days approached, I lost sight of that plan and did not begin to consider it again until those days began to close in, heralding the onset of another winter.

By Christmas I still had not made up my mind but was soon to do so, spurred into action by a conversation I overheard late one January night outside Dooley's Hotel. A brief exchange which even now, all these years later, still has a razor-sharp edge. It was at the closing stages of a Fine Gael fund-raising dance. Flossie and I had come out to the reception area where we had agreed to regroup with the Campions, Sean and Taddy, our lift home. Other people with similar arrangements were beginning to gather, collecting their coats from the cloakroom, standing about, waiting. Slow strains of 'Rosemarie', released every time the ballroom door opened, filtered through the broken, end-of-evening chatter. As more and more people emerged Flossie and I moved forward, ending up nearest the open front door when the music stopped.

Outside, crisp and clear in the night air I heard the voice of Alphie Cusack, a vet who we all knew, the man on whom Flossie had, despite assertions to the contrary, set her sights. And not unreasonably, because while he had the pick of the country it went without saying that he would choose some-one who stood to inherit land. So Flossie, if not the front-runner, was certainly up there among them. And the two of them had begun to talk a bit, joke in a gamey sort of way. I had seen him look at her several times that night, stare to the point of rudeness, but even more significant was the way he asked almost everyone except her to dance.

'Didn't see you inside,' I heard Alphie say, his back turned to us, addressing a man who had just pulled up outside and was opening the door of his car.

'What would I want with dancing?' the man, stout and big faced, replied, awkwardly negotiating his way out of the car 'That's for the likes of young blood like you.' He offered Alphie a cigarette, tossing the silver paper flap from the newly opened pack on the ground.

'With what's in there tonight,' Alphie flung his head back in the direction of the hotel, 'I'd have done better in a bloody convent.' Then, laughing loudly, he lurched forward to take a light from the match cupped in the stout man's hand.

Flossie laughed, a cautious bid to join in from where we stood a few paces away. But too cautious, drowned out by the chatter of the swelling crowd behind us.

'I don't know about that, now.' The stout man hummed speculatively. 'I was in the bar early on, saw a few going in. A few high kickers there all right. Didn't I see the two Mackens?'

'Hardly what you'd call high kickers . . .' Alphie drew slowly on his cigarette which briefly illuminated the paisley pattern on his scarf.

Flossie and I were on full alert, edging out into the porch, on the brink of letting them know we were there. 'I don't know about the older of 'em,' the stout man chuckles, 'but from what I hear there's no breaking in to be done on the other one.' He nudged Alphie, nudged him again, more forcibly, adding in a throaty neigh, 'And, as the fella says, no one'll ever miss a slice of a cut loaf.'

'That's news to me,' Alphie dropped his half-smoked cigarette, twisted it into the ground with his foot and turned around. The instant he saw us he realized we had heard what had been said. It was clear from the minefield suddenly stretching between us and him, from the way we had become visibly immobilized, turned to stone in the doorway with the crowds beginning to pour out on either side. Alphie took a step in our direction, his hand raised as if to say *don't move*. He then changed his mind, turned and guided the other man into the car, making quickly for the passenger door himself.

'Well. All set?' Taddy Campion's voice, directly behind us.

Incapable of speaking, I am relieved to hear Flossie say, 'All set.'

We pile into the car with all the urgency of people fleeing from a war zone. The conversation is intermittent, sudden bursts of talk about nothing, the band, the crowd, the food. And, in between, intense planning on my part, terror mingled with relief as I rehearse what I am going to say to Flossie when we get out of the car. It was an unprecedented chance to speak, one which, as we drove through the pitch black January night, I vowed to seize, boldly preparing one moment, recoiling in trepidation the next. But as it turned out Flossie, no more a trailblazer than myself, was plotting her own course.

'It's as well to have the measure of that Alphie Cusack,' I said as we walked across the gravel sweep to the front door.

'What do you mean?' Flossie's voice was tight.

'The things he and that other man were saying.'

'Oh for goodness' sake, Nora. Men go on like that the whole time. It means nothing.'

'It means everything, Flossie.'

She opens the door, tight-lipped.

'I'm sorry,' I blurted out. And I was sorry, profoundly sorry, believing that I was accountable for the way things were working out. It wasn't just the cruelty of those words or even the loss of Alphie Cusack, which was bound to follow.

We were, bit by bit, being silently ushered into the margins of a world where we ought to have been pivotal. And the truth is we knew it. It was there between us, binding us together in a barbed tangle while at the same time dividing us to the point that we could not reach each other.

'You're tired. It's late.' Flossie was agitated.

'But you heard what they said.'

'You're making a mountain out of a molehill. Now good-night.'

She flung her coat on the hallstand and went directly upstairs, quickening her pace as she got to the top.

I never felt the impossibility of moving beyond it all as keenly as I did then. I sat on the lowest step of the stairs, wish and memory mingling to force the car off the road and into the water at Clonlara, watching the blood pumping from Father Whelan's head, my thoughts racing forward to England and anonymity.

For a long time afterwards Flossie openly held out for Alphie Cusack. And, according to Cassie, frequently had Daddo summon him to treat one of the cattle when there was nothing much the matter. He came, saw to the welfare of the animal, then left, never once coming into the house. He spent years gadding about the countryside, as Cassie put it, finally settling down with a girl fifteen years his junior. A nurse from Galway. 'A doctor's daughter,' Daddo would say in a puzzled sort of way if her name came up in conversation.

'A girl with notions. Hard to please by all accounts,' Cassie would add if Flossie was there. Words of consolation, but too tepid. Far too tepid to thaw the resentment Flossie bore.

Flossie and I saw them a couple of years ago when I was back for a few days at Easter. They were driving in the opposite direction, heading out of the town as we drove in. Alphie appeared much older than his years. I said as much to

Flossie, expecting her to agree, but all she said was, 'I wouldn't know.'

I was offered a place on a nursing course towards the end of February 1949. The letter arrived on the first fine day of that year. Almost summery, it was, the whole world unfurling, hysteria intermittently breaking out among the starlings in the orchard. And Ammie, after a whole winter shuffling between her bedroom and the basket chair on the landing, downstairs, sprightly in her striped lemon dress. On days like that, bright, sunny days at the onset of spring, the windows of Templeard were always flung open, every one of them, a task Cassie took on with a mixture of defiance and celebration. The Mackens conquer another winter, still all there, hail and hearty.

It was against the background racket of that jubilant ritual that I brought my news to Ammie. She was repairing the frayed edge of an ancient deckchair, smiling blithely as she gathered the stray threads together. Her expression did not change when I told her my plans. She just nodded indulgently, closing her eyes lightly. Then, as though escaping briefly from an all-consuming preoccupation, said, 'Nora, you are doing the right thing. I'm sure of it. Certain sure.'

From under a great tangle of wool in her sewing basket she produced a black velvet evening bag and folded my hand around the ornate clasp, holding it tightly until I made a move to pull it away. The bag was full of jewellery, pieces I knew and loved, her amethyst necklace, pearl earrings, silver locket and much more besides. I scooped them up, about to speak when she raised her index finger to her lips.

'Shhh . . .' she whispered, alarm filling her eyes when she saw that I would not be silenced.

'This is your jewellery . . .'

'Nora, please, not now. Just take it, take it.' The begging strain in her voice intensified. 'Please, Nora, no more, not now.'

Forays into the present, like that, were few and far between by then. I think she had to save up whatever it took to make them, hoard her diminishing ability to engage with us until her need to use it was absolute. Though only in her mid-fifties at the time, no older than I am today, she had decided to bow out. But it was such a slow retreat that neither Daddo nor Cassie made anything of it until later, much later, by which stage she was totally out of reach.

If I had the chance to speak with one person, now dead, I would choose her. No question about that. Just an hour or two, walking the low fields listening to her story, telling her mine, knowing that at the centre of both the same events festered.

I left Ammie and walked away with the evening bag, struggling to hold back tears already scorching down my cheeks. Then swung around, prompted by an impulse to rush back, stopping when I saw her there, smiling beatifically, waving as if from the end of a pier, my ship a speck on her horizon.

I then decided to tell Daddo the news, follow him down to Fogarty's field where, shortly before the post arrived, he had gone to inspect drainage work.

I spotted him from the wooden stile at the end of the orchard, stomping along in the distance, flocks of plovers taking flight before him, the squelch of his boots in the soggy ground growing audible as I got near.

'Daddo,' I called out. He swung around, his eyes bright and welcoming, the empty, cold sky a great ark behind him.

'I got an offer. Saint Mary's, Paddington.'

'Well now, that's good news,' he said emphatically. 'Very good news indeed.' He continued walking, slowing to a dawdle as I got near.

'I'm going to take it.'

'And so you should,' he said, a clear ring of pride in the words.

'And so you should,' he repeated a few seconds later, his voice trailing into despondency. 'You may as well.' He spread his arms in defeat, pointing to the soil with his splayed fingers. 'I did my living best, Nora. You know that, don't you?'

I walked by his side in silence, felt the heavy thud of his step on the earth. Heard him draw breath tersely.

'There are those, and I know it full well, that wouldn't want you under their roof.' He bolted ahead, his clenched fists swinging. 'But let God be their judge. Just remember this much, Nora Macken, Templeard is your home and you'll always be welcome here.'

Not far away, Murt Rafter, the drainage contractor, was loading pipes on to the trailer. I prayed he would hear us above the rattle of the tractor engine, turn around, which he did, but not for a few seconds. An eternity, during which I unwillingly returned to the woodland lane, to the rank smell of ragwort, quickly plummeting to the familiar depths of self-revulsion.

He turned the tractor engine off, greeted Daddo, then pushed his cap back a fraction, throwing a glance in my direction. 'Miss Macken.'

Very soon we were back on solid ground, listening while Murt Rafter explained some difficulty or other he was having with the pipes. I stood about until I saw Daddo take a shovel out of the trailer and begin to dig.

And that was as near as we ever came to speaking about it, which, at the time, was nearer than I could bear to go myself.

I pull up at the outer gate in what I figure is plenty of time for the sorting. But I can see that it is already well under way. Figures moving to and fro between the limes. A big van parked in front of the porch, *Rent-a-vec* splashed in large, red letters along its side.

I had decided on the things I wanted from Templeard, and arranged with Flossie to put them aside. A framed print of Daniel O'Connell, the liberator. Ammie's basket chair. Cassie's letter from Eoin O'Duffy. Some photographs. A few other bits and pieces.

Pat, Margaret and Pat junior are dashing in and out of the house, loading armfuls of stuff into the van. Hired, it turns out, for their own use only. The house itself seems peculiarly passive, resigned to a virtual sacking.

Margaret, on one of her forays out, spots me getting out of the car to open the inner gate. She is carrying a fire screen, one of a pair with matching insets, embroidered by Ammie, what seems like hundreds of years ago. She holds the screen in front of her like a great Roman shield, calls back into the house.

'It's Nora. Nora is here.'

Flossie, Ber and Girlie rush out. Flossie first, her cardigan buttoned up to the neck, her smile a mixture of affection and shyness. Directly behind, almost falling over her as they make their way up to the inner gate is Ber, her face slack with relief, her own brand of welcome, tightening to delight as they get nearer. Several paces behind, Girlie prances along, her arms flung dramatically in the air. Margaret, watched by the two Pats who are manoeuvring a wardrobe into the van, cannot decide what to do. Slowly she leaves down her great Roman shield and follows Girlie, quick-stepping along to catch up.

They rush towards me with all the bustle and tumble of a circus troupe, their voices competing across the clover field.

Soon we are all strolling down the last stretch of the avenue and on to the gravel sweep, agreement in every syllable, a shared determination that this, the last gathering here, will go well. We bunch into the porch, tied up in a tangle of unfinished sentences, interruptions, half-answered questions.

'Tea.' Ber tugs me in the direction of the kitchen.

'In a minute,' Flossie answers, pulling me upstairs. She points to a big mound of clothes on the landing, tells me they are to be burned later, tips one of the many overflowing cardboard boxes with the toe of her shoe. 'All for the fire,' she says, pleased with the arrangement.

The whistle-stop tour of the bedrooms is cut short by Ber, her voice rising with urgency. 'Tea. Quick. Come while it's still hot.'

'You go down. I'll be along in a minute.' Flossie seems uneasy, fidgety.

In the kitchen, sitting in Daddo's chair, is a man. No longer an ante-chamber to the world, the place has become the world. He stands up when I come in, leaves his cup and saucer on the table and holds out his hand. He is quite short, but could be classed as handsome if he didn't have long strands of hair dragged across his head in an effort to conceal his baldness.

'This is Mr Rooney, Nora,' Ber says, matter-of-fact.

I imagine, as I shake hands with him, that Ber is just about to tell me what he is doing here. Someone from the auction-eering firm? The new owner? A furniture removal man?

As Mr Rooney turns his back to pick up his cup and saucer, Ber's whole body twists into a paroxysm of gestures. She points first at him, three or four fast finger pecks, then at the door as the clip clop of Flossie's loose-fitting shoes fills the hall. Girlie starts to giggle, partly drowned out by Margaret's ahems. Then Girlie, as though scalded from a gulp of piping hot tea, clamps her mouth with her hand, makes a dash for the door, barges her way past Flossie and lurches headlong into the hall, spluttering.

Margaret follows, po-faced and self-righteous.

'I want you to bring down those boxes. Bring them out to the orchard. We'll have the fire there. The other things on the stairs as well. The clothes.'

Only when Mr Rooney stands up does it become clear that Flossie was speaking to him. No one says a word until he has left, by which time I have figured out why he is here, though I'm by no means certain.

'Flossie, what's going on? Who is Mr Rooney?'

Simple and all as it seems, my question provokes something of a minor crisis. A sudden criss-crossing of glances, with everything coming to a standstill. Direct questions requiring direct answers were never common currency in Templeard. It occurs to me to backtrack, a route I immediately recognize as regressing into silence and isolation, one I will not take. And still I am unsure how to proceed.

'What's got into you, Nora?' Flossie asks, flecks of bemuse-ment breaking through her stern expression.

'What's got out of me, would be more like it.' The laughter prompted by this quip, chipped in unwittingly, escalates very rapidly, each new burst prompting a further bout.

We limber back slowly, loose, open talk already in the air. I take the lead.

'Now, start at the beginning, when and where you met him.'

Flossie grips the hem of her cardigan, stretches it down as far as it will go, and throws her head back in abandonment. 'I met him in a shop.' Straight away we are in the throes of laughter again, more than this kitchen has known for a very long time.

'All right, you met him in a shop, and he . . .' I falter, momentarily seized by an urge to tell them how happy I am to be sitting here with them, talking in this unguarded way. But saying something like that would require us all to stand back, take stock of ourselves. I have had enough of that to last a lifetime.

'All right, you met him in a shop, and he . . .' I repeat, picking up the thread of what I was saying. 'A shop, where?'

'The creamery shop. He's the manager there,' Flossie says impatiently, as if I should have known. I smile at her, more and more sure of my bearings in this world from which I have been distanced for longer than I care to remember.

'I took to buying the dog food in the creamery, three years ago when I found out that there were four-stone bags of it made. Only to be had in the creamery shop. Nora, I tried to tell you about him at Christmas. On the way back, when I went with you. In that hotel we stopped at. But you weren't a bit interested.'

'Well, I'm interested now, Flossie, so go on.'

'I don't want to hear the word marriage mentioned. That's out of the question. Jim is a companion. Holidays, that sort of thing.'

'What sort of thing?' I cut in. There is a very brief pause.

'Nora? Have you lost the run of yourself?' Ber seems genuinely shocked, but swayed by Flossie's hearty laughter, smiles cautiously.

'At least I won't die wondering, if that's what you mean,' Flossie bolts back, frisky as a gelding.

Our laugher resounds around the empty kitchen, filling every crevice, reaching near hysteria when Mr Rooney appears at the door, standing as if summoned for inspection. It seems that the very foundations of the house are shaking, our laughter a force unto itself, exorcizing all that remains of the life we knew in Templeard.

The two Pats appear in the doorway behind Mr Rooney. Stare at us, afraid to come in.

'Time to get the fire going.' Flossie marches out past them, orders them to follow, tells everyone to bring as much as they can, points to the shapeless turf basket, to a pile of magazines on the hall floor, to two old deck chairs in the porch. And off we set for the orchard, joined by Girlie and Margaret who bring token offerings, Daddo's bee-keeping mask and a faded red hot-water bottle.

On the way down, Ber steers me to the edge of the group, grasps my forearm and holds me back until we are a few paces behind the others.

'You should have been here earlier, when Flossie told Margaret and Pat she wasn't going to live with them. Not a meg out of either of them. And you know why?' She nods in the direction of Mr Rooney. 'He was there. All set to tell them what was what. But it didn't come to that. Thank God.'

I examine him from behind, the odd shape of his head, practically no neck, the flap of his blazer moving up and down as he walks, his grey slip-on shoes more dandy than the rest of his get-up. Not by any means a man of presence. Hard to fathom how he could have saved Flossie from anything, let alone Margaret's wrath. It strikes me that she and Pat had probably already got cold feet about the plan, but no point in saying so to Ber. She sees all men, even Mr Rooney, as omnipotent. The great enablers. A view hewn here in Templeard, written in stone as far as Ber is concerned.

'Did you hear the final figure, how much she got?' Ber asks

in a low whisper. 'A fortune,' she adds confidentially before I have a chance to reply.

I wonder, not for the first time, if she will go on being content with stolen moments like this. Or will she, one day, ask why she must always go behind the scenes to speak with her own voice. Either way, I see now that I will have to be careful how I tell her my story. Not because she is a nun, at least not directly. Her view of the world, shaped here in Templeard, has gone unquestioned. To challenge it now, point to the serpent in our Eden, might lead her to re-evaluate the choices she has made, provoke an unnecessary revision of a life with which she seems content. If I were offering a clear alternative, some sort of companionship then it might be different. But I'm not, not enough to justify an assault on her illusions.

Flossie turns around and with a fast scoop of her arm beckons us to keep up. Ber quickens her step. Then, over her shoulder, words smuggled through the side of her mouth. 'You know, she,' pointing furtively at Flossie, 'has a bid on a house in the town. A palace.' And with that she takes her place among the main players.

The orchard, enclosed by a high whitethorn hedge, has a cloistered feel to it. And grass growing so high that it tips the low-slung bows of the apple trees. We spent whole summers sitting on those bows, legs dangling. A world that memory goes on trying to mould as perfect. Stray thoughts from that long-ago cross my mind as Flossie pours petrol on the big mound of household oddments, papers, boxes and the like. Everyone stares down, peering as they might into a large hole in the ground, the occasional, empty phrase tossed in by Pat failing to dent the silence.

Mr Rooney hands Flossie a spivy looking lighter, which she awkwardly tries to ignite before indicating that she wants him to light the fire. We move back, further back as the blue-green flames shoot up, billowing out into great clouds of black smoke, darkening the whole orchard. The low furnace hum broken by the hiss and spit of the burning wood has a hypnotic effect, drawing us back.

When it begins to die down there is an uneasiness, a collective wish to keep it going.

'There's plenty more to be burned in the house.'

A call to arms from Flossie, followed by an instant response, four, five, six people making their way up the orchard, rushing back minutes later with bed ends, wellington boots, the bockety card table, mattresses. And that's just the beginning.

I help Ber tug the parlour curtains from their rails, bundle them into a big ball and run down to the fire with them. Up and back again, more and more stuff until I'm breathless, forced to take a break. I stand near the fire, my eyes beginning to water. I look up, and through a gauze of grey smoke see Girlie stumbling down the orchard, her vision almost fully obscured by an armful of old evening dresses.

'Oh God, I don't believe it. Six yards of tulle from Maloney's went into that. And the netting, just look . . .'

Girlie lets the dresses, seven, maybe eight in all, fall to the ground. She picks out the dark green brocade, a dress we all wore at one stage or other, holds it up to herself, pulls the waist line in with her forearm. Makes a face, lips coquettishly pursed, starts to sway from side to side, singing 'When the swallows come back from Capistrano . . .' Pulls the dress over her head, turns to me in playful panic. 'Quick, fasten me up.'

I pick up the scarlet chiffon, squeeze into it, take Girlie's outstretched hand, spin my way through the tall grass . . . *If I were a black bird I'd whistle and sing and I'd build my nest in the ship that my true love sails in* . . .

Flossie arrives, picks up the turquoise tulle, throws it down in favour of the eau-de-nil satin, all the heat of the fire in her face, her eyes gamey bright.

Through the flames I see the two Pats and Mr Rooney, arms laden, gaping at us, their faces full of boyish alarm. Looks as if they might drop their booty any second, turn on their heels and run. Three boys spotted raiding the orchard.

Girlie is first to throw her evening dress on the fire, me next, then Flossie. They deflate and crumple slowly, wisps of lemony flame rising from the edges, smoke spiralling upwards in neat white furls, each dress slowly losing its human shape. And we watch swathes of silk and taffeta frazzling to fine mesh then to dust, a sense that we are witnessing a cremation, the immolation of a life which had endured long after its force was spent.

Flossie is anxious to go to Campions where she has left the dogs and made arrangements for us to stay. I had planned to spend the night in Templeard, some vague notion of reclaiming it. A test, maybe, to see if the events of long ago might not suddenly rear up again and assume the tyrannical power they once had. But it's over, all over, a deadness in everything; in the embers of the fire, in the trampled grass of the orchard, in the gaping lurch of the house, doors and windows flung open. And inside, an emptiness, paper strewn about the hall, farm ledgers, cattle records, blue cards and the like. Nothing left in the kitchen except a picture of the Sacred Heart and Daddo's chair.

'When you have land, you have life,' he used to say gripping the tatty arm of that chair with his huge, work-ravaged hands. An axiom which no doubt held true for many generations of Mackens but one which Flossie has had the wit and the courage to disregard. There is something humiliating, unbearably wasteful, about lives lived by rules which have ceased to serve them.

We drive away, Flossie and I, the large, framed print of

Daniel O'Connell and Ammie's basket chair in the back, the Eoin O'Duffy letter in my bag, other bits and pieces in the boot. Flossie asks me if I'm happy with the way things have worked out to which I reply, 'I am.'

In the silence which follows I consider that question, extending its scope in a way Flossie had not intended. And I find myself thinking that I am, in the broadest sense, happy enough with the way things have worked out. But if, like Solomon, I were given a choice of gifts, I would not choose wisdom as he did. What I would choose is trust, a gift for which I would gladly trade every whit of wisdom I have gleaned on this journey.

Iwazaru

1

1945. In the centre of the Italian peninsula, a place to which people did not travel at that time because of the devastation wreaked by war, a young boy lay on a narrow bed, his eyes fixed on the ceiling, his arms rigid by his side. His age was known, but it was not known precisely. Some said six, others seven, and there were those who said he was a great deal older but had kept the appearance of a child because of his illness. But those who lived with him, and particularly Padre Ramon who tended him, knew this to be untrue.

'What can they know of the boy's condition?' Padre Ramon would ask. 'They know only what they hear from Donna Chiara.'

Every morning at first light, the blind Donna Chiara, accompanied by her daughter La Sorda, and her granddaughter Maria Stella, set out from their house in the lower part of the town and climbed the five steep hills to the House of Rest. There, Donna Chiara began her day's work, cleaning first the outside walls and working her way towards the great oak door which she polished vigorously with clove and orange-scented wax. On this, the street side, the house had three floors, but there were a further four floors descending to the rear, so it could be entered through a low cellar door from the narrow path which circled the base of the rock on which the town was built.

Donna Chiara had been a servant in the House of Rest long before the arrival of Padre Ramon. As a young girl, she had been sent by her father to work in the household of a miller in a nearby town, a man to whom her father owed a substantial sum of money. From the first moment the miller's wife set eyes on the girl, she feared that her husband would be beguiled by her great beauty. This fear was well founded, so the miller's wife set about looking for grounds on which to dismiss her. But she met with no success because evidence of clumsiness or sloth were never to be found in Chiara's work. Still, the miller's wife was determined and watched her continuously, hoping to find fault with her work. She had resolved that when this occurred she would immediately call her husband, giving Chiara no time to undo whatever damage she had done. When he arrived she would point out the girl's negligence, certain that he would accede to her wish and promptly dismiss her. But a whole year passed and not once did Chiara's work give cause for complaint. Then, for no reason anyone in that household could fathom, Chiara's sight began to fail.

Every day from then on, as the miller's wife sat opposite her husband at mealtimes, she would set about calculating how great a burden Chiara would be to them when she became fully blind. Soon she spoke of nothing else, beginning in her waking moments to list the tasks a blind servant could not undertake and not ceasing until the early hours of the morning when she was overcome by sleep.

Late one night, the miller, listening to her list these tasks, was seized by a great rage. In his torment he roared the name of Chiara and continued to roar it until she appeared at the foot of the bed. As soon as she arrived he ordered her to be gone from the house by morning.

All of this took place before the Great War, a time when it was not easy to find a position. Chiara went from house to house recounting the hapless circumstances of her dismissal from the miller's household and begging for even the lowliest of positions. But nobody wanted a servant with such poor eyesight. After much hardship and humiliation she left that town and made her way to the next one. It was in the course of her journey there that she first felt a child stirring within her. In a loud voice she cursed the miller and his household.

'What will become of me?' she cried, stretching her arms high into the air, cursing the olive trees and the fleeing lizards. And because there was no one there to answer she was obliged to answer herself. 'I will never again,' she vowed, 'speak to strangers of my great misfortunes.'

The first door she came to on the narrow path circling the base of the great rock on which the next town was built was the low cellar door of the House of Rest. The elderly housekeeper, unaware of Donna Chiara's failing eyesight or of the child she was carrying, gave her a position.

Despite her misfortunes Donna Chiara was more than able to carry out her work, and as a result was given responsibilities for which a servant-girl of her origins would not usually be considered. But her sight continued to fail and, long before the daughter to whom she gave birth had left childhood, Chiara was totally blind.

'What will become of me, now that I am blind and can no longer go about my work?' she would say, gripping her young daughter's arm and shaking it as she cursed her blindness. La Sorda, deaf from birth, felt her mother's despair and took pity. Every day she accompanied her to the House of Rest, and guided her up and down the many steps of the steep stairs, standing by in silence while Donna Chiara dusted and polished and scoured and scrubbed.

Their days were spent in this way for many decades, so long that neither Donna Chiara nor La Sorda could imagine any other life. Even the birth of a daughter to La Sorda in her fortieth year made little difference in the beginning. This child, Maria Stella, was from her earliest days brought to the House of Rest and held in her mother's arms while her grandmother dusted and polished and scoured and scrubbed.

The townspeople said that La Sorda's daughter had been conceived in the House of Rest, fathered, they told each other, by one of the newly arrived Georgians. These holy men, prisoners of conscience for many years, had escaped and fled their country. They were given refuge in the House of Rest where they prayed for a restoration of the old ways in their homeland. Some of the townspeople claimed to know which of the Georgians was the father of Maria Stella, furthermore asserting that La Sorda had been impregnated by him in the company of her blind mother whose unremitting ardour for her work was widely known. Whether or not the child had been conceived in this stealthful way will never be known, because La Sorda resisted all attempts made to find this out.

La Sorda, who carried her deafness like a heavy weight, did not possess a single trace of her mother's beauty. When she was spoken to her head would tilt to one side as though she were straining to listen. This led many people to suppose that she was merely hard of hearing and not totally deaf. Consequently, they shouted into her ear, confounding the distress which her condition caused her.

In Donna Chiara's inner eye, her daughter had the bushy eyebrows and the swarthy face of the miller, a legacy which from infancy she had taught her daughter to regret. Donna Chiara considered these features, as well as the shortness of La Sorda's arms and legs, a much greater burden for her daughter to bear than her deafness. It is not surprising, therefore, that when Donna Chiara learned that her granddaughter resembled her in every imaginable detail she was overjoyed.

'The child has been saved from the terrible fate of her

mother,' she would say, frequently calling people in from the street and asking them to describe Maria Stella's appearance to her. And as they enumerated the child's many attributes, her satin skin, her slender arms, her hazel eyes, Donna Chiara would smile with deep contentment, then prolong the account with questions, delighting in every detail disclosed.

Maria Stella was a happy child, whose fanciful speculation on a great variety of topics caused her grandmother to throw her head back and laugh. They would sit opposite one another, each with her hands clasping the other's cheeks, their words so full of the great love they felt for each other that those words lost any other meaning. When Donna Chiara left the house, guided by La Sorda, Maria Stella would follow behind clutching her grandmother's skirt, peeping out wide-eyed at everything as the three made their way up the five steep hills to the House of Rest.

She was a very curious child and would, in spite of her mother's hand-wringing and imploring expressions, wander away, searching out those parts of the House of Rest where even her grandmother, in all her long years in that household, had never been.

Much of La Sorda's time was taken up with schemes to keep Maria Stella by her side, but the curious child still managed to outwit her. So La Sorda tied a cord to the child's leg and held it in her left hand while with her right hand she guided her mother through her tasks. The peace which this brought, however, was short-lived. One morning as Padre Ramon passed them on the stairs he saw that the tethered child, in straining to go further than the cord would allow, had caused her leg to bleed. He pointed to the blood on the newly scrubbed steps and looked sternly at La Sorda before he continued his journey.

Demented by her failure to keep the child in check and already exasperated by her mother's criticisms of her, La

Sorda flew into a rage. A low guttural sound burst from her throat as she tugged the cord and pulled Maria Stella towards her. Then in her torment she clutched the child by the shoulders and shook her until, convulsing with terror, the child began to make the same inverted rasping sounds as her mother. They remained locked in this furious bond, Maria Stella with her nails deep in her mother's thighs and La Sorda with her sinewy hands clamped tightly on the child's shoulders, each violently shaking the other until the anger of the mother passed fully into the heart of the child and the child's fear passed fully into the heart of the mother.

Padre Ramon, who had reached the top of the fifteenth flight of stairs, halted there while Maria Stella, still swallowing her mother's anger in great spasms, began to breathe more freely. But when the child went to speak the only sounds to emerge were the tight straining noises her mother made. In her panic she went to shout, placing her hands over her ears, when instead of a thunderous roar she heard only a dry croaking sound. She squatted low on the ground and backed against the wall of the stairwell, pushing with all her might as if to burrow through it. Her neck stretched out, twisting and coiling until she came to resemble a swan preparing for flight. She leapt high in the air, opening her mouth wide and shutting it abruptly, her eyes rolling in her frenzied attempt to speak. But her words had got caught in her throat and remained stuck there like fish bones until she had used up every last bit of her strength. Then one by one they emerged, coated in spittle and drained of their meaning.

'The child must never again be tethered in this way,' Padre Ramon announced, pausing until his resounding voice, furling down the great stairwell, became a powdery whisper. 'She must be allowed to go wherever she pleases. This is clearly the will of God.'

From then on Maria Stella wandered wherever she wished

in the House of Rest, but was so humiliated by her mutated speech that she did so in silence. The only one to whom she ever spoke unimpeded was her grandmother. Once outside the fragrant warmth of her grandmother's love, Maria Stella's words would begin to thwart and buckle, twisting their way out through the pinched tightness of her throat like dough curling through fingers.

When the people of the town came to know of her terrible stutter they said that La Sorda, jealous of her daughter's voice, had, in a tormented rage, tried to destroy it. The blind Donna Chiara was thrown into turmoil by these rumours and would almost certainly have contradicted them were it not for the vow, made to herself as a young girl, never to speak to strangers about her misfortunes.

Maria Stella's stutter was a source of much entertainment to the children of the town. They taunted her, pushing her from one to the other, intent on making her call out. Battling with her inchoate anger she would move backwards, her head bowed and her chin pressed firmly against her chest, trawling for words which might bring their taunting to an end. Soon she began to avoid them altogether, violently protesting if her grandmother told her to join them at play. And if the matter of her attending the school in the town was raised, she would rush out of the house, throw herself on the ground and thrash the earth until she could no longer be seen in the clouds of dust she created.

So her days were spent roaming at will around the House of Rest, a place which had a great many wonders to engage the curiosity of a child. But her curiosity was not that of a six-year-old. It was neither playful nor meddlesome, but piercing, penetrating intensely the object of her interest. This was noted by several people, some of whom regarded her habit of staring at things as sinister. Her all-consuming curiosity, they said, was the result of being reared by a deaf mother and a blind grandmother, implying that because these women did not have the use of all of their senses, they had recourse to other, uncharted ways of knowing. These rarely trodden paths to knowledge, they alleged, had been passed on to Maria Stella, leading her to examine things in the peculiar way she did. But those who knew her nature well dismissed these speculations as foolish, asserting that Maria Stella had always been a very curious child. And there was, without doubt, a great deal of truth in that.

She would fix on an object for a long time, staring at it intently until it lost its familiarity. She might, for instance, stare at a pitcher of water or a loaf of bread until she managed to abandon the notion of it she already had, concentrating all the while until she formed a wholly different notion of it.

This had begun as a game two or three years before. Maria Stella, then scarcely out of infancy, had devised the game around the belief that there were wondrous treasures waiting to be uncovered here, there and everywhere in the House of Rest. She would search behind books, under chests and settles, high up on ledges, in crevices and corners, anywhere that was not immediately visible to the eye. Angered by how little of value she uncovered, she began to suspect that a different order prevailed in the material world when she was not looking, one in which these treasures could be readily located. To catch a glimpse of that different order she would swing around suddenly, hoping to catch things in a state of unpreparedness. But all to no avail, for the world as she habitually observed it never for one instant lost the semblance of itself.

She would fly into a rage when she failed in this quest. Those who tried to console her quickly learned that their efforts were ill spent. 'Wiping the tears from the cheeks of a child so firmly in the possession of anger is a fruitless task,' they would tell each other.

Then altogether by chance Maria Stella made a discovery which brought an end to this sudden turning. One day, whiling away the afternoon heat, she lay on her bed staring for an inordinately long time at the light bulb above her. In the course of her staring she began to see the bulb as someone might had they not known what it was. In doing so she momentarily lost the notion she had held of it until then. This discovery, that she could see an object on different terms, if only momentarily, was a source of great joy to her.

Having found a way of making objects shed their conventional appearance, catching them in their otherness as she herself explained it, she was never again seized by an urge to swing around suddenly. She did not, of course, unearth any great treasures in the new order she had discovered, but she may as well have, such was her delight in her power to unmask the material world about her

Every morning, seated on the smooth stone sill of the window near the top of the stairs, she gazed down at the passers-by on the winding path far beneath. Everyone who trod that path was woven into the stories she told herself. And like the objects at which she stared, they too were divested of all that anchored them in the known world and given new parts to play in the busy, noisy world of Maria Stella. The women walking out the road to the café where the bus stopped, the soldiers, the children, all clamoured for space on her canvas, distorting themselves this way and that until they had found a place.

Then in the afternoons, when the whole house had taken on the stern quietness peculiar to places of its size, she would tiptoe down to the infirmary room. Standing there, fingering the scalloped moulding of the doorway, she would listen, enthralled by the voice of Padre Ramon as he recited his fabulous stories to the stricken boy inside. These stories of evil manikins, stolen children, frogs and malevolent sorceresses made her heart gallop, made her long to go in and see them in the telling. But ever mindful of her grandmother's warning about the boy she did not dare cross that threshold.

'Never, ever go near the child in the infirmary room,' Donna Chiara had said to her, 'he has the way of a child who has been cursed, a child who will never know anything but ill luck.'

So Maria Stella contented herself with listening at the door, entering Padre Ramon's stories in such an absolute way that hours after they had come to a close she remained adrift in the world they conjured. This was particularly so with 'The Pied Piper of Hamelin', a story Padre Ramon told more frequently than any of the others because of the way it engaged the boy. On her way home in the evenings, Maria Stella would race ahead of her mother and her grandmother, tripping and skipping merrily.

'Stay near. Come back. Come back,' the blind Donna Chiara would call, hearing her granddaughter's footsteps disappear into the distance. But Maria Stella paid no heed. She was on her way to the mountain, following the wonderful music, seeing and hearing only mystery in the world about her.

2

'All the little boys and girls,
With rosy cheeks and flaxen curls,
And sparkling eyes and teeth like pearls,
Tripping and skipping ran merrily after
The wonderful music with shouting and laughter.'

And here Padre Ramon paused, willing the boy to join in as he had done every time since he first heard it a week or so before.

'All the little boys and girls, tripping and skipping ran merrily after,' he repeated coaxingly, eyeing the boy over the rim of his glasses, waiting. Suddenly the boy sprang up and burst out, 'All except one.'

Padre Ramon leapt to his feet. 'All except one, all except one, for he was lame and could not run.'

He drew a deep breath, bracing himself to continue, more convinced than ever before that the boy could be delivered out of the darkness. When he went to continue the story the boy sprang up again. 'All except one,' he said, delighting in the way Padre Ramon pretended to be put out by the interruption. And so it became a game, Padre Ramon attempting to continue the story and the boy interrupting, both delighting in their own, as well as each other's, performance.

Such a happy prospect had not seemed at all likely when the boy first arrived at the House of Rest. Carried in the arms of Padre Ramon up the many flights of stairs to the infirmary room, his limbs were taut and his eyes fixed in an unchanging stare. All, except Padre Ramon, rapidly came to the conclusion that nothing could be done for him. He was, they pronounced, insensible to the world around him, dead without having left life.

'Look,' Guido the disgraced sacristan from Reggio would say to those he brought to see the boy. 'Look, when I clap loudly his eyes do not blink. And his hands, they're so tightly clenched that I cannot prise them open. He has died, I tell you, he has died but death will not take him.'

For three days and three nights the boy had remained like that, his pallor so sickly that even Padre Ramon was intermittently overcome by hopelessness. He watched over the boy for hours on end, praying for an improvement. 'A change for the better, however small,' he was heard to beseech, 'will put our hearts at rest, give us added reason to rejoice in Your goodness.' Strange to say that when, on the third day, such a change did occur, it was not Padre Ramon who first witnessed it.

On that day, as on every other day, La Sorda and Donna Chiara reached the infirmary at noon. During the cleaning of that room La Sorda always took it upon herself to move the enamel bucket from time to time, positioning it within easy reach of the blind Donna Chiara. To her great dismay she noticed that every time she moved the bucket the boy lifted his head and looked about as though he had awoken from a disturbing dream. Unnerved, she ran to the doorway and from there, with one hand placed over her face, watched him through splayed fingers, closing them tightly when she saw that he was sobbing. Fearful as always, La Sorda rushed her mother through her tasks and left the infirmary as quickly as possible.

That night the boy approached her in a dream, moving closer and closer until his face loomed in front of hers, round and pale as the moon. She awoke panic-stricken, full of remorse for deserting him when, in his sobbing, she had plainly seen that he was in need of attention. Straight away she vowed that from then on she would devote herself wholeheartedly to his recovery, assuring herself that her mother would come to regard him sympathetically and so cease to issue warnings about the dangers of associating with him. This, however, did not turn out to be the case. Whenever Donna Chiara heard or even suspected that La Sorda was attentive to the boy she would grip her tightly by the shoulders and shake her violently, mouthing the word *cursed* over and over again, her white, sticky eyes fixed directly on her daughter as though she had the power to see her.

Yet Donna Chiara was in her own way tolerant of the boy. Never once did she complain of the hardship she endured in the cleaning of the infirmary room, though there was without doubt good reason to do so. Many times the boy had emptied the contents of his food bowl on to the floor and from there proceeded either to gobble it up directly or scrape it up with the side of his hand and forcibly push it into his mouth. If anyone entered while he was crouched protectively over the spilled food he stopped with startling suddenness, but did not look up. Instead he inclined his head to the ground, listening with great concentration as though he were tracking their movements.

Word of these habits spread rapidly through the House of Rest. People frequently gathered in the doorway of the infirmary room, speculating about how he would react when one of them opened the door. Then, boldly flinging it open they would pinch their noses while they alerted each other to the stench of urine. Angry that the boy had become a spectacle, Padre Ramon put a notice up on the infirmary door forbidding anyone to enter without his permission. But while this deterred them in the way he intended it to, it gave rise to even wilder conjecture about the boy's condition. He had, they said, fallen victim to a recurring illness as an infant, each new bout of which returned him to the precise age he was on the day he was first afflicted by it. Accordingly, they claimed, he was destined to remain a child for the rest of his mortal life.

The townspeople had fixed on an altogether different story. When they first heard about him they got the notion that he was a war child. There were many such children adrift at the time and this view of his origin took firm root. These children could be found wandering through the streets and among the stumps of houses in empty towns. Some had been reported roaming through places untouched by war, often hundreds and hundreds of miles away from their native regions, drifting alone in fields, racing in packs across plains, huddled in caves at night.

Some of the older people of the town told of one such roving group, forty or fifty children who, one evening at dusk in the summer before the Great War ended, came charging through the narrow streets of the town, screeching like sea birds. Oblivious to the townspeople, they stampeded across the square, raced down the seven hills and out on to the plain stretching westwards. Where they had come from and where they went was never known but their rampage was under-stood in an oblique way, by the very elderly who had seen many wars.

Accounts of how the boy came to be a war child differed. Some held that his parents had been burned alive in an onslaught on their village, a scene they said he continuously witnessed though it happened many months previously. Others claimed that his father had been killed at the front, and his mother, driven to distraction by her loss, had climbed on to a service truck and travelled north with the advancing army. If confronted with these stories Padre Ramon would neither confirm nor deny them. His only response was to aver, always with the same implacable serenity, that the boy, like all other children, was a child of God.

Padre Ramon's lofty speech, his equanimity, even the roundness of his head put minds at rest.

The boy, nurtured by the care La Sorda bestowed on him and the constant concern Padre Ramon showed for him, began to leave the bleak world he inhabited. It was a joyful time in the House of Rest, each day bringing a new cause for celebration as he laid claim to another attribute of the spirited, loquacious and inquisitive boy he would, in time, become.

Curiously, when asked his name, as he often was once he had found his voice, he said he did not know. This perplexed even the cleverest of his interrogators.

'Surely he has a name,' people would say to each other. 'How can he have been on this earth for six or seven years and not have a name? Even the most unworthy soul in God's great creation has a name.' And they might well have gone on posing these arguments indefinitely were it not for the fact that the boy had a habit of repeatedly calling out the name Angelo from the depths of his sleep.

'Angelo, Angelo, Angelo,' he would shout out into the darkness of the infirmary at night.

That was how he came to be called Angelo. Some said and many agreed that his name could not be Angelo. Why would he call out his own name? They speculated that Angelo was the name of someone he knew, perhaps someone in whose care he had been left and from whom he had been forcibly separated. Either way the name took hold.

Padre Ramon, who had initially sought a cure for Angelo by praying over him, progressed once his recovery was underway to celebrating the holy sacrifice of the Mass daily in his presence. Positioned as close as possible to his bed, he projected the ripe succulent words of that ceremony directly at him, convinced that Angelo would find the same luxuriant comfort in them as he himself found. Within a very short time Angelo had begun to hum in accompaniment, beginning at the *Confiteor* and continuing to the end of the Mass. Padre Ramon was overjoyed and doubly so when he realized that whenever he paused, Angelo would continue in his emaciated, falsetto hum to trace with uncanny precision the cadences of the ceremony.

Observing Angelo's love of repetition, Padre Ramon decided that in addition to celebrating Mass by his bedside he would recite a story to him every afternoon, starting with those he knew well from his own childhood. Before long Angelo had mastered the rhythm of these stories, but none more so than 'The Pied Piper of Hamelin', a story he quickly learned to recite from beginning to end without a single flaw.

La Sorda's approach to Angelo's recovery was very different. She went to the infirmary whenever her mother, the blind Donna Chiara, did not need her help. And there she would grasp Angelo's head tightly with her strong hands and look piteously into his eyes until the trepidation she found there turned to trust. She then clutched his arms holding them firmly until they lost their tautness, concentrating fiercely all the while as though she were exorcising the very torment which racked him. Angelo, sensing from the beginning the depth of her goodwill towards him, welcomed her attention unguardedly and in her presence took on the appearance of a child of his age. Whenever he spoke to her, she feigned the antics of a listener, nodding and grimacing as he recited the stories he had learned into her deaf ears.

It was not long before he took to traipsing behind her as she led her mother around the House of Rest, sometimes holding the tail of her skirt as a toddling infant might. And never far away, tracking them from behind pillars, from dark alcoves or from her outpost on the top landing, was Maria Stella. It was her intention to lure Angelo away from her covetous mother and bring him to play in the loft room, the only place she knew they would not be followed because of her grandmother's great fear of bats.

Decades before, while she still had some sight left in her eyes, Donna Chiara had undertaken the cleaning and ordering of that loft room. If in the course of her cleaning she disturbed any of the many hundreds of bats which clung to the rafters, she would, despite herself, begin to move in unison with them, throwing her arms out as if to fly and then swooping and diving with them. On seeing her mother toss this way and that, La Sorda – a young girl at the time – would try to restrain her. But this was an impossible task, for the limbs of the blind Donna Chiara would become supple and pliant as she moved among the bats, losing their usual rigidity. And besides Donna Chiara could not always be easily located, because once one cluster of bats had been disturbed the others would leave their perches in their hundreds, darkening the room until nothing except an occasional gap in the flickering blackness of their movement could be seen.

Padre Ramon, as well as many of the others who lived in the House of Rest, heard the great clamour whenever Donna Chiara and La Sorda went into the long loft room. But he did not consider it necessary to go up. 'Listen to Donna Chiara,' he would say. 'Such is her ardour for her work, that she stirs up a great tempest in carrying it out.'

He might have gone on saying the same thing for many more years were it not for the appearance of La Sorda, one winter morning, as he prepared to celebrate the holy sacrifice of Mass. Her choking cough, which he heard as she thundered down the stairs from the loft room, ended suddenly when she spat a flapping bat on to the white linen cloth he had laid out. At first Padre Ramon thought she had, in some inexplicable way, swallowed it and so he grasped the water cruet and began pouring water into her mouth, certain that she would want it cleansed. But she did not, and she spat the water out just as she had spat out the bat, struggling to speak despite her inability to form sounds accurately. In this offensive way, spitting out what remained of the water and gesticulating towards the upper part of the house, she managed to convey her alarm. Soon, wearing only his corded alb, he was following her as she bounded up the many flights of stairs to the loft room.

Once there, La Sorda left Padre Ramon in the doorway, deeply disturbed by the sight of so many bats in motion. Watching her searching for her mother in the flickering blackness, he became filled with remorse for the harshness with which he had judged her up to that point. Clearly she was a courageous person who cared deeply about her mother and was therefore deserving of his forgiveness for the blasphemous act of spitting a bat on to an altar cloth.

Hearing the great commotion overhead, others came up and stood in the doorway with him, no less disturbed by what they saw than he was. And there the group remained, gazing in bewilderment for a long time, waiting for the bats to settle. Shapes shifted and merged in the thinning blackness like shadows cast by flames on a wall.

As these shapes took on a more substantial form, each of the onlookers gave an account of what he thought he saw. Before long they had reached agreement, declaring that Donna Chiara was, as one of them had speculated at the outset, high up in the rafters and was being guided down by her daughter who stood beneath her.

As the two women approached the group in the doorway, Padre Ramon said, 'This blind woman does the work of three sighted women, risking life and limb as we have witnessed, to complete the tasks assigned to her. Surely she is deserving of great praise.' Everyone immediately acknowledged that what he said was true and applauded the efforts of Donna Chiara. Although she heard their words of praise, she was not moved by them. The great fear which had gripped her among the bats had left her stunned, her eyes bulging so far out of her head that its whole shape appeared to have changed. On observing this, Padre Ramon examined her in a detailed manner and saw that the fluid which permanently glazed her white eyes had begun to drip and flow down the furrows of her cheeks like tears. This he said was a sign, indicating that Donna Chiara had endured much suffering in the course of her work in the loft room. And feeling great pity for her he declared that she must not be asked to carry out this work in future. The blind Donna Chiara's gratitude for this kindness was evident to all.

The townspeople said that her blindness gave her an under-standing of bats and caused her to behave like them whenever she was among them. But while there could have been a degree of truth in this, there was decidedly no truth at all in their belief that she was drawn towards bats and had to be forbidden by Padre Ramon from entering the loft.

Whenever Maria Stella wished to avoid her mother she would go to the loft room. There she would devise games around the extraordinary things which Donna Chiara had stacked in an orderly fashion many years beforehand. Maria Stella, long used to her grandmother's warnings about the consequences of undoing her good work, was careful to preserve that order, even though she knew her grandmother would never again be in that room. So when she examined the curious implements or used them as props in games, she would always replace them in the exact position in which she had found them. The crutches first, resting against the wall in a long line, the callipers next, hanging from hooks, then the wooden limbs placed on the open shelving and so forth until she had replicated precisely the order the blind Donna Chiara had created all those years ago.

3

Every morning of his first summer in the House of Rest, Angelo stood on the steps under the great entrance awaiting the arrival of La Sorda. When she came into view, which she did at the top of the fifth hill, he ran towards her, his arms open ready for her embrace. And she, delighting in his joy, would leave Maria Stella to guide Donna Chiara the remainder of the way.

All day long La Sorda lavished affection on him, sometimes clasping him so close to her bosom that he all but suffocated. These extravagant displays of devotion did not, of course, go unobserved and before long there were those, meddlesome people in the main, who began to predict that Angelo would tire of La Sorda's attention. And while it is true to say these same meddlesome people foretold many things that did not come to pass, in this instance their prediction turned out to be correct.

As the summer grew heavier, building up to the great storm which every year ravaged the region, Angelo found La Sorda's incessant kissing of his face, her clasping embraces and her compulsive caressing of his hair, increasingly irksome. It was these excesses of affection, coupled with the growing confinement he felt in her company, which prompted him to steal away from her one afternoon and go in search of Maria Stella. By this time, Maria Stella had all but given up hope of enticing him away from her mother and was taken by surprise when he approached her in her observation post at the top of the stairs.

Each surveyed the other quizzically before any words passed between them.

'Why don't you speak?' he asked, disarming her with his forthrightness.

Maria Stella went to reply, but the muscles of her throat clutched the forming words like clamping irons and would not release them. So she continued to stare at Angelo, growing angry when she saw nothing in his eyes but her own reflection.

'Why will you not answer?' he continued.

With her mouth wide open and her eyes tightly shut Maria Stella tried to speak again, stretching her neck like a hissing goose. He watched her as if she were a street performer, unwittingly imitating her by extending his head from his shoulders.

'What is it you wish to say?' he asked, his voice softening.

For the third time she tried to reply but met with no success. Her humiliation mounted and would almost certainly have caused her to run away were it not for the intervention of Padre Ramon. On overhearing Angelo from the landing below, he grasped what was afoot and took it upon himself to reply on Maria Stella's behalf.

'She will not answer because she cannot,' he said as he made his way up. 'She stutters. That is why she points. She asks you to join her in play.'

Breathless after his climb to the top of the stairs, Padre Ramon smiled at Maria Stella, who did not smile in return. Instead she scrutinized his face, penetrating the goodwill she found there until she unearthed the deceit nestling at his core. But she was not distressed, at least not in the way a person unused to seeing things clearly might have been. She turned to

Angelo and, gripping him by the arm, led him up the three wooden steps into the loft room.

In the furnace-like heat of the room, they began to build a fortress with the crutches, callipers and wooden limbs. Very soon, Maria Stella was speaking unimpeded just as she spoke to her grandmother, and giving instructions which Angelo followed without question. When their fortress was complete, she urged him to take cover inside and then roused the bats until they swarmed around in their thousands. Hurriedly she took cover herself, huddling up close to Angelo whose terror at the sight of legions of swooping bats suddenly gave way to an excitement so intense that Maria Stella was moved to calm him. And so they played on until the end of that day, the first of many days stretching over the happy years which followed.

Over those years their games grew in complexity, absorbing Angelo and Maria Stella to such an extent that for long periods they lived more wholly in the fabulous world of their own creation than in the one woven around them by others. They used the callipers to join the wooden limbs together and so constructed make-shift people which became the audience for their performances. They sang and they danced, composed stories and acted out the stories they had heard from Padre Ramon. He himself often came and stood watching them play from the doorway. Sometimes he joined in, disrobing himself in the heat of the loft room and falling about with them until he was exhausted by his gyrations. Stretched on his discarded clothing he would still try to direct their play. On such occasions Maria Stella lost the power of speech entirely and had to sit among the audience, a position she deeply resented.

These years of absorbing play were also years of prodigious learning, for Padre Ramon was an able teacher, and without ever taxing the patience of Angelo, or indeed of Maria Stella, taught them to write and read. But that, in Padre Ramon's own estimation, was of secondary importance, for his true ambition lay in anchoring Angelo firmly in the Great Story, the one in which he himself dwelt and about which he knew all there was to be known.

He embarked on this formidable task with exemplary skill, planning the best course of instruction. So when, for instance, Angelo asked where all the crutches in the loft room had come from, Padre Ramon did not, as an ineffectual teacher might, attempt to tell him the whole story at once. On the contrary, details were sparingly meted out, each one given over carefully like a piece of a mosaic passed from master to journeyman.

'The crutches,' he confided, 'were abandoned many, many years ago by the physically disabled, those who had suffered the loss of a limb or had been born without the use of one.'

Angelo's way of thought, in many ways no different to that of most children of his years, led him to accept that explanation as complete in itself. However, several weeks later he broached the topic again.

A less astute teacher would almost certainly have regarded such a lengthy gap between questions as indicative of a lack of interest. But not Padre Ramon, for his long years of training, and subsequent practice in spreading the Word, taught him the true ways of learning.

'Why,' Angelo asked, 'did those who had suffered the loss of a limb no longer need their crutches?'

'Because,' Padre Ramon explained, 'they were miraculously cured by Santa Rosa.'

This answer, like the answers Padre Ramon had given to Angelo's previous questions, satisfied him for a while, and once he had assimilated it fully, which he did over the days that followed, he naturally wanted to know more about the saint.

'We shall go and see her tomorrow,' Padre Ramon

announced when Angelo began to question him again. 'And if Donna Chiara and La Sorda permit it we will bring Maria Stella with us.'

The following morning, wearing his biretta, which he only ever wore when he journeyed beyond the House of Rest, Padre Ramon led Angelo and Maria Stella up the two hills to the main square of the town and into the church of Santa Rosa. There, the saint's embalmed body lay in an open coffin in the centre aisle, dressed in the brown robes of the order to which she had belonged, to which, indeed, she still belonged.

'How long has she been here?' Angelo whispered, his urgency bringing a smile to Padre Ramon's lips, though smiling was not permitted within the confines of the church.

'Many centuries. Ever since the time of the great pilgrimages.'

The children stared at her tightly joined hands, her hollow cheeks and black sunken eyes.

So great was their interest in her and the many colourful scenes depicting her life on the church walls, that when Padre Ramon announced it was time to leave, they begged him to extend their stay. He refused but they clung to the pew ends, resisting his efforts to usher them out. Aghast, they pointed to demons hurtling out of the mouths of portly burghers, to heavily clad women tumbling out of towers, to wailing throngs entering great furling flames.

The people of the town, though they had speculated at length about the origin of Angelo had never seen him before and they gathered outside the church, telling each other as he emerged how little he differed from other children. 'Not at all,' many said returning to their work, their disappointment evident in their faces.

On the way back to the House of Rest, and afterwards in the infirmary, Angelo plied Padre Ramon with questions about Santa Rosa. True to his purpose, Padre Ramon replied sparingly, sometimes merely shaking or nodding his head. Consequently Angelo's curiosity remained unsatisfied. He avidly sought out information about the embalmed saint from those in the House of Rest, and later when he was permitted to go further afield, from the people of the town.

In this circuitous way he strode eagerly into the Great Story, in time coming to dwell so wholly within it that even Padre Ramon who had led him there with such canniness was troubled by the intensity of his zeal. It was at this stage that Angelo again became the subject of widespread speculation among the townspeople. Many of them insisted that he was happy during that time, going about seeking out details of the miracles attributed to Santa Rosa. They reminded each other of his cheerful chatter, his earnestness, and above all his remarkable faith. But there were also those, a small number, who held that, like all growing children, Angelo had entered a world of stories and play, seeking refuge there for the seven years it takes to gain the strength necessary to embark on the journey after childhood. That he was not, in truth, safe in that refuge and therefore unable to acquire that strength during those seven years, was, they claimed, largely accountable for the fate which befell him. Certainly when the time came to leave childhood Angelo could not be persuaded to do so.

By that stage Maria Stella was no longer his great companion, no longer the cornerstone of his world as she had been for so long. Unable to hold out against her grandmother's pleading, she had agreed to attend the school in the town. And that marked the demise of the wondrous world in which she and Angelo had dwelt so happily.

On the day she disclosed this news he was crestfallen, and not in the least consoled by her promise to spend the time she was not required to attend school in the House of Rest. It was a promise she kept without fail, but instead of mollifying his distress it served only to aggravate it. Her absence took on a poignancy it had never had in the past, her presence a preciousness which inhibited their play. For many wretched months in the spring of what people generally agreed was his fourteenth year, he wandered around the House of Rest, dejected. He longed to tell Maria Stella of the depths of grief to which her absence drove him but was unable to bring himself to do so. And on he trudged into summer, only saved from the fatal strangle of loss by the hope that Maria Stella would once again defy her grandmother and spend her days with him.

During one of her visits, his distress triggered a complete abandonment of all self-stricture, a recklessness which led him to describe the depths of grief to which her absences drove him. Before long, Maria Stella was moved to tears by his words.

For hours they foundered in hopelessness, Maria Stella torn between her wish to please her grandmother and her wish to bring an end to Angelo's suffering. And Angelo himself wept copiously, his dilating nostrils and inflamed face a pitiful testament. They turned to the past, unaware that while they pored over this and that event of their seven happy years together they were building a bridge over their grief. Soon they were trampling boisterously across that bridge, unsure if their tears were tears of sadness or of joy. They pledged loyalty to one another, swore on their young lives to remain eternally true, each wiping the tears from the other's face while in quick succession they found and lost and found each other's lips.

No longer in the grip of uncertainty, they decided to seek out Padre Ramon and ask him if Angelo could enrol in the school in the town. Their laughter and rapid chatter filled the great stairwell and resounded throughout the entire house as they scampered hither and thither in search of Padre Ramon, swept along on the cusp of a spiralling hope which, when they eventually located him in the vestry, left them ill-prepared for his response.

'Under no circumstances,' he said, kissing his vestments one by one as he disrobed after Mass. 'Under no circumstances will you be permitted to do such a foolish thing.'

'Why?' Angelo demanded, a tremor in his voice.

'They have nothing to teach you,' he said forcibly. 'There is nothing they know that you do not already know, nothing of value that I have not already taught you.'

They left the vestry, devastated by Padre Ramon's refusal, plummeting back into hopelessness as rapidly as they had risen out of it.

The following day when Maria Stella did not arrive at the House of Rest as she had promised Angelo, he found himself in the depths of a darker despair than he could ever have imagined. Paralysed with anguish his breathing stopped for several minutes. Drifting in and out of consciousness, he saw before him the face of Santa Rosa, round and smiling as it was depicted on the church wall. He begged her to deliver him from the torment that gripped him, praying furiously as he struggled to keep her image before him. He continued to pray, fearing that if he stopped he would again be visited by these vile and wretched scenes.

Unknown to Angelo, the evening before Padre Ramon had taken Maria Stella aside as she left. 'You are no longer a child,' he had said, 'and therefore ought to know your place. You are the daughter of a servant and must not seek to influence the course of events in the way you do.'

In a single instant, a whole world unfolded before Maria Stella, a great tapestry of injustice, deceit and subterfuge, filling her with such anger that she spat directly into Padre Ramon's face, strenuously craning her head and gulping in spasms as she did whenever she tried to recover her lost speech.

Padre Ramon allowed the viscous spittle to remain on his cheek.

'To spit at me as you have done is to spit at God for I am the carrier of His Word. It is a profanity too abject for forgiveness. You will never again enter this house.'

Maria Stella hung her head in shame and began to weep.

The following morning he called Donna Chiara into the vestry and while he prepared to celebrate the holy sacrifice of the Mass, gave her an account of Maria Stella's conduct. Pointing with his long, scrupulously clean index finger, he located the position on his cheek where the spittle had landed.

'Look,' he said, at once aware of the folly of asking Donna Chiara to look at what she could never hope to see. Without hesitation he took her finger and placed it firmly on the spot while he impressed on her the grievousness of her grand-daughter's sin.

Desperate to make amends, Donna Chiara knelt before him, imploring him to make her culpable and so exonerate Maria Stella.

'Even if I was willing to take such a step, it would not be possible, for how can a sin, grave or otherwise, be transferred in this way?'

Now fully prostrate before him Donna Chiara apologized for her ignorance and begged for guidance. 'What will become of her?' she asked. 'To whom can she go to have this sin forgiven?'

'Only the Almighty can forgive this sin,' Padre Ramon announced, lifting the chalice and stepping over her as he made his way into the chapel.

Though profoundly troubled, Donna Chiara considered her granddaughter's exclusion from the House of Rest a blessing, and in her prayers gave thanks to God for delivering her out of the company of Angelo. But she did not reveal her satisfaction at this turn of events to Maria Stella, nor did she impress on her the grievousness of her sin. Instead, guided by intuition as she was, she set out to discover why Maria Stella had responded with such vitriol to what in her estimation were truthful, if harsh, words.

'He has shown you nothing but kindness and consideration, nothing but goodwill. You have lived safely in his protection and learned much under his guidance.'

Donna Chiara spoke lovingly, holding Maria Stella's face in her hands. But Maria Stella was herself horrified by what she had done and, much as she tried, she could not account for the grossness of her behaviour.

'He has shown me nothing but kindness and consideration,' she repeated, 'nothing but goodwill. I have lived safely in his protection and learned much under his guidance.'

She would, Donna Chiara eventually concluded, have to live with her sin until Judgement Day.

But, as with all encounters between Maria Stella and Donna Chiara, it was not long before the overflowing love they felt for each other made all else that passed between them seem trivial. It was a love so unreserved and powerful that it seemed to illuminate the space around them. As the townspeople said then and would continue to say down through the years, it was the salvation of Maria Stella. This was, without question, the truth.

[4]

Whenever Maria Stella reflected on the circumstances of her banishment from the House of Rest, as she did a great deal in the course of her life, the change in Angelo when he was refused permission to attend the school in the town took precedence over everything else. All the life drained out of his face, leaving him with the yellow, oily pallor of the dead, that same pallor which, when he first arrived in the House of Rest, led people to say that he had died but death would not take him.

'What are we to do?' she had asked him on that fateful afternoon, so perturbed by his appearance that she grew alarmed. And all the while, her grandmother's words chimed like church bells in her ears. 'He is cursed, I tell you, destined for all the unhappiness in the world.'

But then, to her surprise Angelo had replied calmly, allaying her fears, though not wholly dispelling them. 'I will ask Santa Rosa to intercede,' he said, clenching his fists.

Naturally Maria Stella found no cause for concern in this resolution. Many people, including Maria Stella's grandmother, prayed fervently to Santa Rosa. Maria Stella had often done so herself. She had spent many blissful hours enraptured by the scenes depicting the saint's life on the walls of the church. It was some time, therefore, before she came to see that Angelo's resolution to turn to Santa Rosa for help that day was of a different order, that it marked a new departure in his devotion.

Before it became apparent how ill-fated that departure was, great changes had taken place. The House of Rest, which had offered shelter to the needy for centuries, lay empty, the shutters of its tall windows slapping noisily against its flaking walls, its once gleaming wooden floors corroded by pigeon dung and the steps of its great stairs caked with rotting leaves.

Not long after Maria Stella's banishment, perhaps no more than a few weeks later, a delegation from the Holy See – five high-ranking members of the Uffizi, each with a black satchel – arrived in the town square and sought directions to the House of Rest.

The traders, keen to know what was afoot, closed their stalls and set out after them down the hill. They were joined by their wives and children. Others followed, swelling their numbers to a garrulous crowd. Rife with speculation, they gathered outside the House of Rest. Inside, the five clerics conducted the business which had brought them to the town. One rumour which circulated among the crowd was that clerics had come to investigate reports of the mistreatment of Angelo, whose peculiar ways had of late given cause for concern. This died down when it became known that he was in the church. He would, they said, surely have been summoned were he the subject of the investigation. A second rumour took hold, again not for long, that Padre Ramon was to be given an award, an order of merit for a heroic deed. But as no one could say what that deed was, the rumour ceased to circulate. And all the while, slowly gathering credence and destined to stay current indefinitely, was the belief that Donna Chiara, for a reason which remained unspoken though it circulated in laden glances, had cursed Padre Ramon, had used her powers to bring about his downfall.

These speculations came to an immediate halt when Donna

Chiara, guided by La Sorda, walked out of the great oak door for what Donna Chiara knew was the last time. Straight away they were plagued with questions by the waiting crowds but disclosed nothing, La Sorda because she had heard nothing and Donna Chiara because she had vowed never to speak of her concerns publicly.

No sooner had they left the scene than four of the five clerics appeared, their mouths tightly closed, their expressions grave. They surveyed the crowd as one, commanding silence with their solemn gaze. When that silence was absolute, the fifth cleric emerged followed by the three Georgians, rubbing their eyes, their hoary beards a wonder to the gawking children. And, in their wake, Guido, the disgraced sacristan from Reggio, smiling at the crowds as though a civic reception had been prepared in his honour. Others followed, perplexed old men who squinted into the sunlight, drawing back when they saw the size of the crowd. Then the singer, a distraught, emaciated woman whose grief-stricken arias had filled the House of Rest since her arrival following the death of her two sons some months previously. She, supposing the crowd had gathered to hear her sing, cleared her throat and stepped forward. But before she had voiced her first note, their attention was abruptly diverted. Padre Ramon, laden down with two enormous portmanteaus, stumbled out the great oak door. Haggard, and looking much older, he glanced despairingly at the onlookers before allowing himself to be escorted down the steps by the five clerics.

As these men of purpose made their way through the crowd, one of the traders summoned up the courage to ask them why the House of Rest had been evacuated.

'It is an anachronism,' one of the clerics proclaimed. But as no one knew what an anachronism was they remained in ignorance. Perhaps other questions would have followed, leading to a composite view of what was going on, but their attention was suddenly arrested by pounding footsteps. Angelo. The crowd divided as he charged down the hill, creating a direct route to Padre Ramon, through which he sped as if pursued by wild dogs. Padre Ramon dropped the two portmanteaus, in preparation – the gaping crowd assumed – to embrace Angelo. But they were wrong. When he raised his hands he did so in protest, a gesture so clearly intended to keep the boy at bay that Angelo ground to an unsteady halt. And there, with the townspeople on either side bearing down on him with expressions of tenderness and pity, he looked towards Padre Ramon, searching his austere face for an explanation for this humiliating rebuff.

Padre Ramon began, his voice sour and insinuating, 'You have in the course of your seven years under my tutelage come to consider yourself a child of God. This, I vainly hoped, and for a time ardently believed, would spare you from the fate ordained by your birth. But you are –' Padre Ramon paused, his entire head taking on a purple hue, while Angelo, bristling with attention, strove to anticipate what was to follow. And all around, written on every face in the crowd was the hope that Padre Ramon was about to change course and speak with kindness to the bewildered boy. But this hope was violently dashed to the ground by an allegation so venomous in its tone, so damning in its charge that many people in the crowd clutched the person nearest to them just as they might if there was an earth tremor.

'You are a child of Satan,' he hissed, 'conceived by his design and born in defiance of God's wishes. In taking pity on you, I failed to see that your need was a cunning ruse of your evil begetter. And now I must make amends for my blindness and those sins to which it led.'

Padre Ramon bowed humbly at each of the five clerics in turn, then took up his two portmanteaus and allowed himself to be led away, never again to return to those parts.

Insensible with grief and confusion, Angelo watched the defeated padre walk down the hill, his head hanging, his shoulders sloped from the weight of his bags. A few paces behind him, the Georgians struggled to keep up, scratching their heads and stroking their beards. Following them and herded together like oxen by Guido were the old men, many of whom had suffered in the Great War and had not been out in the streets since that same war ended some thirty-five years before. And finally the singer in full song, a plaintive aria requiring gestures which slowed her down, gradually detaching her from the rest of the group.

Angelo continued to watch as the motley procession trailed away into the distance, unaware that the crowd around him, like a broken ripple in a pond, had edged back to form a wide arc. Some still clutched the arms of those on either side, others clasped their mouths in shock at Padre Ramon's vicious words.

Little by little they began to grapple with the meaning of those words. Some argued that Padre Ramon had lost his reason, tapping their heads with their index fingers while offering a variety of implausible reasons for this turn of events. As these were people who, whenever they failed to comprehend what was said, always questioned the speaker's soundness of mind, their judgements were generally ignored. However, on this occasion men of insight sided with them. A blind fury must have led to Padre Ramon's rash words, they said, a momentary dementia brought on by the closure of the House of Rest.

That explanation, though far from satisfactory, served a very worthy purpose. It enabled the crowd, terrorized by Padre Ramon's allegations, to disregard them and approach Angelo. In that way he came to be consoled, surrounded as he soon was by reassuring voices. But no sooner had they left the scene than Padre Ramon's words, like booty to be sorted, were tossed this way and that between them until all that remained was one highly prized nugget, the words, Child of Satan, over which they would argue vehemently for a long time to come.

Now there were, if the truth be known, few very truly ignorant people in that town. And this, more than anything else, can be seen to account for the paucity of numbers, no more than four or five, who believed that Padre Ramon had spoken literally. These credulous folk, recalling stories told to them by their grandmothers, passed on, no doubt, from previous generations of grandmothers, held that Satan could and sometimes did assume a human form. And, in that assumed form, he could and sometimes did beguile and lure into sexual union not women of low calling as might be supposed, but those of renowned virtue. Furthermore, the true nature of this seducer, these foolish people claimed, was never known or even suspected by the woman until his seed, always as cold as ice, was spilled inside her.

Perhaps there were more than four or five who subscribed to this primitive interpretation of Padre Ramon's charge, but observing the ridicule to which those who voiced it were subjected, they decided to keep their views to themselves.

The most widely held opinion, similar in many ways to that literal one, differed in one essential respect. Those who forwarded it emphasized that Satan, in bringing about the birth of a child, did not assume a human form or indeed take possession of the body of whoever he selected to carry out the perfidious task. This notion, they said, was concocted for the simple-minded, those who did not have the ability to grasp the complex ways in which he deployed his powers. It was clear to people of enlightenment, people like themselves, that his field of prey was always the human spirit and so it must have been with the conception of Angelo. Satan had not, as the ignorant and simple-minded claimed, participated directly in that conception but had contrived to bring it about by exploiting the spiritual weakness of those whose sin had led to Angelo's birth.

While there was general concurrence on this issue, there was, stemming from it, a plethora of other issues on which no agreement could be reached. In this way the perception of how Satan had brought about the conception of Angelo, far from being the concluding point, came to be the starting point of a lengthy debate. It serves no useful purpose to elucidate the various strands of that debate, suffice to say that it centred on the notion of salvation and can be condensed to a single question. Was the kingdom of God closed to a child in whose conception Satan had played a part? Applied to Angelo's lot, the question gave rise to two opposing factions of opinion, one which looked on him with compassion, the other determined to rid the town of his presence for ever. The first group believed, and strenuously argued, that the circumstances of his conception had no bearing whatsoever on how he appeared in God's eyes. His salvation, they insisted, was solely dependent on his faith, adding that in this respect he was, owing to his unceasing devotion to Santa Rosa, far better placed than even the most pious among them.

'Look at how he spends his days. In the church, praying by the open coffin of Santa Rosa. In the square, proclaiming her virtues. At the foot of the hill, recounting her miracles to all and sundry. Surely this cannot be called the work of Satan?'

Their argument failed to move their opponents.

'It is but a disguise,' they would retort. 'He feigns devotion to our saint in order to draw goodly souls towards him. Why even Padre Ramon was duped, becoming as he did a victim of this artful ambassador from the underworld.'

And so their arguing would go on, often taking place in Angelo's presence. His benefactors, those who brought food to him in the House of Rest where he continued to dwell, made every effort to save him from these painful ordeals but only with occasional success. His persecutors would accost these generous benefactors at every turn, taking particular satisfaction in doing so when they were giving Angelo whatever food they had taken from their own tables, calling them agents of Satan and other odious and incriminating names. Scuffles broke out between the two sides from time to time, earning the townspeople a reputation for unruliness among the other towns in the region. Angelo's persecutors held him culpable, asserting that his work would not be complete until chaos reigned supreme.

Strange to say, throughout the period when the town was in the grip of conflict, there was, in addition to the persecutors and benefactors, a third body of opinion, impossible to gauge because it went unvoiced at the time. But even if it had been voiced, it is doubtful that it would have had any impact on the dispute. It posited a notion of the scheme of things which lay beyond the Great Story and therefore would not have been visible to the vast majority of the townspeople who dwelt within the bounds of that story.

The adherents of this unvoiced view, who did not emerge until many years later, held a notion of the world in which a man and woman whose sexual union leads to the conception of a child are, in an absolute sense, the begetters of that child. They outrightly rejected the interplay of unseen, extraneous influences, both good and evil, claiming it was absurd and profoundly injurious for a child to hold such a perception of their origin.

This was the view which Maria Stella came to embrace, but not for some time to come. She had thrown her lot in with her schoolfellows and spent long periods sauntering about the town with them, whiling away the time in laughter and chatter. Their concerns had become her concerns and though the corollary was not the case she still came to resemble them in so many ways that, were it not for her striking beauty, she might have been indistinguishable from them. And happily she exerted a degree of influence over them, ensuring they did not taunt Angelo as they were wont to do, indeed as some of them had been encouraged to do by their parents and grand-parents.

As for Angelo himself, his lot was more pitiable than ever. He continued to depend on the generosity of his benefactors for every morsel he ate and would sit crouched at the base of the great oak door of the House of Rest, sometimes for hours on end, waiting for one or other of them to show up. When they did, he was frequently so demented by hunger that he would snatch whatever was brought before it was offered and ram it into his mouth without acknowledging that it was a gift. This alienated those of his benefactors who required the reward of gratitude, thereby reducing to a handful those on whom he could rely for daily nourishment. These brave, good-hearted souls did not judge him on any count. They responded only to what they saw, a youth, barely out of boyhood, who might well perish were it not for the meagre alms he received.

La Sorda, though often hostile to her own daughter, Maria Stella, continued to seek opportunities to indulge Angelo, to lavish affection on him as she had done ever since his earliest days in the House of Rest. Her interest in him made his lot more bearable, but only intermittently because Donna Chiara, as averse as ever to any involvement with Angelo and aware of La Sorda's engrossment in him, scrupulously monitored her movements.

Still, irregular and fraught as La Sorda's visits were, it has to be acknowledged that there were occasions when they saved Angelo's life. None of his other benefactors, for reasons hinging on a variety of superstitions, ever went into the House of Rest. When he was ill, which he frequently was, they left the food they brought for him at the foot of the great oak door. Sadly he was, in the course of the many illnesses which plagued him, often too unsteady on his feet to go to the door. Or he might, with effort, make his way there, only to discover the remains of what had been left by his benefactors, scattered about the place, the rest having been eaten by the hairless dog who scavenged for food in that part of the town. La Sorda, fearful of alerting her mother, never brought food herself. But if she saw food at the foot of the great oak door, she would pick it up, race up the fifteen flights of stairs and deliver it to Angelo in the loft room. That was the only room he ever occupied in the House of Rest. And he kept it just as it was when he and Maria Stella played there, the make-shift audience arranged to witness all that went on.

5

Scarcely a night went by when Maria Stella's sleep was not tormented by the spectre of Angelo's stark, bewildered face. Many times she tried to lay claim to the friendship which in her heart she felt certain still existed between them, but neither she nor anyone else in the town could engage him in conversation. He was, to all intents and purposes, lost to the life that went on about him, consumed as he was by an all-enveloping devotion to Santa Rosa, prepared only to speak to her or about her.

When he was not in or around the House of Rest, he was most likely to be found in the church, where, close to the embalmed body of the saint, he prayed feverishly, or at the base of the great rock where he tried to engage passers-by with an account of her powers of divine intercession. And because this was a place his persecutors did not normally frequent, he was spared the suffering and humiliation of their assaults whenever he went there. Naturally, it was not long before the greater part of his time was spent in this spot and his visits to the church confined to the late evening, a furtive hour at the end of the day, passed in the presence of his beloved Santa Rosa.

In this way a routine was established and people grew so used to it that if a visitor to the town had asked who the youth holding forth about Santa Rosa was, the townspeople would simply have said 'It is Angelo.' As though naming him was an explanation. And if that same visitor looked to know more, they probably would have been informed of the controversy surrounding him, but not in a way to make it seem peculiar, because the townspeople did not consider it as such.

Throughout this whole period Angelo's lot remained a wretched one, though his persecutors became less dogged in their determination to hound him from the town, contenting themselves with spitting or hurling insults at him whenever they came in contact with him. But wretched as this existence was he did not succumb to the obsequious ways of the destitute, continuing instead to proclaim confidently the sanctity of Santa Rosa. Every day he brought the evidence of her intercessionary powers, crutches, callipers and wooden limbs, down the fifteen flights of stairs of the House of Rest and out through the low door leading on to the path at the base of the great rock. And there, close to the entrance portal to the town, he lined them up for all to see.

What most intrigued those of the townspeople who took the time to listen to him was not the trouble he took to arrange the discarded implements of the disabled but his speech, which in every imaginable detail resembled that of Padre Ramon's. His gestures too, they noted, were remarkably similar to those of the padre, flamboyant, angular and strikingly at odds with the taut stoop in which he otherwise composed himself. They compared him to an actor who, empowered by the part he was given to play, found depths of strength within himself to which he did not in other circumstances have recourse.

'So great were her powers of intercession,' he would begin in a loud, commanding voice, 'that as well as the multitudes of able-bodied people who thronged this town in search of salvation, the physically afflicted, those who had suffered the loss of a limb, came in great numbers hoping for a miraculous release from their suffering.'

Occasionally, passers-by might stop and listen but as often as not they would lose track of the story and proceed with their journey. This did not discourage Angelo. On the contrary. He continued to hold forth in the impassioned voice of his erstwhile teacher, even more forceful, more self-assured.

'The merchants of this town, who profited greatly by the influx of people, built large houses for themselves but began to fear for their prosperity when it became known that pilgrims of means, afraid of being beset by the many poverty-stricken cripples in the square, were avoiding the town altogether, paying homage instead to lesser saints in the region.'

And here, with a flurry of gestures, gathering his supposed audience towards him, Angelo would assume the indignant voices of the burghers whose prosperity was threatened.

'The day is drawing near when we will be hosts only to the diseased and the disabled. For who would choose to seek his salvation in a town where the enfeebled outnumber the able-bodied? A town filled by day with the plaintive pleas of beggars and by night with their groans as they sleep their tormented sleep in the doorways of our houses?'

At this point Angelo would spin around on the heel of one foot, returning to his imagined audience with all the aplomb of a street player.

'To avert this decline in their fortunes, these merchants passed a law banning all infirm people from the town square, thereby forcing them to enter the church of Santa Rosa from a side street lower down the hill. Furthermore, they took it upon themselves to build a shelter in the vicinity of that lesser entrance, a place where the disabled could be accommodated at night.'

As soon as Angelo uttered the word 'shelter' he would throw his arm back vigorously, pointing at the House of Rest. 'See with your own eyes,' he would say, animated by the prospect of their seeing what he saw. 'See where the building has undergone change, a great deal of change through the centuries. This side has been refashioned, but,' he would confide 'if you take the trouble to approach it from the other side you will discover, above the portal, the five coats of arms of the families who provided for its construction.'

It was not unusual, indeed not unusual at all, to hear Angelo challenge his audience, attributing questions to them and anticipating their responses.

'And how, you might well ask, did the disabled fare now that they were denied access to the square by statute? Perhaps someone among you would like to answer this question?'

'Ah, it seems not,' he would say after a moment or two, replicating the particular inflection Padre Ramon employed when he wished to convey disappointment.

'They did not fare at all well. And why not? Because, on entering the church of Santa Rosa from the side street they were, unfortunately, forced to descend the many steep steps to the crypt before climbing the long, winding staircase leading to the trap door behind the altar. That was the only route. From there they were guided by a team of waiting seminarians around to the front where they could see but could not touch, as the able-bodied, prosperous pilgrims could, the sanctified remains of Santa Rosa. But –' and here he held his hand up, pointing skywards with his index finger, 'but the occurrence of a miracle in that very spot, witnessed by many people, prosperous pilgrims and destitute cripples alike, changed for ever the way future pilgrims would approach the open coffin of Santa Rosa. A seven-year-old boy, carried in his father's arms from a distant region because he did not have the use of his limbs, asked to be let down as soon as they were ushered out from behind the altar and saw for the first time, after many weeks of arduous travel, the coffin containing the body of Santa Rosa. Reluctantly his father obeyed him and with great care eased him on to the cold marble floor. To the astonishment of all, including the team of seminarians who ran hither and thither trying to keep the enfeebled in line, he walked directly up to Santa Rosa. His father wept for joy and in a loud voice, which resounded around the church, exclaimed "Mirabile dictu" and in the same breath pledged life-long devotion to Santa Rosa. His son kissed the lips of the embalmed saint, while all that were gathered there fell on their knees in prayer.'

Now, even if Angelo had a listener, such a person would in all likelihood have ceased to follow the story by this stage in the telling, for the rapid pace at which he spoke coupled with his copious weeping, turned the teller into the tale.

'How is it he weeps in this way every day?' the towns-people had asked each other when he first began to bring the crutches and callipers down to the foot of the hills and regale passers-by with the great feats of Santa Rosa. That question, like the many others they asked, was answered in a wide variety of ways. Some said that his tears were tears of jubilation, that every day he shared in the joy of the miraculously cured boy and his grateful father. Others claimed that he wept for all those who were not cured, those whose journeys had been in vain. Others, wise in their own way, but rarely heeded, claimed that his tears were tears of hopelessness. He wept, they said, because he had no story of his own.

'The avaricious merchants, fearing that this great miracle would attract even more cripples, made little of it. They shrugged their shoulders if asked about it by the able-bodied pilgrims who gathered at their stalls. However, their efforts to depreciate it were in vain. Not only did the number of crippled visitors increase a hundred-fold but everyone, able-bodied pilgrims and cripples alike, who came here to pay homage to Santa Rosa, wanted to take the exact same route to her open coffin as the boy who had been miraculously cured.'

Angelo smiled beatifically.

'And, as this meant entering and leaving the church through the crypt door, the great majority of them did not bother to climb the last two of the seven hills leading to the square. Consequently they left this town without examining the wide array of goods offered for sale by the merchants.'

Angelo, his face filled with the wonder of his story, would spread his arms out to invite applause, whether there was anyone there or not.

'It was during this period of decline in the fortunes of the merchants that the most spectacular miracles took place. Scores of people who had entered the town on crutches or dragging themselves along the ground by their callused elbows, left better able to comport themselves than many of the able-bodied pilgrims who had stridden past them on the route a day or two before.'

In advance of nodding his head, which he habitually did as he entered the next stretch of his story, he would glare at his audience, intently searching their faces for doubt; an inquisition so prolonged and concentrated that when it was directed at an actual group, as it very occasionally was, they found it deeply unsettling.

'Shouts of joy raced ahead of the cured as they left the town, echoing back and forth until the whole land resounded with their jubilation. Men would stop their hammering as far away as the great marble quarries in the north and bid each other to listen. It is, they would say, the joy of the cured, those who have been given back the use of their limbs.'

And so Angelo would continue throughout the day, stopping briefly to drink from the flagon of water he brought with him or to eat whatever his benefactors might have left nearby.

La Sorda would have been a more frequent visitor were Donna Chiara less attuned to her movements. When she did manage to steal away, in the afternoon while her mother was resting, she would race down the seven hills at a perilous speed, violently pushing aside whoever got in her way. Then, breathless, she would place herself directly in front of him, feigning the antics of a listener. But Angelo did not acknowledge their former intimacy.

He could not be stopped telling the story. Good-hearted people who tried to persuade him to abandon his post when a thunder storm threatened met with the same frantic resistance, reporting that he was visibly overtaken by panic and would accelerate the already rapid pace at which he spoke as if the story in itself was a refuge.

Maria Stella was deeply troubled by it all. She often approached him at the foot of the great rock, pleading with him to speak to her.

'Why,' she might ask, 'do you tell of these same events over and over again when there is nobody here to listen?'

Sometimes, by way of response, he paused momentarily, as though he was formulating an answer. But then his eyes, without moving, became distant and before long he was once again deeply immersed in the story.

Crestfallen, Maria Stella would walk away.

She would have asked her grandmother for an explanation, asked her why Angelo had become a prisoner of the story he told, but she could not because never once in all those years had Donna Chiara wavered in her contention that Angelo was cursed. 'Destined,' she continued to remind Maria Stella, 'for all the unhappiness in the world.' And while this warning had not threatened Maria Stella's friendship with him in the past, it had – in an insinuating way – taken root. So whenever she thought about him, her grandmother's terrible foreboding echoed loudly in her ears, frequently thwarting her efforts to entice him beyond the boundaries of his devotion to Santa Rosa.

Still Maria Stella persisted. She would periodically set out full of purpose, determined to challenge him. But even then her resolve might easily come to nought, because it often happened that in the course of her journey to him, the worthlessness of her quest would loom in front of her, leaving her powerless to complete it. And so she might be found sitting on the edge of the pavement or on a doorstep, her face buried in her hands. Those passers-by who offered assistance made little or no headway because in her distress Maria Stella lost her grip on speech, making such convoluted sounds in her effort to explain her plight that even the most persistent of these kind people came to the conclusion that she was beyond help.

There was, however, one occasion when she did meet with some success in her quest to engage Angelo.

'I do not know,' he had answered one languidly hot afternoon when she asked him, as she did every time she confronted him, what possessed him to speak at such length about Santa Rosa.

Her delight in hearing him answer was instant but it was short lived. No sooner had he spoken than he drew back and, full of ire, began to shout the story at her, entering it at a point considerably ahead of that at which he had left it.

'The widows, the widows, the widows,' he roared, his nostrils dilating until he came to resemble a panic-stricken horse, struggling, as he did frantically, to find his place.

'The widows of the five merchants thought . . . they thought that by bequeathing what remained of their wealth to the House of Rest, they might, the widows thought they might bring an end to the misfortune that had befallen them and their families ever since their avaricious husbands passed the law forbidding . . .'

Maria Stella, frightened by his fury, began to fear for her safety and did not attempt to engage him again. Only very gradually did his fearsome shouting begin to tail off, his twisted features unfurling as he found his way back safely. She feigned attention, all the while waiting for an opportunity to leave the unhappy scene.

'The widows' wealth, though a lot less than it had been, was still great and endowed the House of Rest with an immense fortune. And this, beyond doubt,' he said with an extravagant hand flourish, 'was brought about by Santa Rosa.'

Once fully back on course, Angelo re-entered the animated, trance-like state in which he habitually spoke and Maria Stella walked away listening with a heavy heart to his voice thinning out behind her.

'Among the many valuable relics in the possession of the five widows was a thorn, a thorn reputed to be from the crown mockingly placed on the Lord's head in his final hour. When this became known to the bishop in whose dioceses this town was at that time, he decreed that the entire estate bequeathed to the House of Rest, having in it so many precious objects, ought to be administered by the Holy See. And so it was for many centuries . . .'

And on he continued, on and on until nightfall.

Much later the townspeople would look back on that era in an attempt to understand Angelo's attachment to Santa Rosa. What prompted them to do so was the astonishing test to which he would subject her, a test which immediately gave rise to a whole host of questions.

Why, they asked, did he need to test her love for him at all? He had every reason to believe that a saint to whom he was so devoted cared deeply for him. And moreover why did he put so much at risk?

6

Angelo's bid to measure Santa Rosa's love for him is, to this day, a topic of conversation not just among the people of that town but among those who live in the neighbouring towns too. There is scarcely a person in the entire region who would not, at the mention of his and Santa Rosa's names, cease whatever they were about and readily hold forth on what had happened. But for all that, only a fraction of the many accounts on offer look beyond the test itself, formulated as they are to convey the astonishment of the teller. So it is not surprising that another event, which may in a circuitous way have precipitated the test, is now only rarely discussed, though at the time the townspeople could talk of little else.

That event had its beginning on the coldest day of the year when there came to the town a young attorney, a man whose handsome appearance was not at first noted because the hat and scarf he wore to protect himself against the wind concealed all his features save his eyes. Straight away he began the enquiries which had brought him to the town and, before long, found himself being directed to the house in which Donna Chiara, La Sorda and Maria Stella lived.

The three resounding knocks which announced his presence caused disquiet within. A visitor to that house was a very uncommon occurrence. Donna Chiara told Maria Stella to find out who was there before answering, but Maria Stella ignored her grandmother's instruction and opened the door directly.

The stranger who stood before her went to speak, but was so captivated by Maria Stella's great beauty that several moments went by before any words passed his lips. Eventually, he brought himself to ask if he was at the house of a blind woman, who many years before had been a servant in the household of a miller in a nearby town. Maria Stella, sure that Donna Chiara's long and arduous working life had been spent entirely in the House of Rest, informed the stranger that while her grandmother was most certainly blind, in no other respect did she fit the description of the person he sought. And with that she wished him success in his quest and bade him farewell.

But he made not a single move to leave. Instead, he looked directly into her face as though pained, unable to disguise or in any way negotiate the fierce desire he felt. Maria Stella, for her part, was overwhelmed by his attention and curious to know how she could have provoked so immediate and intense a response in a stranger.

They dallied in the timelessness of that first exchange, making no attempt to regulate the mix of mutable sentiments dashing back and forth between them.

'Who is it? Tell me now, who it is?' Donna Chiara demanded, her ancient voice quivering through the enchanted orb in which they lingered. 'Who is it? Who is it? Who is it?' she repeated with the irascibility of old age.

'I do not know,' Maria Stella answered, smiling at the stranger. 'This man is searching for a blind woman who at one time served in the household of a miller in this region,' Maria Stella called in to her grandmother in a clear, kindly voice, her patience with Donna Chiara a testimony to the great love she felt for her.

'Who is searching?' Donna Chiara shouted, noisily making her way out towards them. But before Maria Stella could ask the stranger his name there was a tremendous commotion. Donna Chiara in her rush to the door had overturned a chair and was swiping the air with her sticks and swearing vociferously.

'Who are you and what is it you want'? she demanded when, distraught and agitated, she finally got there.

'My name is Umberto Agustinelli,' he replied. Then in a firm and forthright manner he proceeded to tell Donna Chiara and Maria Stella of his mission to find the blind servant of the miller. He explained that he had visited almost every town in the region and spoken to a great many people in the course of his search. 'But all,' he said despondently, 'to no avail.'

'It was the express wish of the miller's wife,' he continued, 'recorded in her final testament and reiterated many times on her deathbed, that this particular servant be found, because . . .'

'I am she,' Donna Chiara pronounced, raising her hand and allowing him to proceed no further. 'Your search is an end.'

And with that she began to tell the story of her dismissal from the miller's household, breaking for the first and last time the vow she had made. In doing so she provided the attorney with incontrovertible proof that she was the one he sought.

In a moment of reckless celebration he took both Maria Stella's hands and drawing her towards him began to rejoice. His jubilation was short lived, because Maria Stella, angered by the injustice of her grandmother's dismissal from the miller's household and deeply saddened by the suffering which that dismissal had caused her, began to weep. The attorney's joy turned to concern, and before long he was offering consolation. Kind, comforting words which Maria

Stella embraced fondly, savouring each as though it were a potion which could banish the sadness her grandmother's story had provoked in her.

La Sorda, curious as to what was afoot, approached the group from the inner room only to be pushed, then beaten back inside by her mother who feared that her beloved granddaughter might be compromised by the presence of such an ugly mother.

The tenderness with which Maria Stella was comforted by the attorney rapidly restored her equanimity and soon she was in the warmth of the house, seated close to him, listening attentively as he recounted the sequence of events which had brought him there.

'One year ago today I was approached by an old woman in poor health whose husband had died many years previously. He had devoted his whole life to the accumulation of wealth and had been a man of vast means. But he did not wish to be regarded as such so he had gone to great lengths to conceal the extent of his wealth from everyone, including his wife. Theirs had been a childless marriage so his widow came to inherit all of the great fortune he had secretly built up. But it brought her little contentment because she carried the weight of a loathsome misdeed which, committed early in her married life, was a source of terrible torment to her. Through the use of a poison made from a woodland parasite, she had brought about a gradual deterioration in the sight of her servant. It was a crime committed in desperation, she alleged, a crime provoked by the fear that her husband had fallen under the spell of this woman's great beauty.'

The attorney paused and took the old, work-ravaged hand of Donna Chiara in his, sure that these revelations were a source of great anguish to her. This, however, was an erroneous assumption. At the mere mention of her beauty

Donna Chiara was overcome by joy. In addition, it can be asserted that while she did not know the precise manner in which her sight had been robbed, it can hardly have come as a surprise to learn that the miller's wife was to blame. At any rate, she happily accepted the succour the attorney was offering and, smiling fondly, told him to continue with his story.

'Consumed with remorse, the miller's wife vowed to make amends for her sin before she died. She instigated a search, hopeful that the servant whom she had wronged could be brought before her and would, on learning how contrite she was, forgive her. But that was not to be. When her final hour came, the miller's wife died in torment, loudly lamenting her sorry lot and pleading with God for forgiveness.'

Donna Chiara withdrew her hand from his and held the parched tips of her fingers to her eyes, thereby drawing attention to her loss.

'She shall have no forgiveness, neither from me nor from God.'

The attorney, unsteadied by her anger, looked to Maria Stella for guidance, finding in her eager expression ample encouragement to continue.

'But even on her deathbed the miller's wife did not give up the hope that one day the servant whom she had so grievously wronged would be found. And, in anticipation, she bequeathed all her worldly possessions to her, having first set aside a reward for whoever found that servant, a fortune by any standard but only a negligible portion of her great wealth.'

'Your news, though welcome, will not restore sight to these eyes,' Donna Chiara said with profound regret, searching the space around her with her outstretched hand until she found her granddaughter's face. 'And I will never have the good fortune to look on this, the beautiful face of my Maria Stella.'

And she tarried with her sorrow a while, uniting Umberto and Maria Stella in her sadness.

'Nevertheless, it is a happy day,' she said, with a sudden change of humour. 'A happy day because, in bringing the bearer, the news is worth a great deal more than all the riches of the world put together.'

Then, with the palm of her hand still resting on Maria Stella's cheek she raised her other hand in search of the attorney's face. And he, in anticipation, leaned forward, placing himself in the path of that hand, eager to be drawn into the great torrent of love flowing between her and Maria Stella.

'This,' Donna Chiara announced, gently guiding their faces toward her own, 'is a fitting end to a life that would have been lived in darkness were it not for the great joy you, my Maria Stella, have brought to it.' And with that she died.

Several moments passed before either the attorney or Maria Stella realized that the intimacy into which they had been drawn belonged to them alone.

Maria Stella's grief over her grandmother's death was boundless, at times so profound that it would almost certainly have led to an impairment of her senses were it not for the persistence with which the attorney repeated Donna Chiara's dying words. And that grief was furthermore compounded by La Sorda's response which was one of total devastation. She shook and vigorously poked the corpse of her mother, imagining, or so it seemed to those who witnessed it, that she could bring her to life. Eventually, she had to be forcibly restrained from approaching Donna Chiara and confined for considerable periods to an unused room at the back of the house.

In all of this Umberto was of great assistance to Maria Stella. He proved himself a good deal more skilful than either she or her grandmother had ever been in the management of

La Sorda. His treatment of her was marked first and foremost by kindness and never more so than at the burial of Donna Chiara, when La Sorda lay down on the earth, believing that she too was to be buried. He explained to the mourners that it was a thwarted expression of grief, thereby saving La Sorda the ignominy of ridicule, which though well-contained at that particular point would doubtlessly have found expression at a later stage.

Sadly, La Sorda never recovered her wits.

Now in possession of the fortune bequeathed to her grandmother by the miller's wife, Maria Stella naturally wished to make her mother's unenviable lot as easy to bear as possible. But this was by no means a straightforward undertaking because La Sorda, unable to grasp the extent to which her circumstances had been bettered by the wealth in her daughter's charge, fixed on trivial comforts whenever Maria Stella managed to engage her on the subject, an elaborate confection she had seen in a patisserie window, for instance, or some fad in vogue with the children of the town, spinning hoops or yo-yos.

Even when she began to understand the scale of her new wealth, there was still cause for concern. At any moment she might implode with laughter and run away swallowing her half-formed words in great, mirthful gulps, as if it was a game. Or she might pretend to follow what Maria Stella was proposing, only to reveal her absolute incomprehension at a later stage, thereby forcing her to begin all over again.

At any rate, having endured much exasperation, confusion and misunderstanding, Maria Stella and the attorney eventually succeeded in forming a picture of how La Sorda wished to spend her days. At the outset, it greatly puzzled them and understandably so because what La Sorda gave them to believe she wanted most in the world was to be ill.

'Absurd,' the attorney declared when Maria Stella, interpreting the sounds with which her mother conveyed her thoughts, first explained this to him.

If they had not been so devoted to discovering her wishes they might easily have given up at that point. How could a daughter knowingly bring illness on her mother? And yet it was a wish they could not persuade La Sorda to relinquish.

In the end it transpired that La Sorda, in wanting to be ill, merely wanted to be treated as an invalid. It was a notion she got from observing a woman in whose household she had been occasionally employed since the closure of the House of Rest. This woman, an invalid, was cared for by a bevy of servants all of whom were answerable to her husband. And he, because he was wholly devoted to her, spent the greater part of his day ensuring that they did precisely as she dictated. La Sorda envied this woman and wanted nothing more than to spend her days in the same way.

And so it came to pass that a house on the square was procured and fitted out to serve as a small sanatorium. A team of nurses was hired, and a doctor who, as well as tending to La Sorda's medical needs, acted as general super-visor.

La Sorda had her bed, with its many feather pillows, placed close to the window of the first-floor room where, for the rest of her waking life, she watched the comings and goings of the townspeople with unflinching interest. Every morning she was, by her own request, extensively examined by the doctor who then prescribed some medicament or other, always precautionary, because La Sorda enjoyed singularly good health.

If, at that point, Maria Stella's only concern was her mother's contentment then hers would have been a happy lot. In the attorney's love she had found love itself, had come to possess it as she might a great power, enabling her to see all that was glorious in the world. But there was one remaining obstacle to the completion of her happiness and that was the grief Angelo's wretched circumstances continued to cause her. He lived in squalor in the House of Rest, each day bringing the discarded implements of the disabled down to the town gate where he told the story of Santa Rosa. Some observed that he did so less animatedly, contending that he had begun to doubt the efficacy of the story, but that is of little consequence because he remained as unwilling as ever to enter into discourse with those around him.

Maria Stella confided her concern about Angelo to Umberto, giving him a full account of the many hardships to which Angelo had been subjected, including his public denunciation as a child of Satan by Padre Ramon. But she also dwelt on the happy times they had spent together in their childhood. She spoke of their games in the loft room, of the audiences they used to construct from the discarded implements of the disabled, of Angelo's inventiveness, his mimicry, his laughter.

The attorney, whose affection for Maria Stella intensified whenever she spoke of her childhood, was overwhelmed. He pledged himself to do everything in his might to free Angelo from the story in which he was imprisoned. And, by way of preparation, began to ply Maria Stella with questions.

He broached the question of Angelo's origin many times. If it could be established where he had come from and how he had spent his earlier years, the attorney said, it would throw light on his present conduct. Maria Stella told him what the townspeople had said when Angelo first arrived some twelve years previously, emphasizing that their accounts were entirely speculative. 'Padre Ramon is the only one who knows where Angelo came from and as we do not know where he is now, there is nothing to be gained by dwelling on the question of Angelo's origin.'

When, after much deliberation, the attorney fixed on a

strategy to bring an end to Angelo's isolation, he outlined it to Maria Stella, adding a question, in effect a proposal, the full import of which did not strike her at the time.

'If it can be impressed on Angelo that he need not estrange himself from the world, that a fate other than that of an outcast can be his, then the last obstacle between you and a future of your choosing will have been removed. Is this not so?'

'Yes, certainly, but . . .' she paused, about to continue when the attorney drew her towards him and, gasping as though the breath he drew was his last, clasped her firmly to him. It was, Maria Stella would recall many years later, a rapturous blending of desires, sensation and sentiment, mingling to transport them beyond their individual selves into a single spirit.

Late into the night, long after they had parted Maria Stella remembered what she was about to say when the spell cast by that transcendent moment took hold. Suddenly she became alarmed, realizing that in failing to speak she had unwittingly accepted that their destiny would be determined by the outcome of his efforts to release Angelo from the tyranny of his story. She had, in short, allowed Umberto to believe that her love was conditional. And this was not the case. Not the case at all.

The only happiness she could imagine was the supreme happiness she had found with Umberto. And, while she might ardently hope to see Angelo's circumstances change for the better, she was deeply distressed to realize that her destiny had now come to depend on such an eventuality.

So great was her anguish that she did not sleep for the remainder of that night. Instead she paced the hours away, planning how she would disabuse Umberto of the lamentable misapprehension with which she had allowed him to leave.

At first light she set out for the pension where he lodged. By the time she got there he had already left for the day. In an attempt to find out which direction he had taken, she questioned the taciturn keeper but he just shrugged his shoulders and walked away.

Maria Stella rushed to the town square but found neither sight nor sound of him there. And none of those she questioned, herdsmen on their way to tend their flocks, children loitering on their way to school, merchants setting up their stalls, could enlighten her. She ran hither and thither, each moment spawning a new array of concerns, exacerbating her anguish and leaving her more disconsolate than ever.

By the time the first of the town's visitors entered the square Maria Stella was nearing absolute despair. But she put the same question to them as she had to many of the townspeople in the course of that tempestuous morning. To her relief one visitor reported that he had passed a man answering the description she gave, adding that he was to be found at the entrance to the town listening to a youth holding forth on the miracles brought about by Santa Rosa. Pleased to find himself conversing with a woman of such remarkable beauty, the traveller went on to embellish his account, but before he could utter another word, Maria Stella was racing down the first of the seven hills, full of self-reproach.

The scheme Umberto had devised to lure Angelo beyond the bounds of his story required that he himself should first become thoroughly familiar with it. By so doing he hoped to learn to see the world through Angelo's eyes, then, once in possession of the same vision, planned to expand it until it overlapped with that of other people. It was, in short, a ploy to merge Angelo's story with that of the world at large.

The next stage in the attorney's scheme centred on persuading Angelo to leave the decaying House of Rest and go to live in the well-ordered house set up for La Sorda on the square. There, he would be more than adequately provided for and could, with the assistance of a sizeable indenture fee, be apprenticed to one of the many guides providing tours of the town to visitors.

When Umberto first outlined his plan to Maria Stella she had marvelled at its loftiness and was unreserved in her praise for his cleverness. But now, racing frantically down to where she hoped to find him, greatly disturbed by the unsteady course onto which their love had been directed, she gave no thought whatsoever to Angelo. Indeed she did not even look in his direction when, out of breath and convulsed with tears, she arrived. She just abandoned all self-possession and thrust herself straight into Umberto's arms, repeating his name several times. And there, well within Angelo's hearing, she told Umberto he did not have to concern himself with Angelo, that her love was absolute and not in any respect conditional on Angelo's redemption.

Angelo stopped telling the story of Santa Rosa, but neither Maria Stella or Umberto paid any heed to him, so absorbed were they with each other.

Motionless, Angelo looked on. His stare, at first vacant and bewildered, slowly began to register what was taking place before him. Little by little, his pallor reverted to the oily yellow colour which, in the past, had led people to say that he had died but that death would not take him. Gathering up the discarded implements of the disabled he trudged over to the cellar door of the House of Rest.

'Why are you going?' Umberto called after him, abruptly releasing himself from the prolonged embrace in which he and Maria Stella had remained.

Very slowly, Angelo rested the instruments on the dry, cracked earth, then turned to speak to Maria Stella and Umberto. 'Santa Rosa. What is her true power?' he asked quietly, his voice almost unrecognizable.

'I cannot say. Who can say? It is not possible to know the

power of a saint.' Umberto spoke decisively, his extravagant gestures belying his great satisfaction in having drawn Angelo into discussion.

Angelo bent down and picked up the implements, defeat in his every move. 'A way will have to be found. I must know the extent of her power. It must be known.'

Maria Stella, silenced by her astonishment, watched as he entered the House of Rest, then turned to Umberto. 'You have won his trust,' she said in awe. 'He has spoken in a way he has not been known to speak for many years.'

Her face shone, incredulity, love, gratitude, admiration, all finding a place in her ebullient expression. 'This is but the beginning,' Umberto confidently declared. 'Tomorrow I will return and within five days, you have my word, no more than five, Angelo will have left the confines of his story, never to return.'

Maria Stella foraged for words to express her joy but could find none.

'The future is ours to shape as we wish,' Umberto whispered, taking her hands and pressing the open palms and splayed fingers against his cheeks.

7

The townspeople followed Maria Stella and Umberto's court-ship with unremitting interest. So voracious were some for information that they instructed their children to pry on the couple and report back whatever they could glean. Consequently, Maria Stella and Umberto were rarely seen without a trail of children behind them, all of them set to flee should Umberto suddenly swing around as he often did in a playful ploy.

The extraordinary fascination he and Maria Stella held for the townspeople can be explained, though only in part, by their striking appearance. They were an uncommonly handsome couple. In whatever setting they found themselves they would have aroused the curiosity of those about them. There was also the matter of Maria Stella's newly acquired wealth which, on the day the townspeople first learned about it, brought all transactions to a complete standstill. For weeks they talked of little else, leading to a proliferation of theories as to how she had come to possess it. But while wealth and beauty can be seen to account for the townspeople's insatiable interest in the couple, those were by no means the only attributes to arrest their attention. Indeed, for many, Maria Stella and Umberto's generosity was a source of interest every bit as compelling.

'Look how they treat Angelo,' those people would proclaim. 'They have provided him with every comfort. La Sorda too. Is it any wonder that they have been blessed with happiness?'

Angelo had been coaxed into leaving the House of Rest by Umberto and installed in La Sorda's elegant house on the square, though the only way he ever entered or left his quarters there was through a back door, thereby hoping to avoid the various attendants who busied themselves about the house.

On the rare occasions when he was drawn into conversation, usually by those intent on showing him kindness, he would respond to their well-intentioned enquiries in a hesitant, almost inaudible manner. 'I do not know,' was his most frequent reply, which discouraged people from befriending him, as he intended it should.

However, he no longer brought the discarded implements of the disabled down to the portal and, if he held forth about Santa Rosa, which he sporadically did outside the church, it was not to proclaim her greatness as he had done in the past. On the contrary, it was to question her power, a procedure which invariably ended with his resolving to find a failsafe way of measuring it.

When this ambition was reported it led many to conclude that Angelo had lost faith in Santa Rosa, leading them to suppose that she had, in some matter of great importance, failed to intercede on his behalf. And, as was always the case, there were those who brought conjecture a step further, citing the intimacy between Maria Stella and Umberto as the matter in question.

'Her love for Umberto, displayed for us all to behold, is a source of unending torment to him,' they said, claiming furthermore that despite his recalcitrance, Angelo was deeply attached to her. However, to most of the townspeople, his spirit was far too downtrodden, his heart too obdurate to harbour such an attachment.

At any rate, all musings on Angelo's attachment ended the day she and Umberto decided to marry.

It was an evening in early summer, with a great many more people than usual ambling around the square, the warm weather creating an air of easy cordiality among them. And there, strolling up and down in their midst were Maria Stella and Umberto, as much a spectacle as ever, perhaps even more so because for many of the elderly it was their first evening out of doors after a harsh winter and an unpredictable spring. Several of them, eager to see the couple about whom they had heard so much, stopped and stared unabashed at Maria Stella and Umberto. One old woman, said to be a hundred years of age and too infirm to walk further than a few paces from the front door of her house, demanded that Maria Stella and Umberto be brought to her for inspection. This caused consternation among the bevy of ageing daughters who danced attendance on her, all of them too self-effacing to approach the couple. But Umberto, alerted by the panic-stricken way those daughters glanced at them, guessed what was afoot and went directly over to where they were gathered. And there, with great to-do and flourish, he presented himself and Maria Stella to the old woman, prompting a protracted hiss of gratitude from her fawning daughters.

'You must marry and soon,' the old woman said boldly. 'Look at me, look at how God has punished me, seven daughters who might have married if I had not stood in their way. See how foolish they have become.'

But neither Umberto or Maria Stella looked at the unfortunate women. Instead they turned to one another, finding in each other's eyes a fusion of love and expectancy. Then, seized by a sudden impulse, Umberto bolted away and, pushing his way through the evening strollers, made for the great, circular fountain in the middle of the square. A loaded silence fell as the crowds watched him wade through the gurgling water and climb the central plinth to where Neptune languished.

'Maria Stella,' he bellowed, raising his sodden arms to form a wide, imploring arch. 'Maria Stella, will you marry me?'

The crowds followed the question across the square and watched it alight on a smiling Maria Stella, there, more beautiful than ever in the thinning, incandescent light of that summer evening. She nodded, not once but a dozen times, each more affirmative than the one before.

'You must answer, you must say the words,' Umberto pleaded, but Maria Stella could not bring herself to shout her response and so began to nod again. At this juncture the crowds, overcome with delight at what was unfolding before them, began to answer on her behalf.

'Yes,' some roared in his direction, others bellowing 'I will,' and so on until the square became a sea of voices all pledging themselves in marriage to Umberto, none louder than the seven daughters of the old woman. And it did not stop at that. Far from it. Lost in careless merriment the townspeople celebrated into the early hours, happiness gusting through their extravagant dancing, their mirthful calls to each other lost in the great, jubilant swirl of the night.

Preparations began almost straight away. The wedding was fixed for the late summer, nine weeks away. Three whole days of celebration and feasting were planned and every man, woman and child in the town, over a thousand in all, was invited to attend. The town would be closed to visitors and the square cleared of trading stalls in order to accommodate the great spread of tables and chairs required for the occasion.

It was a summer of ceaseless joy, with all sights firmly fixed on the great event. The young girls of the town, swept along by the lavish preparations, draped themselves in improvised bridal garb and paraded about clasping bunches of bougainvillaea. Their mothers dallied in the course of their errands, never finding enough time to say all they wished to say about the wedding, about Umberto and Maria Stella, about love, about hope, about happiness.

As the great occasion drew near, Angelo was frequently to be found high up in the church belfry, from where he monitored the elaborate preparations in progress down below in the square. He watched the stringing of bunting from the fountain to the hauling pulleys set into the façades of the houses. He watched the enormous banners, vermilion emblazoned with gold, being unrolled from the parapet of the mayoralty. And according to some he took particular note of the movements of Umberto, there tirelessly directing the decoration.

It would be a mistake to assume that in observing the preparations and generally lurking about as he did, Angelo gave cause for concern. Indeed, the reverse. There was ample reason to suppose that the future augured well for him too, because each day he appeared more at one with himself and less hostile to those who sought to befriend him. This led Maria Stella to hope that it was only a question of time before he was fully assimilated into the life of the town. So, in drawing up plans for the wedding, she decided to seat him at the bridal table, thereby giving him pride of place among the dignitaries.

On the glorious morning of the wedding day, there was an air of great quiet about the town. Everyone was busy, not least Maria Stella. Resplendent in swathes of cascading white silk and attended by five maids of honour, she was as beautiful a bride as there ever had been.

The room in which these preparations took place was the one in which Maria Stella had whiled away a great many happy hours with her grandmother, Donna Chiara. It is not surprising, therefore, that the happiness she felt was occasionally dampened by the regret that her grandmother was not there to share in her joy. At one stage, no longer able to contain the swell of tears prompted by that regret, Maria Stella began to weep, provoking a rush of colliding voices as the five maids of honour vied to remind her of the prophetic blessing Donna Chiara had given to her union with Umberto.

Before long, the room was again full of cheer, laughter abounding as the final preparation got underway. Then, a sudden wave of concern swept the room.

'Even those who are late will have arrived at the church by now,' one of the maids of honour said. Another urged Maria Stella to consider Umberto's position while a third pleaded for calm.

Maria Stella had elected to make the journey to the church on foot. This, she explained to those who had tried to dissuade her, Umberto in particular, was her way of ensuring that Donna Chiara remained firmly in her thoughts and in her heart, the route up the seven steep hills being the same one they had taken together day in day out for many, many years.

And so she set out, accompanied by her five maids of honour, two bearing her vast, shimmering, silk train while the others strewed the path ahead with rose petals. Their every word resounded in the emptiness of the streets, leading them to whisper how peculiar, how unfamiliar, the town appeared without the usual bustle and clatter.

When they reached the square they came to a sudden halt, each looking for words to express the awe and wonder prompted by the magnificence of what they saw. The scene, like that in a port harbouring a great armada of ships, was a blaze of roaring colour with flags and banners all billowing and flapping in the fresh morning breeze. And the mass of tables, set for a thousand guests, had in the absence of those guests a ghostly beauty, each glass catching a fleck of pale blue, a reflection of the garlands of entwined anemones running the length of every table. So overcome were they by the wonder of the spectacle that they had almost reached the steps of the church before the stillness, the profound quiet flowing from the open doors, struck them.

Their pace quickened, with Maria Stella leading the way, only to come to an unsteady standstill when she saw that there was not a soul in the church. Not a single person, anywhere. Bewildered, she walked down the aisle, stopping every few paces as though expecting the scene, as she had often envisaged it, to burst into life; the triumphant sound of the wedding march, people stealing a sidelong glance at her as she sailed down the aisle, Umberto standing at the rails.

If at that point she had turned around and looked out through the open doors of the church she would have seen some of the guests skulking out from their hiding places, hoping to catch a glimpse of her as she discovered what they themselves had discovered an hour or so beforehand.

Her silent journey down the aisle ended at the open coffin of Santa Rosa. There, still clutching her bouquet of yellow roses, she struggled to comprehend the sight which confronted her. In panic, she turned to where she supposed the maids of honour were. But they were already out of the church, racing through the lavishly adorned tables, frantically pulling off the veils which impeded their flight.

Maria Stella edged back from the open coffin, slowly at first, keeping her eyes fixed on the sight which would remain with her for the rest of her life. Umberto, the pleated lining of the coffin sodden with his blood, his limbs jutting through the raw flesh of his dismembered body, his severed genitals pushed into his mouth, splinters of his broken teeth embedded in his swollen lips, his face and head bludgeoned almost beyond recognition.

The townspeople, most of them dressed in their wedding finery, watched Maria Stella back out of the church in silence, her pace so slow that to some she did not appear to be moving at all. They thought that once she reached the first of the assembled tables, the bridal table, she would turn around and face them, thereby revealing the unfathomable depths of her devastation. Perhaps some of them intended to approach her to offer the comfort of their companionship. But before Maria Stella reached the bridal table, the square began to resound with mocking laughter, a hollow, contrived sound which drew all eyes up to the belfry. All, that is, except Maria Stella's. She kept her head bowed, already resigned to the terrible truth that it was Angelo and Angelo alone who had done this.

As his laughter ebbed, his voice, more triumphant, more powerful than anyone could have thought possible, filled the square, resounding in the ears of every last one of them.

'Now, you have seen what the child of Satan has done.'

And, surveying them contemptuously, he leaned forward, his chin jutting out, his hands tightly gripping the belfry ledge.

Suddenly, the crowd bolted back, a great gasp of horror rising from them as Angelo lifted the sacred corpse of Santa Rosa from the floor beneath him and draped it carelessly over the side of the belfry. Then in a single sweeping movement he clasped it by the neck and held it up for all to see, roaring out, 'The power of Santa Rosa shall now be tested.'

With that he climbed up on to the narrow ledge, prompting several of the women in the crowd to cover their children's eyes. Barely holding his balance, he reached down and hauled up the small shrunken body of the saint, managing to maintain a steady stance only for as long as it took to reaffirm his mission.

'Now it shall be known,' he bellowed, clasping Santa Rosa to himself and, in one great surge of effort, leaping out from the belfry.

There were those in the crowd who would later claim that his fall was not direct, that he and Santa Rosa remained suspended in the air for a few moments before falling to the ground at a pace considerably slower than might have been expected. Furthermore, they asserted that it was the injury Angelo sustained when his head violently struck the church wall which killed him. Otherwise he would, they said, have survived the ordeal to which he subjected himself, thereby demonstrating beyond doubt Santa Rosa's power of intercession.

At the time, however, neither these nor any of the hundreds of others who witnessed that terrible scene could find their voices. And so it was that they began to disperse in silence, each in his or her own way sensing the inadequacy of the story in which they dwelled and thereby carrying the weight of Angelo's death away with them.

As for Maria Stella, both on the day and for a very long time afterwards, the ordeal was altogether beyond her endurance. Angelo, clasping Santa Rosa, had fallen to within a single pace of where, still holding her bouquet of yellow roses, she stood motionless. And there she remained, paralysed with grief, incapable of responding to the comforting words of the townspeople courageous enough to approach her.

Not until several hours later, with the scalding sun beating down on her head, did Maria Stella allow herself to be led away. Beyond that she showed no sign of emerging from the grief-stricken stasis into which the terrible events of that morning had thrown her. Nor was there any reason in the weeks and months which followed to suppose that she might regain her wits and take full cognizance of what had befallen her. Indeed, the reverse was the case. Maria Stella lost her power of speech almost entirely, often reaching the point of asphyxiation when she tried to form words. The outlook, according to the physicians in whose care she was placed, was far from good.

But what they and the many others who observed her during that time were wont to overlook was that Maria Stella had loved and been loved and harboured the seeds of her own recovery. And that was certainly borne out by the course her recovery took. The first words she managed to say with ease were *Umberto* and *Donna Chiara*, words to which she returned again and again whenever her speech failed her.

In time she regained her voice, a process which was accelerated by the growing realization that all the great events of her life had already taken place, and the only way forward, a quest for understanding of those events.

Mizaru

1

Our road, as I still call it, spins out from a big, bustling roundabout and, after a mile or so, just when it seems to be losing momentum, loops directly back into another. It's one of the main routes in and out of the city so nowadays it's chock-a-block most of the time, traffic snailing along all day. It's not a suburb, at least not in the sense that it has a life of its own. There are shops all right, several of them at both roundabouts, some quite large. But most people still think of the city centre four miles away as the real heart of the neighbourhood.

The only shop on the road itself is Reedy's, a converted garage with a galvanized lean-to stretching out as far as the pavement. Inside, two narrow aisles, dug out like tunnels through a mountain of stock, lead to a fluorescent grotto of cooked meats and dairy products.

There are two funeral parlours on the road, built about ten years ago by rival brothers, Ernie and Toss Galvin. One of them, Ernie, is currently building a crematorium nearby. It's on the site of what we, the Ace Commandos, used to call Saigon, a disused farmyard from which all our military man-oeuvres in the neighbourhood were conducted.

My father likes to joke about the crematorium, likes to tell people what he said to the two members of the residents' association who called asking him to sign a petition objecting to its construction.

'A crematorium? Sure it's a godsend at my age. Why would I want to object to it?'

He laughs at the good of it. Laughs heartily as he describes their reaction.

'Stood there, they did. Dumbfounded. Didn't know what to make of me.'

'Dumbfounded,' he says again more forcibly, using the word to hike his laughter to a higher pitch. 'Didn't know what to make of me.'

It's a story he has told me several times over the past few months. I think what he enjoys most is the false impression he gave, the idea that they thought him morose and fatalistic. The opposite in fact of what he is. Difficult to see what other opinion they could have formed of a man in his mid-seventies delighted to have a crematorium on his doorstep.

He gets a big kick out of misrepresenting himself, out of masking his true intent. 'Outfoxing them,' as he would put it. It's a skill in which he has prided himself for as long as I can remember. And beyond that too, because whenever he talks about his youth, about escapades with his brothers, almost all his stories end in triumph. Victory won by some last-minute ploy in which they outwitted the other side. And there was no shortage of 'other sides' in the small Tipperary town in which he grew up. Anyone of any standing qualified; shopkeepers, the local garda sergeant, Colonel North, whose estate, with its savage dogs and man traps designed to catch poachers, was a perilous no-man's-land into which they often ventured.

I loved those stories. Still do, though not in the same way. They carry a sense of power, of possibility, passed on like ancestral weaponry; my father there telling me that whatever the odds, *we always managed to hold our own*. And we did it by *keeping our mouths shut, by not letting on, by keeping the trump card up our sleeve until the time was right to slam it down for victory*.

My uncles roamed fearlessly through those stories, each of them every bit as magnificent in real life. They came to Dublin whenever Tipperary were playing, which twenty, thirty years ago was quite a lot. My cousins, most of them around my age, travelled with them, all bunched into Uncle Frank's green Vauxhall. They insisted on squeezing us in too, my father and I. And off we all drove to Croke Park, seven or eight of us on board, all roaring 'up Tipp' through the open windows.

My father's *trump card* in the crematorium episode remains *up his sleeve*. He knows there is no need to play it, at least not when he tells the story to me. It goes without saying that he has no intention of being cremated. None whatsoever. He will be buried where my mother is buried, in the small, hillside cemetery about a mile outside his native Derryveigh, a place he visits at least a half dozen times a year. Meanwhile he has every intention of outfoxing death and is making a first rate job of it.

2

My mother's family are different. They have little or no lore, no ancestral weaponry. And even though they too are from Tipperary, they did not come to Dublin for matches, let alone roar 'up Tipp' through the open windows of a car.

In the main, they came to visit, to sit for an hour or two in the sitting-room, drinking tea and talking to my mother.

Aunt Girlie, my mother's youngest sister, was the exception. She came up on shopping trips, usually accompanied by her daughters, Rachel, Constance and Olwen. She parked her car, a sleek, black BMW, in later years a bottle-green Jag, outside our house. Then, after a hurried cup of tea they'd set out for the city centre by bus.

Their return journey, late in the afternoon, was made by taxi. The four of them emerged from under a mound of shopping, lurched to our door and stumbled in. At the first opportunity they dropped their carrier bags and boxes, feigning collapse and sighing competitively.

Showing my mother what they bought was a big part of the day, a part she enjoyed no end. She encouraged them to try on their new outfits, suggested different combinations, told them how well this or that would go with something she recalled them buying on a previous trip. Before long the whole house was humming, a sleepy harbour roused by the arrival of an exotic cruiser, my cousins running up and down the stairs, tissue paper strewn everywhere, 'gorgeous' hissed in breathless admiration. And my mother, suddenly girlish, her enthusiasm and excitement conjuring up a person I hardly recognized.

I spent the greater part of those visits hanging around the car, leaning against it, opening it, sitting in it, closing it. Its presence more than compensated for my mother's family's lack of lore. It set us apart from our neighbours, showed us in our true light, because while that neat, well-maintained, pebble-dash house was home, tightly woven into our view of ourselves there was the belief that we were heirs to a worthier legacy.

It would be easy to attribute that fancy to my father's 'up Tipp' bravado, to his belief that his native Derryveigh was second to none, a connection of immeasurable value. But lots of households on our road had fathers from rural towns like Derryveigh, and sons who, like myself, identified with the county of their father's birth, fiercely loyal to the county team throughout their childhood. The big defection to our native Dublin did not come until we, these city-born sons, were in our early teens, something many fathers saw as a rejection of all they stood for, which I suppose it was.

But my father took a very different view. The Dublin team was on a roll at the time, I was right in there, part of Heffo's army, and I think he regarded my defection as clever, a canny move which had me on the winning side. And he valued that as much, perhaps even more than he valued my loyalty to Tipp.

'His crowd,' he would say to his brothers when talk turned to the Dubs. The careless toss of his head in my direction, the grudging tone in which he said 'his crowd', had all the hallmarks of disappointment. But I knew there wasn't a whit of criticism implied. That careless toss of his head acknowledged that I had made a smart move. It was a language my uncles spoke every bit as fluently as my father. Their contentment at having a Dublin supporter in their midst was made very clear to me in the way each of their well-scrubbed faces became fixed in an approving scowl the minute my father said 'his crowd'.

Complicated as that disguising of sentiment could sometimes be, I was still much more at home with it than I was with the way my mother operated. A lot of the time it was impossible to know what was going on. That was the case even with Girlie. My mother might enter enthusiastically into the excitement of those shopping trips, more buoyant with her sister and her nieces than she ever was with us. But then, within minutes of their leaving, she would begin to criticize them.

'The truth is some of the things Girlie buys are ridiculous. Rachel and Constance have the figure, Olwen too. But she definitely doesn't.' I wasn't much of an audience, but that rarely seemed to matter. 'Of course, Girlie always does exactly as she pleases. Selfish. Always was.'

Occasionally I got the impression that my mother would say these things even if I wasn't there. It was as if she was in constant discussion with her family, never reaching any kind of resolution.

'Girlie is the last person I'd turn to if there was trouble. The very last.'

Before long Girlie's fall from grace is complete. The mysterious scent of my cousins has been usurped by cooking oil, their discarded tissue paper and carrier bags all gathered up. The ironing board, out of the sitting-room for their visit, is back in place, a heap of clothes beside it. Not a single trace of their visit remains except for my mother's mood, her unexplained anger, that sense of grievance she seems unable to keep to herself.

[3]

My mother never took any steps to protect herself from whatever it was about those visits that upset her. For years I followed her blindly into the fray, stumbling behind, trying to keep pace with the jump of her indignation. But as I grew older I learned to keep my distance, to look to my father when she was in the grip of that reckless anger, watch the masterful way he diffused it. His opening tactic was to delay. Wait until it was in full swing, then begin by agreeing wholeheartedly with the harshest of her criticisms.

'You never spoke a truer word, Margaret,' he would pronounce.

It was a convincing mask, one that made him appear every bit as critical of her sisters as she was herself. Then they would compete with each other in the scramble for faults. Any attempt on my part to defend my aunts was instantly scotched. 'It's none of your concern.' Or, 'Stay out of this, you.' Words which carried all the weight of a prison sentence.

I don't know when I figured out that there was some sort of private ritual in progress. But somewhere along the line my father began to draw me in. With a behind-the-scenes gesture, more often than not a quick cheek-twitch of a wink, he'd let me know that he did not mean to be taken too literally.

'She comes here to cause trouble. She does it for spite. She's always just waiting to have a go at you,' he might say to my mother

'Well, I wouldn't go that far, Pat. I mean, she has her good points . . .' she might reply, stalling while she prepared to defend the sister in question.

And so, disarmed by his tactics, she would start to take back what she had said. My father too would begin his retreat, tiptoeing away with her anger, as if it was a pair of scissors or a blade taken from a small child. But the last word, always his, and usually pitched from behind his newspaper, did not follow for at least ten or fifteen minutes.

'They're not the worst, not the worst at all.'

In steering her back, my father restored the ease which marked our lives together. But regardless of how put-out she had been by any of those visits from her sisters, and some of them knocked the jiz out of her for days, the prospect of another prompted a spate of cleaning, of cake-making, of excitement which did not sour to hostility until they had left. It was as if she was drawn towards them and rebuffed by them in equal measure.

My father never objected to their visits, at least never in my hearing. He may even have enjoyed unravelling the tangle in which they left my mother. It called for strategy, for delicacy. A bit like a formal wooing. Maybe that was it, maybe he lost her to them and won her back over and over again through-out their forty years together.

[4]

My Aunt Ber's visits had an air of comic espionage about them. Her insinuating 'hello' and her contrived calm set the agenda from the outset. She had important matters to discuss, make no mistake about it. Her first objective was to get my mother to herself in the sitting-room, which involved getting rid of me. That would have been easy enough if she hadn't gone in for extravagant, hammish gestures, never quite out of my field of vision, indicating to my mother that what she had to say could not be said within my hearing. Once alerted, I dug my heels in, unwilling to be pushed around by someone who seemed to consider her claim on my mother greater than my own. Just to impress on her how mistaken she was on that score I often hung about longer than I would have done, once or twice stubbornly sitting through an entire session.

Ber had joined a convent in the nineteen forties, directly after she finished secondary school. *Entered*, as my mother always put it, without ever saying where or what she had entered. Some twenty, twenty-five years later, the rules changed. The enclosed life she and the other nuns led was ended. Free to re-enter the secular world whenever she wished, she set about re-establishing herself in the family, thinking her place there secure. Sadly, that belief was consistently eroded down through the years only to be dealt a crippling blow by the sale of the family farm in 1978. But the full impact of these displacements did not become apparent – at least not to me – until she was well into her sixties. Then it was as if all the important decisions she had ever made were called into question. She lost all sense of direction and with it her breezy confidence.

Years of part-time courses followed, all with a philosophical bent. Equally caught up and equally lost in the maze of undergraduate ideas around at the time I was singled out as a sounding board. Flattered by the eagerness with which she accepted what I had to say, I spent several family get-togethers, funerals in the main, rambling wide-eyed among the ologies with her.

In the end, Ber's search for a new foundation was fruitless. If anything it only left her more displaced than ever. She remained, first and foremost, dutiful at heart, a position which seemed at best old-fashioned, at worst foolish.

Advancing age has allowed her to sidle back into community life and she has done so with an obsequiousness painful to observe. Sometimes I visit her, bringing my own children Conor and Aoife with me. Her attempts to reach them lock us all into rigid embarrassment. I take refuge in talk about world events, make pronouncements which straight away seem to lose their meaning in the tidy drawing-room of that suburban bungalow she shares with four other nuns.

Of the many different themes she and my mother fixed on in their heyday, all involved their sisters: Flossie, Nora and Girlie. Flossie, their eldest, unmarried sister was by far the most frequently discussed.

There never seemed to be enough time to say all they had to say about Flossie's running of the family farm, 'the place', as they always called it. The smallest adjustment she made, new curtains in one of the bedrooms for instance, would be reported by Ber and discussed by both in minute detail. In that way the place – Templeard – took on an importance which diminished that of our own house and made the life that went on in it seem uneventful, at least while the visit lasted.

Flossie's so-called moods, her relations with the neighbours, the Campions, her appearance – everything had to be considered and assessed. Ber's departure often took as long as the visit itself. Swept along on a great torrent of talk, they clung for as long as possible to every fixed point on the course, the mantelpiece in the sitting-room, the hall door, the garden gate, the car. Then finally overpowered, they separated, each watching the other return to a life which could never be charged with the same intensity as the one they shared.

The high-tide mark of those sessions extended from the period just before my grandfather died in 1975 until the farm was sold about three years later. From when I was twelve until I was almost sixteen. There were any number of crises. At some point during my grandfather's final illness there was a question of his going to a nursing home, or a hospital maybe. Either way, the proposal prompted a series of heated conferences and frantic phone calls. The outcome was a campaign, coordinated by my mother and Ber, to impress on Flossie my grandfather's right to spend his final days in his own home. This and the many other campaigns they waged to impress on Flossie the responsibilities that went with the place, had the tacit backing of Nora, who lived in England – who still lives in England – and Girlie, who probably allowed herself to be roped in to avoid trouble.

The hostility which the sale of the place caused made life impossible in our house for months. There was talk of Flossie coming to live with us after the sale, a plan to which I objected vehemently.

Nora was held almost as responsible as Flossie for the sale.

My mother said she was bitter, that she had persuaded Flossie to sell out of spite. Spite. Bitterness. These words were not followed by question marks. I had no reason to question them at the time.

5

Flossie was never fully forgiven for the loss of Templeard. But when my mother suffered a second stroke in the summer of 1995, there was a softening, a thaw in relations. Flossie and Nora came to visit twice during Nora's annual holiday. On their first visit, on the way from the airport, they stopped briefly. On the second visit, they stayed for a long time talking with my mother in the sitting-room, which had been converted into a bedroom because she could no longer climb the stairs.

Despite that, the outlook for a full recovery was good. 'Excellent', my father and I had been told, both by the consultant and the physiotherapist. They had repeatedly stressed the importance of 'a positive approach', which by and large my mother seemed to be taking. Every day, helped by my father, she did a series of exercises and had recently reported the partial return of sensation to her left shoulder. It was with more resentment than I could contain that I watched Flossie and Nora emerge from that room after the second of their two visits, downcast and silent. There was no doubt in my mind that they were dramatizing my mother's illness, Flossie in particular, carrying on as though it was the last time she would ever see my mother.

I hummed and hawed as they set about leaving, annoyed by my failure to challenge them.

'Keeping her spirits up is a big part of her recovery,' I eventually say to Flossie.

'It's to her you should be saying that, not me,' Flossie replies, tipping her head in Nora's direction. This is followed by a determined, tight-lipped rush for the front door, with Nora following, calling after her, asking her to wait. Flossie just stomps ahead, forcing Nora to break into a trot to keep up.

In the room I find my mother crying, though I can hardly bear to look. The second stroke had left one side of her face slack, her left eye half-closed, a dribble of saliva leaking out the side of her down-turned mouth.

'Rooney,' she says, her voice stalling. A smile breaks awkwardly over the right-hand side of her face. 'He's in the car. Outside.'

'Waiting all this time,' I laugh, relieved to be on familiar territory, laughing with my mother at Flossie's treatment of Rooney. She does not want to talk about her sisters' visit. And, for the moment, neither do I.

Rooney is Flossie's companion, though unpaid driver and general dogsbody would probably be a more fitting description. He made his first appearance about twenty years ago, around the time Flossie sold Templeard. He was there the day we all went down to clear the place out. There was no question then in my mother's mind about his motives. 'After her money, nothing else,' she insisted, making no attempt to disguise her anger. But Rooney turned out to be what my father calls 'a nervous nellie', a singularly ineffectual man who, to this very day, Flossie keeps on probation. Encouraged by my father, my mother learned not only to laugh at Flossie's humiliating treatment of Rooney, but to specialize in reporting its worst excesses.

'He's been there for hours,' I say, lifting Nora's lipstick-rimmed tea cup from the mantelpiece and placing it on the tray. 'He's well used to it,' I continue. 'When she went in for those tests last year, remember, she made him wait in the hospital car park all night.'

'Pat, I haven't been fair to Nora.' My mother's voice is crystal clear, every word separately emphasized – or maybe that's just how I remember it now.

I lift the tray, leave it down again when I realize I can't hold it and open the door at the same time. I'm intent on what I'm doing. I do not want to hear what my mother has to say about Nora. She and Flossie have caused enough distress with their defeatism, all that death-bed stuff. I open the door and when, seconds later, I turn to collect the tray, see that my mother's eyes are firmly fixed on something on the wall facing her. I look across, see only the familiar zigzagging lines of the wall paper. Look back. Her face is blank, head slumped slightly forward.

I bring the tray to the kitchen, prompted by some absurd notion that if I do everything correctly, all will be well. But I'm losing ground rapidly. I go to the front door, look out for my father. When I see no sign of him I approach the half-opened door of my mother's room, knock, listen intently, then ring for an ambulance.

I begin to rehearse what I will say to the ambulance crew. I imagine one of them, see him there listening to my account of what happened, interrupting to tell me what I am unable to say to myself.

The siren bellows up our street, continuing to fill the house well after it has been turned off. My father arrives at the gate just ahead of the ambulance men. It is the first time he has been out of the house in a week.

Nobody says she is dead. We just stand looking at her, my father and I at the front, the two ambulance men restless in the background.

'Flossie and Nora,' I half whisper to him. 'They were here until ten minutes ago. She was fine until then.'

My father does not reply which, as the seconds pound by, comes as a relief. My foolish words fall slowly through the heavy air, the childish fear that I might be held responsible for my mother's death laid bare.

As it turned out, my father was much more prepared for her death than I was. He seemed to grasp it in its entirety, sink with it to the depths to which it brought him, whereas I seemed only able to catch it in snatches. In some way that's how it has remained, with questions about her life suddenly bringing her back, her death somehow incomplete.

6

Of my mother's four sisters, Nora is the one I have seen least frequently in recent years. And never once without Flossie. Still, whenever I think about those sisters, which at present is a great deal more than I have ever done before, Nora is the one on whom my thoughts settle, her mild reserve welcome midst all the bluster of the others. But long before I became conscious of that reserve, I had formed an altogether different opinion of her, one I still hold in the main, shaped as it was during the long Christmas holidays we spent in Templeard every year until I was twelve.

She was the opposite to Flossie in every sense. Within minutes of our arrival Flossie would begin to list all the things she hoped I wouldn't do that year. This involved tut-tutting references not merely to last year's crimes but to all the crimes I had ever committed in Templeard. The worst involved chasing a hen to its death, or more accurately chasing a hen who stopped suddenly, causing me to fall. My right knee landed full force on its splayed wing, which remained splayed as it hobbled away. Fearing that Flossie would discover the injury, I got one of my grandfather's walking sticks and in a wild frenzy, intensified by the hysteria of the other hens, clobbered it to death. Flossie caught me burying it under a mound of straw in the inner yard. She would not accept that it was a mercy killing, that the hen had been all but dead when I decided to finish it off. She told me I was on the way to becoming a criminal and would one day have human blood on my hands if I did not mend my ways. She reported the crime far and wide and reconstructed it tediously every time I met her for years afterwards.

Nora's greeting on our Christmas Eve arrival was unassuming, shy even. She stood back, allowed the others to clamour and fuss, then when things had quietened down a bit, took me aside and gave me the first of a series of presents, always a box of books. These she read with me over the days that followed, her slender white fingers pointing at men falling from the sky in parachutes, elephants sitting eating at tables, ships floating in the night sky, Nora every bit as delighted by them as I was.

Her Christmas-day presents, left in the dining room grate, were different to the useful presents, jumpers and the like, left there by the others. Cars, big sleek American models, complete with elaborate wings and chrome finishes, the latest Scalectrix sets, self-assembly space stations with rockets that projected as far as the ceiling – presents I was not allowed to open until after breakfast. Then, down on my hands and knees and closely observed by Flossie, Nora, Ber, my mother and father, I started the unwrapping, never fully sure if my gasps of astonishment lived up to expectation.

'You needn't be looking up at me. There's nothing there from me,' Flossie says flatly. 'I wouldn't see you spoiled.'

I look to my father, wonder if I'm supposed to be grateful to Flossie. Straight away he is down on his knees too, marvelling at everything, asking me to demonstrate this and that, his gaping amazement a spur to look for new tricks, to speculate, to tell him I think the batteries in the gold Cadillac are everlasting. Behind us the others take on a photographic stillness now, over-exposed at the edges, their red eyes investing me with an importance that hangs like a heavy cloud over my every move.

In the changing perspective, brought about by the events which prompted this long backward glance, I see Nora traipsing around Hamleys or one of the other big toy shops in London, and wonder if her mission to buy toys for me was a sad part of her own journey.

As for Flossie's announcement, I wonder about that too, wonder who those words were directed at. My parents? The whole group? Was it a warning, a crude statement to everyone that she had no obligations to me?

7

Nora's absence from the pickle of her sisters' lives dates from the sale of Templeard and her marriage two years later in September 1980. Her annual return visits, always alone, had the hallmarks of duty about them, her subservience to Flossie, so absolute as to appear intentional, adopted for the week. She continues to come, always for the first week in August, still drawn by duty it would seem.

My mother often spoke of how inseparable Flossie and Nora were as children, always regarding her as a nuisance, 'a tag along' they went to the rounds of the earth to get rid of. And later, when Nora's singing began to attract serious attention, the whole house was organized around her going to lessons and competitions. My mother never went so far as to say that Nora was the favourite, but she implied as much. Nora had 'everyone wrapped around her little finger, with them all waiting on her hand and foot'.

Even in my mother's rosiest stories about her childhood Nora appeared as a show-off, someone who left her and the others in the shade, 'parroting all Daddo's talk about the history of the place, reading Ammie's books and talking about them as if she was the world expert'. And her trophies, won at Feis Ceoils, displayed on the sideboard in the parlour in Templeard, were always gleaming, 'polished by you know who', my mother would say pointing at herself.

I wonder now if, under all the rubble, there was an un-excavated voice, my mother on the point of saying, 'Nora was on course for a fall . . .' A voice that might have lost its sharp edge, its childish intolerance if it had all been spoken about.

Nora sails into view, her peach-coloured suit with its lace trimmings the focus of wild admiration on her wedding day. The others, Flossie, Ber, Girlie and my mother are gathered around, examining her suit's every seam and tuck, laughing and clinking glasses, their intimacy on show to everyone gathered on that sunny lawn in Kent. It was the last time I saw the five of them in a devil-may-care mood, declaring their unity to the world.

For weeks beforehand they had been in a panic, Flossie, Ber and my mother, conferring with each other so frequently and with such authority that it seemed they could call the marriage off if they wished. There were many questions to be considered. Malcolm Hapworth, Nora's husband, was a divorcé, a point which Flossie considered in his favour, though she was hard put to know why Nora could not opt for the same arrangement as she had with Rooney.

'Every man isn't as flexible as Jim,' I heard my mother respond. And in the background my father's earnest 'Indeed,' so loaded with irony that even Flossie, self-absorbed as she was, sensed a jibe.

It's difficult to know whether Ber had serious reservations or not. Perhaps she felt she ought to. When pressed for an opinion by the others, she said she'd prefer not to discuss the matter. Flossie considered this position intolerable and challenged it in a way Ber found embarrassing.

'For mercy's sake, Ber, what's to be said against it? What of it if there's sexual intercourse going on, married or not married, divorced or not divorced. I mean who or what would she be holding out for? Or any of us, if it comes to that?'

My father attributed these views to her fondness for a series of daily tell-all radio programmes. To this day he is unable to contain his laughter when he recalls Flossie's own participation, years later, in one of those shows, every detail of her arrangements with Rooney discussed on air.

The difficulties of Malcolm Hapworth's being a divorcé were – though my mother never said so explicitly – more than adequately offset by the fact that he was a doctor. Her acceptance hinged on the reassuring fact that his children were grown up, that his wife was already well settled into 'a new relationship'. That became the catch-phrase during the weeks running up to the wedding. 'A new relationship.' It was passed from one to the other and then back again, all laying claim to it in their different ways, pleased to find themselves moving forward together into a different climate.

8

Our return flight to Dublin after the wedding marked a return to ourselves. A regrouping, with my mother taking the lead.

'It was the worst wedding I was ever at. The worst.' She shook her head solemnly, defying my father and me to take any other stance.

'A dull old affair,' my father replied, 'a dull old affair.'

'I'm glad she didn't ask me to be a witness. Flossie said the registry office hadn't been cleaned in a year.'

'Is that so?' he asked wearily.

'I didn't see a person under seventy from beginning to end.'

My father glanced in my direction, brows briefly raised in warning.

'Something very dead about the whole thing, all right.' He stretched up and adjusted the air vent directly above him, twisted it this way and that, then angled his face to catch the stream of cool air gushing out.

'And that Malcolm Hapworth, smiling like a Cheshire cat, nothing to say for himself.'

'Hard to know what to make of him.' My father's eyes are closed, all his concentration focused on the gush of cool air.

'A fool, if you ask me.' My mother's voice is heard over the background hum of voices. A woman across the aisle leans out from her seat and peers inquisitively in our direction.

'Bit on the bland side, no doubt about that.'

'And all those ones with the hats, whispering. You'd think it was a funeral they were at. Then asking us to sing, like we were a band of tinkers that had just turned up.'

Suddenly my father opens his eyes. 'What sort of place was it anyway?'

'A country club. It's the fashion.'

'More like a glorified pub. What killed me was the sandwiches, a wedding with nothing to eat except sandwiches. Can you credit travelling to England for a sandwich?' He is in full swing now.

'Canapés, they were canapés.'

'What's the difference? Either way you have to stand up eating them.'

'I prefer that, it means you don't get stuck with the same person for three hours,' she says defensively.

There is a lull, a moment or two, while my father takes stock.

'Champagne is all right for the toasting, but the wrong drink to serve all afternoon.' His distaste is shown in a rapid bunching of his nose and lips.

'Well, tell that to the Queen. It's what was served at the royal wedding.'

'I don't care where it was served, no drink is surer to give you indigestion.' He digs his fingers into the centre of his chest.

'I didn't see you refusing it.'

'How could I? There was nothing else. What other way would I have got through the bloody thing?'

'Well, it mightn't have been the liveliest affair, but there was a fair bit of style there all the same.'

My father nods, glints of contentment flickering across his face.

But it didn't end there. Two, three minutes later, my father, stretching across to give the stewardess his tray, turned to my mother.

'Still, Nora seemed happy.'

'Yes,' she said before she had time to think about it.

'As happy as I have ever seen her. Happier,' my father added, but my mother had already drifted into thought, carried away, perhaps, by a vision of Nora on that sunny lawn in Kent, happy.

9

I went to London the following summer with a group of friends, most of whom had been in my year at school. A job as a hospital porter had been lined up through Nora. The intention was to use it as a base from which to find a better job. But work, work of any kind, was impossible to get so I remained there until a week or two before college reopened in the autumn.

Plans for a summer of everything had soured rapidly. Most of the others ended up leaving London, heading either for the canning factories in the East Midlands or home.

Earlier that year, Malcolm and Nora had moved to Folkestone. He had taken on some sort of retainership as medical officer with a shipping company. It was a stepping-stone to retirement, following a career as an anaesthetist in the hospital where Nora had been an administrative officer. They decided to keep Nora's flat in Lambeth for the overnight trips they envisaged making to London, but those trips turned out to be infrequent. They were considering selling. I was given the use of it for the summer.

The order in the flat was oppressive, everything in its place, folded, wrapped or laid out as if on exhibition. Even the box of matches on the small pottery dish beside the cooker had a symmetry to it that said, 'Do not touch.' The highly polished mahogany chest of drawers and the matching wardrobe in the bedroom were full of Nora's clothes, some wrapped in tissue paper, others in plastic covers.

The record collection, stored in a series of long, black spiral containers with chrome handles, must have contained every musical ever recorded. There were dozens of operas too, glossy sleeves with pained tenors and distraught sopranos.

Despite the array of clothes, books, records, ornaments, there was an anonymity about it all. It was no different to how I now imagine a hundred thousand other flats of its era must have looked. A bid for sameness on Nora's part maybe, facelessness sought in the sentimental figurines on the mantelpiece, in the frothy seascape hanging in the hall, in the pink of the bathroom walls, in the willow patterned cups and saucers, in just about everything except for the large portrait of Daniel O' Connell, the Liberator, hanging over the mantelpiece in the sitting-room. I knew that puffy smirk well. It had hung in the dining-room of Templeard and had a place in my Christmas morning memories. Flossie, Nora, Ber, my mother and father, and O' Connell looking down at me on the floor of the cold dining-room opening those presents.

I never understood why the good fortune I felt in having the flat was not shared by my mother. She made her position clear in the course of one of the regular, Sunday night calls she made that summer. Her voice, full of concern about my arrangements as always, tightened when I began to tell her how lucky I was to have the flat. I think it followed a discussion about where Ray Mullin and Beeze Ward, friends she knew well, were living. They worked the night-shift in an adhesive factory and had a bed share with two Poles who worked the day-shift. The landlady lived on the ground floor, and spent her day monitoring the comings and goings of the tenants. They entered and left like thieves, whispering whenever they spoke during the nine illicit hours they spent there every day. Weekend sleeping was paid for by the hour, available only when the Poles went to the pub.

'So in comparison to Ray and Beeze, I'm steeped.'

A very doubtful 'well' followed, a far cry from the rush of agreement I had expected.

'I've Nora to thank,' I went on.

'Nora to thank? What do you mean?' Her voice was spiky.

'Nora to thank . . .' I faltered, then limped through a restatement of my case. 'Nora to thank for lending me the flat.'

'You have no such thing,' she paused to gather pace. 'That flat was bought for her by Daddo. Why wouldn't you have the use of it?'

I waited, thinking there was more to follow. But there wasn't. As far as she was concerned what she had said was self-explanatory.

10

There was no sense of beginning at what I have since come to regard as the starting point of this long look back.

Saturday morning. We are on familiar ground, my father and I, Flossie's latest escapade the talking point, broached in such a low-key way by my father as to make it seem a matter of little importance. Conor and Aoife are watching TV. Our arrival five, ten minutes earlier greeted with surprise by my father, reluctant to acknowledge that we come every Saturday morning.

'Flossie is on the war path.' He is moving around the kitchen, looking for something. 'Against the nuns,' he adds.

I wait, laugh a little in anticipation of the quip I expect to follow.

'And she'll have her way if something isn't done about it.' He looks in my direction, an earnestness in his expression. For a moment he appears tired. 'She's trying to serve an injunction on them.'

I'm preoccupied by how unmoved Conor and Aoife are by the frantic efforts of the TV presenter. Getting in and out of a box, screaming.

'On the nuns.' He opens the drawer in which everything which hasn't got a particular place in the house is kept. Jumbled string, fly swat, ancient holy water bottle, brass wall hooks, yellowing household appliance manuals, jam covers, coupons, unrecognizable gadgetry. He begins to fooster.

'What are you looking for?'

'There'll be trouble unless she's stopped.'

'An injunction for what?'

'Hanley rang during the week, asking if there was anything I could do to stop her.'

Ever since the sale of Templeard, over twenty years ago, Flossie's solicitor has looked to my father as the voice of reason. The closure of the sale had been delayed because of some of the conditions Flossie wanted written into the contract at the last minute. She got cold feet just before the final documents of transfer were due to be signed and demanded a change of mind clause, the right, for a year I think, to declare the contract void if she so wished. Hanley was in frequent contact with my father then, trying to devise ways of bringing the whole business to a close.

My father decides to sort the contents of the drawer, placing all the things he intends throwing out on to the table.

'What can I do to stop her?' he asks. A disc from a hand-operated mincing machine lands on the table, spins in my direction.

'What is she taking the injunction against?' I ask again.

He raises his eyes. 'God knows. It could be anything.'

Somehow that seemed satisfactory at the time. A likely intermission in another Flossie episode, a promise to keep me posted implicit in the loose wrap-up.

Conor and Aoife leave the chair they have been sharing and sidle over to where I'm sitting. They back slowly into me, each appropriating a knee without taking their eyes off the TV. I draw them towards me, hold them tightly until they wriggle out of my grip.

My father stops foostering, pulls the drawer out and empties the entire contents on to the table.

'I think I'll throw the bloody lot out,' he says, pleased with the plan. 'Nothing you want there, I suppose.'

I shake my head, open the newspaper I have brought and scan the TV columns, noting the matches I know he is planning to view that afternoon. Soon his whole face is alert, his eyes narrowing as he predicts a win here, a walkover there, words blending in the rush to say all he has to say about the afternoon games, the twists and turns of his Tipperary accent sharpening with every breath.

[11]

I arrive back an hour or so earlier than expected. Straight away Conor and Aoife begin to describe the TV programmes they were watching, prompting Claire to ask them questions which, though not devised to establish that they spent the hour and a half watching junk TV, end up doing precisely that.

In her place, I might have taken advantage of this in a light-hearted sort of way, maybe tossed in an observation about TV and quality minding in a bid to put myself ahead in the Saturday play off for time. But all Claire does is laugh as Conor and Aoife lie down on the floor to demonstrate one of the daft games they saw.

What kills me is the way she still manages to clock up points. Lots of them.

I proceed carefully. I know Claire will probably have Conor and Aoife on board for the rest of the day. And there won't be any junk TV. She'll have something planned, something that will have them all fired up, pleading every two minutes to get going.

'Dad wasn't in great form. I was thinking of going back this afternoon, maybe watch one of the games with him.' A problem. Our problem.

'Fine,' she hums, deftly appropriating whatever points I have left.

Claire brings a mountain of files home at the weekends. Her failure to make any inroad into them has somehow become my failure too. They sit on the hall table, marking my exits and my entrances, noting how long I intend staying out. And, on my return, quick to tell me I always take more than my fair share in the time stakes.

My father is not in the least surprised to see me, making me wonder if I told him I would be back. Positive I didn't, I begin to see his antics as part of that outfoxing game he plays. The assorted contents of the drawer are still splayed out on the table, lifeless, like creatures unable to adjust to a new habitat. He lifts his lunch plate from the space cleared among them, dallies with it at the sink for a while.

'Flossie will have to be stopped,' he announces.

He turns around, no trace of his playful self in evidence. There is a food stain on his tie, a blob of gravy at which I stare for too long, triggering a volley of cross-fire, fumbling old age noted and rejected in the fast interchange of glances between us.

'The injunction?' I rush the words at him.

'Yes. Against the nuns, stopping them from contacting the child.' Words hurled out recklessly. 'They wrote saying they had had enquiries. They never answered them. But they're answering them now and want information. On account of the way things are.'

'What child?'

My father turns on the TV, looks for a few seconds at a snooker game, flicks channels rapidly, then turns it off.

'The child,' he insists, demanding I go along with him. 'I didn't hear about it until after you were born,' he eventually says. Then points at the kitchen table as he tells me that the Moses basket in which I was brought from the maternity hospital was placed there. He seems to have no idea how unanchored this information is.

'Your mother couldn't take her eyes off you. Not for a second.'

I don't know where this is leading but I disguise my confusion, make little of his inability to be straightforward. He is keenly aware of this himself, struggling as though with a physical affliction, unable to muster the authority to say what he wants to say. All his hand-me-down wisdom about keeping the trump card up your sleeve, keeping your mouth shut, utterly redundant now.

He turns the TV on again. We watch one of the snooker players chalk his cue, hunch slowly as he lines the shot up.

'Then she starts crying. Looking at you in the Moses basket, with it all pouring out of her. Every bit of it. It was the way she heard about it, that's what upset her the most.'

'Whose child . . . ?'

'It's not known who the father was. It wasn't said.'

'I mean the mother. Who . . .'

He allows a few seconds to elapse then turns away from the TV, mildly exasperated. 'Nora,' he says impatiently, as if my not knowing was a form of stupidity.

'When did this happen?'

He registers my question, but ignores it. 'It wasn't the child your mother was crying over. It was the way she heard it.'

He then begins to settle into the story, his awkward vault over the beginning receding as he recounts the events more or less in sequence. Without batting an eyelid he tells me the child was born in the secondary school where my mother and her sisters had been boarders, that it was all shrouded in secrecy, so much so that my mother and Flossie, one a year ahead of Nora at the time, the other two behind, did not know.

'It wasn't until your mother was nearing the end of her time there that she heard about it, a rumour that a girl had had a baby in the sick room.'

'In the sick room,' I repeat, charging the words with

outrage, willing him to do the same. But he only shifts about a bit, looks at me in a resigned sort of way.

'So it wasn't a secret,' I say.

'Well it was, and it wasn't. Your mother was as quick as the next to pass on that rumour, not knowing it was her own sister she was talking about, not until this friend of hers, God knows I should be able to remember her name.' He pauses while he tries to recall it. 'Anyway, whoever she was said she couldn't stand listening to your mother making a fool of herself, and told her, as I say, it was her own sister who had the baby.'

Lagging behind, I whisper, 'Nora,' say it again as my mother might have said it, then watch as her incredulity gives way to shock.

'Nora,' my father repeats, then draws breath tersely. 'Aye, Nora.'

'Surely there was talk of the father?'

'Well, like the rest of it, whatever talk there was, was all in whispers. There was a farm-hand all right, a young fellow your mother said Nora was brazen with. But when there was nothing said about any of it, that didn't get said either.'

'They all knew and they said nothing?'

'They didn't all know. Isn't that what I'm after telling you. Your mother didn't hear until three years after, and didn't tell me until after you were born. What's more, neither Ber nor Girlie know to this day.'

He looks at me, considers my amazement, then adds. 'At least if they do, they've never let on.'

'The whole thing is just crazy. Ridiculous.'

'You have to know the times that were in it and the sort they were. They had a fierce tip about themselves, the Mackens did. It couldn't have happened to worse. It would have had to be kept quiet. The disgrace of it would have been the downfall of them.'

I catch a first glimpse of how malignant that secret was, see it rotting the centre of my mother's world, there spawning mistrust for decades, a great deal more corrosive than disgrace.

'Well, the long and the short of it is that the nuns who had the child adopted . . .' he pauses, his expression softening. 'Your mother, don't ask me how, was convinced it was a boy.'

'The nuns?' I prompt him to continue.

'They went looking for Nora a while ago. There was some kind of committee set up after all the trouble they've had with people blaming them. They're answering all the letters they got these past years. The letters from people looking to know about their mothers. They wrote off to whoever it is that's looking for Nora. Not telling them anything as far as I know, just . . .'

'What did Nora say?'

'No, no,' he shakes his head emphatically. 'Nora knows nothing about it. They looked for her in Templeard first, wrote to her there, only to be told that Hanley was the one to know where she could be got. Course he never had any truck with Nora, and didn't know, so he gave them Flossie's address, told them she could be got through Flossie.'

My father knows he need not tell me what happened next, need not tell me that Flossie opened the letter, read it and rang Hanley, probably straight away, demanding an injunction to stop things going any further.

'Well the first thing is Nora will have to be told,' I say, convinced this is the only course to take.

In the quiet which follows, it occurs on me that my father has knowingly passed the mantle to me, steered me to a point where I will take over. Ring Hanley. Take Flossie on. Tell Nora what's happening. I could, I suppose, hand that mantle back, tell him I think he has a tough one on his hands, but I don't.

'I'll ring her.'

All the life rushes back into his face. He beams 'would you' as though it had never occurred to him.

'Why not?' I add with less gusto, certain now that he has backed me into this position, that I have been outfoxed.

12

If I had felt in full or even part possession of what I had heard I would have told Claire as soon as I got home. But long after I left my father, the story was still unravelling in my mind, chunks of it moving through the past like great boulders, changing a lot of what I saw when I looked back.

Every time I began to plan what to say to Nora a deluge of questions descended, each in itself a reason to postpone ringing. All weekend her story spun around and around in my head. Efforts to pin it down were hampered by the appearance of my mother at every turn, her resentment clearer than it ever was when she was alive. Her last words, 'Pat, I haven't been fair to Nora,' demanding to be understood, forcing the whole business of Flossie and the injunction into the background. But more important, eclipsing Nora's own place at the centre of her story.

I stayed in the office late on Monday, the decision to contact Nora alternately gathering and losing momentum all day. I eventually rang at about six-thirty. Thought of my father as I tapped out the numbers, all his negotiating antics, his Flossie and Rooney stories, his up Tipp bravado, his unceasing determination to make things work, all familiar landmarks on the path I go down whenever I think that I'm getting out of my depth.

'Patrick, what a pleasant surprise,' Malcolm's welcome is

disarming, forcing me to change pace, ask how he is, answer his enquiries about my father. He takes a long time to get Nora.

I begin by telling her that my father had been going over things, 'Family stuff, a lot of stuff I didn't know about my mother and you and Flossie and all the things that happened.'

'Quite a lot,' Nora laughs mildly. 'Quite a lot.' Her Englishness is always a surprise, her voice a light version of my mother's but for the tightly clipped 'ts'.

'Quite a lot,' I repeat in the expectation that it will lead forward.

'Patrick, is there something in particular?' Nora's voice is steady, the note of enquiry struck so clearly that it continues to sound after she has spoken.

'Well, there is. Yes. On the day you and Flossie came, the last time you saw her, I was wondering what . . .' I stall at the precipice, in the cowardly hope that she will come to the rescue, which she does, more decisively than I could ever have imagined.

'The baby. Is that what you mean?'

I want to say Yes, loud and clear, charge it with gratitude. But I can't. The self-assurance in her voice forces an on-the-spot reappraisal of the Nora I know. And that's where I remain for the first few minutes of that call, foundering in my own astonishment.

She tells me that my mother had demanded a full account, adding that this was because she probably had a sense of her approaching death.

'But she had begun to recover,' I insist, aware of how out of place it sounds.

'Maybe so, Patrick,' Nora replies.

I sink with the thought that my mother could have anticipated her death in such a private, isolated way.

'I never saw Margaret more at one with herself than she

was when we were leaving that day. Never. I've often said so to Flossie.'

I do not like how closely she is tracking my thoughts. But I'm powerless to do anything about it. My voice is stifled by the tight clench of grief in my throat, all my concentration directed to shutting out an image of my mother lying, day in day out, in the darkened sitting-room in our house, her sisters and Templeard the backdrop to her unquiet thoughts. Something of the cold-tea smell of that room mingles with the whiff of soot gusting from beneath the dining-room door in Templeard, a fusion which promises some kind of insight, suddenly out of reach as I re-enter Nora's story.

She is talking about Flossie. Flossie, on that fateful afternoon, did not even then – fifty years down the line – want to hear what was being revealed. She tried to sabotage the telling, an impulse with which Nora is sympathetic. 'Poor Flossie,' she says, conjuring up the image of a distraught child outrightly refusing to accept what is happening.

As Nora speaks I wait for the meek, self-effacing person who hovered in Flossie's shadow on her annual week-long holiday to take over. But nothing of the sort happens. If anything, she becomes even more self-possessed, leading me to ask her why she had not told my mother before, why she had waited all that time.

'I didn't even dare tell myself until I was goodness knows what age, certainly into my fifties.' Only later did it occur to me that she meant it literally, that for decades she had been too frightened to confront the fact that she had given birth to a child.

The peculiar thing is that many of the on-the-spot responses to what I heard in the course of that call are impossible to locate now. They have been swept away on the great swell of questions which followed. I imagine, for instance, that I heard a hollow note when Nora touched on the question of the child's conception. 'I was young . . .' she said blithely. But those words only began to seem suspect later when I was trying to account for the complicity of the nuns, their willingness to allow the birth to take place in the school infirmary. Claire was adamant that this could not have happened unless the nuns themselves had had a reason for concealing the birth. 'She would have been sent to one of those places,' Claire insisted, listing the names of two or three institutions currently in the news for their cruelty to children and unwed mothers.

But one aspect of that conversation with Nora which has not been lost in the blurry moil of all the subsequent revision is the part played by Malcolm. Nora drew him into her story at every opportunity. He was the first person to whom she spoke about the birth of the child. He had made it possible and her gratitude to him was boundless. I point out that anyone hearing it would have been equally sympathetic.

Nora draws breath, on the point of saying something which she decides to withhold. After a few seconds, she says, 'No, Patrick, they wouldn't.' Words weighed down with the implication that I am underestimating Malcolm, which in all probability is true.

Laced through the telling, appearing almost as often as the good soldier Malcolm, is the issue of secrecy, the clandestine atmosphere in which that baby was born. Nora speaks about it with an urgency which prompts me to tell her that I do not need to be convinced, that I understand just how far-reaching the conspiracy of silence had been. But, in truth, I don't. It's almost impossible to go along with the vast conspiracy she is outlining: family, church, school and, by default, the state. The circumstances in which that child was born seem to belong to a very distant past, understandable only in a limited way. But now and then the story bolts out of the past, comes rearing through the centuries and shoots straight to the core of my world, to a place I had in some remote and inexplicable way always kept open for it.

Jolted through time I lose sight of some of the threads Nora is drawing together and fall back on stock responses. I tell her how upsetting I think it must be for her to look back at these events. Say so again, or something to the same effect, a minute or two later. She replies, 'No, not now. It's not upsetting now.' She pauses. 'The opposite really, talking to you like this. It's something I should have done . . .'

'Well, maybe this is the time, the best time. Things have a way of working out . . .' I say, buoyed along by the closeness I feel to her, images of her quiet kindness at Christmas in Templeard flowing back. 'Hanley, you know Hanley, Flossie's solicitor. He rang my father about an injunction she is taking.'

'An injunction? Who on earth against?'

Suddenly I want to stop, want to backtrack. The U-turn options flash to mind. Make a joke of it. Flossie at seventy-something, still taking on the world. I have no choice but to say, 'The nuns,' aware as I do that I am sounding a call to arms in territory which less than a minute ago seemed calm, even serene.

'It seems that there are, were, enquiries. Flossie wants to stop the nuns from giving information.'

'What information? Information to who?'

'They are giving out all the information now. It's a policy not to withhold information about children who were adopted. It's the law. It's been changed I think. I'm sure it won't come to anything. Not at this stage.'

I wait for a response but hear only my own words resounding in the great gulf I have opened up.

She clears her throat. 'Patrick, you understand I need to ring Flossie straight away.'

'Of course.'

I dally, still hoping for a reprieve, but find myself saying, 'It would probably have been better if I hadn't said anything.'

'No. I'm . . .' she pauses, each second filling the space of a minute as she forces herself to say, 'glad to know what's going on.'

There is a deadness about the roofscape at which I'm looking, nothing in the grey monotony to distract me from the thought that I have made a complete mess of this.

13

Just about everything I hoped would not happen as a result of that conversation with Nora happens. And more to boot, much of it in such quick succession that it all appears to be taking place at once. By the time I get home, my father has already been on. He rang to tip me off, as he put it to Claire, intent on alerting me to Flossie's rage at my 'meddling in her business'. When, well into the call, Claire managed to get across to him that she didn't know what he was talking about, they had to go into reverse, work their way right back to the beginning.

This is the first hurdle I have to leap. Explaining to Claire why I had not told her.

There is no beer in the fridge. And I know, before I look into the overhead cupboard, that there is none there either. There is just this peculiarly shaped bottle of Aegean plum brandy we brought back from a holiday years ago, and a German liqueur Claire's sister gave us. All the same I open the cupboard, wondering if this is the moment for the Aegean brandy.

Claire keeps interrupting her account of my father's call to talk to Conor and Aoife. She is leaning over them as though to protect them from the monsters they are drawing.

Still looking into the cupboard, I begin to piece an explanation together, rehearse it to myself before I begin. 'I intended telling you . . .'

'What frightens me about you, Pat,' she cuts in sharply, 'is that you have been here, going about this house all weekend with this in your head. Anything could be going on with you. Anything. And I wouldn't know.'

The Aegean brandy scorches my tongue like a hot iron. Conor and Aoife stare.

'All this is as new to me as it is to you.'

Things begin to loosen a little. It has to do with knowing when we are close to the edge, something Conor and Aoife spark off, which forces us to search for a way of rowing back. I take the lead, lob an exasperated 'sorry' into the quietening fray, then follow through with the explanation. 'It's just that I couldn't get my head around it. I wouldn't have known where to start.'

'What? What can't start?' Conor demands to know, skewing his head to examine his drawing from a different angle.

'Nothing,' we snap at him in unison.

'Those are about the scariest teeth I have ever seen,' Claire is looking at Conor's drawing, baring her teeth, her eyes popping.

They both laugh. Aoife leaps in, points at Claire's goggle-eyed expression with one hand and scribbles excitedly all over the page with the other.

Suddenly I'm in a clearing, quietly exhaling. I empty the Aegean brandy into the sink, throw the bottle into the bin.

'Back in a few minutes. Just slipping down to the off-licence.'

Claire nods. Tells Conor and Aoife they'll be in bed by the time I get back. Then promises them I will go up to say goodnight, maybe tell them a story.

'Yep,' I say. 'Ten minutes. I'll be there.'

The late August evening is still warm, pockets of balmy air trapped in the side slip I take to the shops. People plod along clutching videos and bags of take-away food, all tired, as though waiting for the day to end was sapping all their energy. Conor's question comes to mind. What can't start? Straight away I think about the stories I tell him and Aoife. Stories about my own childhood, a lot of them set in Templeard at Christmas. I wish I could untell those stories now, knock those Christmases off the pedestal I have placed them on in Conor and Aoife's imagination. But what stories will I tell in their place?

When I get back I go directly upstairs. Conor wants me to tell the 'you killing-the-chicken story', but Aoife objects. She puts her hands over her ears and begins to chant. 'No, no, no, no, no,' rocking back and forward in her Teletubbies pyjamas.

'OK. Something different,' I say, but neither are listening. Conor pulls her hands away from her ears, tells her to shut up, twists his round, freckled face way out of shape as he accuses her of always getting her way.

'You know granddad's house, where I used to live years ago. There was an old place with sheds there, back a bit from the street behind us. It used to be a farm. There's building going on there at the moment.'

'What's being built?' Conor asks. His trust in me is un-settling. I manage not to say 'a crematorium', which is about the only pitfall I successfully dodge in the short, very short, telling of that would-be story. I am unable to strike a single spark of magic, thoughts straying everywhere, to Nora, to Flossie, to my mother.

Downstairs, I potter around for a bit. Claire is sitting at the table. It is as though I'm already sitting opposite her, beer poured, talking. I don't like set pieces. I'd prefer to line things up for myself, pour my own beer. There's a low-intensity battle of wits in progress before I even begin to tell her about Nora.

Instead of accepting how incomplete my account of Nora's lot is, I fill in the gaps with possibilities which Claire finds unconvincing. She follows Nora's every emotion at such close range that even the slightest inconsistency becomes a glaring gap. Before long she has become the teller, appropriated the story to herself, flooding it with great bursts of sympathy, charging it with her own anger. She flatly refuses to believe that the child was conceived in the way my father implied, 'a farm-hand Nora was brazen with'. She insists that the nuns were protecting the father in some way, keeping the whole thing under wraps for his sake. She mentions incest but promptly rules that out, not because of the shock I register, but because it doesn't add up.

Somewhere in the pick-and-mix of it all, the idea that someone very influential had fathered the child emerges. Then almost immediately Claire fixes on the notion that it was a priest. Clutching this as though it were a hard fact she rushes back over the story, filling the gaps she has spotted, her certainty gathering pace at a dizzying speed. Mercilessly critical of the nuns until then, she begins to consider them in a different light. Her outrage turns to sympathy in the blink of an eye. The nuns become victims of a bullying church, 'left to do all the dirty work, clean up the mess of some rapist operating with a dog collar', as she puts it.

'Rapist?' I say.

'Yes. It had to be. No matter what way you look at it. She was fourteen, for God's sake.'

Claire leaps from one conclusion to the next, propelled by an anger which places her out of reach. At one stage she gets so het up that she all but blames me for what happened, asserting that I go in for 'the sort of silence in which this kind of thing happens'.

We have unexpectedly looped right back to where we were earlier, poised for a re-run of earlier accusations. I cast around for a different angle, shake my head as I return to how surprised I was by Nora's directness. Claire appears not to be listening, which makes her response seem all the more pertinent.

'The up-front stuff is a shield, she told you the greater part of her story without any reservations so that she could hide the nugget she did not intend telling. Hide it better, I mean.'

'What nugget?' I ask, so taken by the notion itself that I fail to see what she is implying.

'The father, of course.'

Comfortably in control she then strikes a more tentative note.

'But it could be something else too.' Her voice trickles away as she gathers her thoughts. 'You know, with something, something that serious, a person – especially if they didn't speak about it for a long time – can, even after they have spoken about it, hang on to the idea that what happened to them is still untold.'

That strikes me forcibly, Nora destined to carry the burden of her secret long after it has been disclosed just as prisoners are said to experience the sensation of confinement long after their release.

14

My father's response to my handling of the whole thing is very uncomplicated. He just tells me I made a complete haimes of it. He is concerned about Nora, but only to a point. His main reaction is one of annoyance. It irks him that passing the buck to me failed so miserably, that Flossie, whom he schemed to keep at arm's length, is now on to him night and day sounding him out on what steps she should take next, telling him how much trouble I have caused.

'What on earth were you thinking of?' he asked, his voice straining with incredulity, the first time we spoke at any length about it. That was on the Saturday morning, a week, though it seemed more like a year, after the whole thing first came to light.

I should have responded honestly, said I was thinking of my mother. But I didn't. There is a hard edge to his sense of loss which makes almost all my references to her seem intrusive. He doesn't want her conjured up in conversation, not by me at any rate. In comparison, the loss I feel is restless, fitful, alive with regret, often sharper now than it was in the immediate aftermath of her death.

At home later on in the day I idle over the conversation with him, answer his opening charge directly. Tell him straight out I was thinking of my mother. Say it again, louder. And again louder still, forcing him to see precisely how she came to be at the forefront of my thoughts during that call. Then I watch, nodding with satisfaction as it begins to dawn on him how ill served she and I were by all that secrecy, how ill served everyone was. But my imaginary success ends there. I cannot persuade him to let go of the belief that secrecy and silence are inherently worthy. His blank, uncomprehending expression remains fixed in my mind's eye as I tell him that they are commonly used weapons of oppression, employed to alienate and intimidate, to protect the depraved.

His advice has always been, 'Keep your head down and your mouth shut.' It is as if he believes there is some greater authority out there, constantly monitoring everyone's conduct, waiting for an opportunity to catch people out. Keeping your head down and your mouth shut is a way of ensuring you are not the one who comes to the notice of that greater authority.

It's not that he is advocating some kind of mindless passivity either. Not at all. When the coast is clear, when you are absolutely sure you are not being observed you drop that mouth-shut, head-down mask of subservience and dash into battle. Then, agenda met, spoils secured, or whatever, dash out again, mouth shut, head down. Life lived as one long guerrilla war.

Even his dealings with the post office, collecting his pension, organizing his savings, buying postage stamps, renewing his TV licence, call for strategy. He dallies in the queue, lets people go ahead of him to make sure he will not be attended by the post office official who attended him on his last visit. It's one of a number of tactics devised to keep the officials 'off the scent', keep them from building up a profile of his affairs.

Nothing in the world could persuade my father that he is part of whatever authority there is. He is and always will be a stowaway on his own ship.

But then he would probably tell me that I have been duped into thinking I have a say in things. Tell me I have turned taking responsibility into a religion, that I'm no good for a laugh. There's a certain amount of truth in that. I see him with my uncles, their laughter smarting in Dolan's, the pub they go to in Derryveigh. That laughter swells slowly in the course of an evening, merriment crackling through their every exchange as closing time approaches. The last-minute jokes, told in snatches, the three of them drawn into tight, subversive laughter, never more content than when they feel they are under siege.

Mine is a wide-open plain, a world full of choice. I can laugh all I like. But my laughter loses momentum faster than theirs. It has little to bump against, except the boundaries I have put in place myself. Still, I can go along with my father's humour. Laugh with him, particularly when it comes to Flossie. He is keenly attuned to this and even at the lowest ebb in our conversations about her and Nora, he takes a few light-hearted swipes at her.

'Well by the sound of it, you have been written out of the will,' he says, irony percolating through the words. He is moving towards the fireplace, studying my response in the large, oval mirror from Templeard. There is a slight flaw in the glass, a ripple which momentarily exaggerates the size of his eyes, then as he moves closer, swallows them up altogether. I wonder if he can see me.

I smile as he regains his features. The will, Flossie's will, the old chestnut. No laughing matter as far as my mother was concerned.

There was a time when Flossie was very wealthy. 'Montezuma's daughter', he used to call her. The price she got for Templeard was a talking point for years after the sale.

But even then, when she had all that money, there was no

aura of wealth about her. At least that's how it seemed to me, aged fifteen the summer Templeard was sold.

She didn't look like a rich person, always buttoned up in those cardigans she knitted for herself. Fawn, steely grey, dull pink, bumpy where the stitching puckered. And to make matters worse she had a habit of stretching the ends, tugging them down with her round, shiny hands until the whole cardigan lost whatever shape it had. Her complexion, occasionally just ruddy, but mostly scarlet, marked her out as a hard-working, country woman in my book. And that coupled with her prissy, old-fashioned turn of phrase, 'Not so much as a by your leave', 'Mark my words', made it almost impossible to imagine she had a quarter of a million pounds in the bank.

If someone had told me then that she was setting out on a new path, consciously trying to change the course of her life, I would have thought it ludicrous. She was in her mid-fifties, older in her ways than she is now, twenty years on.

My mother watched Flossie squander what she always called 'the Templeard money', angry, not only because none of it came our way but because it was another link with the place gone, a whittling away of the evidence that she came from people of consequence. She would talk of Templeard to the neighbours, more eager to sing its praises than ever before. By the time I left home in the mid-eighties, the kind of talk which had once earned her the reputation of being a bit on the lawdy-daw side had become unreservedly boastful.

Nothing engages my father like the disappearance of the so-called 'Templeard money'. There is a part of him which takes a stubborn delight in the dissipation of that fortune. He never fully got over the first impression he made in Templeard: 'a shop-boy with too much to say for himself'. Words spoken by the old aunt, Cassie, and repeated down through the years by Flossie, often following directly on the me-killing-the-chicken story.

I remind him of the first greyhound Flossie and Rooney bought.

'Hope,' he chuckles. 'They'd have been better off calling it "Disaster".'

'And that box they had made to bring it around.'

'That crock of a yoke. You know he made it himself.'

'Made from an old Fiat cut in half, wasn't it? No wonder it came off the tow bar.'

My father shapes an impression of the greyhound trailer flying across the road behind Flossie and Rooney on their way to a race in Limerick. He mimics Rooney's gomish surprise when they arrive in the car park to find the trailer gone. He scratches his head, pulls a baboonish face.

They never found it. 'Stolen by the tinkers', Rooney told everyone.

Hope was followed by Speedy Sir, then Templetuohy Bolter, Handy Boy, Sure Thing and a string of other dogs, all of whom were bought for what my father called a 'tidy sum'. But it wasn't the money the dogs cost, two or three thousand each at most, that made inroads into Flossie's fortune. It was the bets she and Rooney placed on them, and on other dogs running in tracks as far afield as Derry and Cork.

They came to Dublin almost every week, sometimes stopping at our house on the way to the track in Harold's Cross. I can see my mother looking out the window, her face tightening with anxiety then slackening into an expression of mourning as Rooney parks the greyhound trailer outside our house. Its presence there was an assault on everything we stood for, a crude spoiler to the lace curtains and the flowers in the china vase on the window sill. I remind my father of her annoyance.

'Aye,' he says, with quiet resignation.

'What was the name of the fellow they hired to walk the dogs?'

He does not reply, just tilts his head a little, a half-hearted attempt at remembering.

'Still she sometimes laughed at the good of it.'

'The good of what,' he asks, impatient.

'Rooney and the dogs,' I say limply, tussling with an impulse to say I'm sorry I brought my mother into it.

Flossie's other ventures and escapades – the share they bought in the steeplechaser, the cruises they went on, Flossie's taste for litigation – all took their toll on the Templeard money. Claire says every penny Flossie spends is spent in anger. It is a bid to be rid of every last trace of Templeard, a world she served well, but which served her poorly. And there's certainly something in that because after Flossie sold the place she didn't take one single item from it. She and Nora just drove away the evening the sorting was finished. They didn't even close the front door or the inner gate. The Campions, who were renting the land at the time, rang to tell us the following day, in a complete state because their cattle had trampled through the gardens and the orchard, and some had got into the house itself, leaving a trail of dung in the hall and across the drawing-room.

Over the years, Flossie has gone to great lengths to let it be known that I'm not in line for her money, not even a quarter of it, were she to leave it to be divided between my cousins and me.

Ber was always her main messenger, inadvertently tormenting my mother with details of Flossie's will. Ber may have been sworn to secrecy, but as Flossie well knew, that merely increased the value of the information, made Ber more rather than less likely to pass it on. It was seen as Templeard news which meant that it was collectively owned. Its passing from one to the other wasn't a breach of trust.

Claire maintains that my exclusion from the will comes from Flossie's desire to see the dynasty destroyed. But I'm not so sure that it can be reduced to that. I think the loneliness and isolation Flossie suffered has as much to do with it as anger. I see her reckless spending as a bid to make amends for all those days spent looking after my grandfather and the others.

Either way, it's been a romp since the sale, her and Rooney flying around the countryside with those dog trailers bouncing up and down behind them, her bad form a sauce to his whimpering. I would probably cheer them on, wish them another twenty years on the loose were it not for the distress it caused my mother.

There was a time when my mother believed that Templeard ought to be kept for me. All hell broke loose when it was put up for sale. Far from looking after what my mother called my own interests, I balked at the idea of a future there, treated it with outright derision. I was in a garage band at the time, Frantic Feast. We had just made a demo tape and somebody's brother had an 'in' to a recording company in Manchester. I was almost there. In contrast, Templeard seemed like a prison, a place to which I could be sentenced for life unless I fought hard. And that's exactly what I did. All summer I fought my mother tooth and nail until she dared not mention it.

At a glance, it would be easy to suppose that in marrying and having a son, she had ventured further from Templeard than Flossie, Nora, Ber or Girlie. But nothing could be further from the truth. In many ways she remained in the lonely keep of that house, tied in by its secrets, dazzled by the reverence it commanded.

Now and then I find her drifting around the desolate

landscape Nora's story has opened up, waiting for me to assign a place to her. A sense of guilt, sometimes vague, sometimes definite, hangs over my efforts to do so.

15

I have had no contact with Nora since my call over a month ago.

Whenever I bring up that ill-fated call, which is quite often, Claire says more or less the same thing.

'There wasn't a right or a wrong way for you to tell Nora. It's just that you were the last person to be in possession of the information before it reached her. That's all.'

If I didn't know her as well as I do I could easily imagine that this sympathetic version of the part I played is just a bid to rescue me from the regret I feel. But Claire doesn't go in for that kind of minding. Unwarranted sympathy just isn't part of the package. She tells me this quite often. So often, in fact, that I occasionally wonder if she has doubts about it herself. Anyway, the point is she isn't offering mammy-type sops. She genuinely believes that the moment I heard about that child I became part of its quest to track down its parents.

There is a nun out there, whose name I do not learn for some time. My father keeps me posted on what's going on. He calls her *the nun*. I imagine her to be young and competent, but also naïve because she seems to have allowed Flossie to become an intermediary between Nora and all else concerned.

My father sees this as a smart ploy on Flossie's part. 'You have to hand it to her,' he says, eyes dancing with boyish glee.

'She has herself where she can serve her own injunctions now.' Advised and encouraged by him, Flossie is using this position to make sure that things will proceed no further.

In the course of a meeting with the nun and the social worker on the case, Flossie was shown two letters from a woman living in Chicago. These letters had been acknowledged six weeks previously by the nun but the woman had not got in contact since. The most recent of the letters was received earlier this year, the first, almost twenty-five years ago. They are, Flossie told my father, very similar. The woman states in each that she is trying to make contact with a Mrs or a Miss Macken, mother of a child taken into the care of the nuns in 1939. In the first letter she emphasizes that she is not the child in question.

The social worker and the nun do not take this claim at face value. They have explained to Flossie that many adopted children setting out in search of their birth mothers are fearful that things will not work out. To protect themselves from disappointment, hurt or shock, some begin their search by pretending they are looking on someone else's behalf.

Flossie, predictably, has put her own spin on this. In her view the nun's belief that the woman *is* in fact Nora's daughter has become a hard fact; and the woman herself, 'a sly bitch, nosing around to see if there is anything to be got out of Nora'.

My father shook his head when I suggested that Nora might actually want to make contact with her child. He didn't even bother to reply, just forged ahead, keen to report on what Flossie had to say about the nun and the order to which she belongs. 'Bitches, every one of them, out to save their own skins, day and night on the television saying they're sorry, rounding up the mothers and the babies just to get themselves off the hook.'

My father cannot see Nora's child as a person at all.

This became particularly apparent when, during one of our conversations, I was going through the options open to Nora at the time of the birth. He ruled out every one of them, but none more vehemently than my suggestion that the child could have been brought up in Templeard.

'There's a lot that could be said against Old Macken,' he pauses, creating a big space for the 'but', which then comes full force. 'But I wouldn't wish that on him. Or anyone else for that matter. Why would he let another man's bastard be brought up under his roof?'

This is totally inconsistent with his usual generous self. He has none of that gritty anger which makes for cruelty. But something stops him from looking at Nora's child with his own eyes, kindly eyes, well able to see her as a person and not just a spanner in the Templeard works.

Nora's own position becomes more and more difficult to fathom. Several times I have been on the point of ringing her. But the prospect of Flossie's wrath is more than enough to stop me. Anyway my father has it all worked out, with victory for Flossie 'almost in the bag'. He thinks that if she persists in telling the social worker and the nun that Nora wants no hand, act or part in it, they will drop the case. 'What choice have they?' he asks, his voice full of confidence.

I tell him he has been too quick to accept Flossie's account of Nora's position, point out how at home Nora seemed with her story. I try to get it across to him that even if Nora were going to refuse to become involved she would not go about it in this histrionic way. But he just shakes his head solemnly, akin to telling me I'm talking nonsense. And that's more or less where we stand on the issue until late October.

Then news of some sort of showdown between Flossie and the nun begins to filter through, bringing Nora directly into the fray. Angry because things were not working out as she hoped, Flossie had given the nun what my father knowingly refers to as 'a piece of her mind'. A dose of vitriol which at some time or other she had given just about everyone with whom she has had any dealings.

I wasn't altogether surprised to learn that Nora had been in direct contact with the nun and social worker all along. Two or three short calls. That's all, because there was still no reply to the acknowledgement letter they sent to the woman. Nora made it clear to my father that she was a willing participant and was following the advice given by the nun and the social worker. Malcolm was on the job full-time, a buffer between her and the rest of the world. Together they had arrived at a wait-and-see position.

Nora's main concern throughout was for Flossie. Her one request to the social worker and the nun was to be tolerant with Flossie, to include her whenever and wherever possible. That's precisely what they had tried to do. They encouraged her involvement, sought her advice and approval, tolerated her interference which, as the weeks went by, turned to full-scale harassment. And still they tried to bring her around to the idea that contact between Nora and her child was a worthy goal.

Claire is quick to challenge my impatience with Flossie. She fears that the coming together of Nora and her daughter, should it happen, will destroy Flossie altogether. She points out that Flossie's whole life has taken shape in and around a conspiracy to deny the existence of Nora's child. Keeping her at bay, as Flossie has been so intent on doing in recent weeks, is a last-ditch effort to hold on to the life she knows.

'It's late in the day,' Claire says. 'Too late for Flossie to start anew.'

I nod, unable to say, 'It's never too late,' because I know in Flossie's case it is. There is no redemption for her in meeting this woman. No new truths to compensate for the abandonment of the old ones.

Claire misinterprets my nod, thinks I need more convincing. 'It's a bit like one of those tumours they discover in old people,' she says. 'Removing it would do more harm than good.'

16

When my father visits Derryveigh, which he does about a half-dozen times a year, he stays with his brother Frank and his wife Aideen. They live over the butcher's shop Frank ran until his retirement five or six years ago.

There is a definite pattern to his Derryveigh trips. He takes the mid-morning train from Heuston Station, still Kingsbridge to him though the name changed over thirty years ago, and arrives in Thurles two hours later. Frank meets him at the station and, after a slow pint and a round of ham sandwiches in a pub nearby, they travel the ten miles to Derryveigh in Frank's car.

Regardless of the season, my father wears his gabardine overcoat and the newer of his two peaked caps. He carries two bags, the heavier gripped tightly in his right hand, making him look lopsided. As well as his clothes, this small tightly packed bag often contains some mechanical part or other Frank has asked him to track down for the Ford Prefect he is restoring out the back in the killing yard. In his other hand he has a plastic carrier bag containing a small fork and a trowel both wrapped in the tatty square of sacking he kneels on when he tends my mother's grave in the cemetery outside town.

The only set visit is the November one: the first and second of the month, All Saints' Day and All Souls' Day. Not that he is religious. Far from it. He sees these days as given over to the memory of the dead and accordingly marks them out to spend with my mother.

Aware of how often in recent weeks we have collided, I offer to accompany him to Derryveigh, take some time off, drive him down and stay with him for two or three days. I imagine that he will be pleased, but he isn't. He tells me he is well able to manage, that he enjoys travelling by train. And I have to admit that that's true. Nobody enjoys the free train travel for over sixty-fives as much as he does. He gets an enormous kick out of sitting there watching the countryside flitting by, knowing he is surrounded by people who have paid for their tickets. It has nothing to do with saving money, and everything to do with his delight in stealing a march on the world.

After quite a bit of agitated thought on his part I find myself being allowed to drive him to Derryveigh. This turning of the tables is, of course, very familiar, with him assuring me he'll fix me up, make arrangements for me to stay with Frank and Aideen, see to it that it all works out. Vaguely amused by his shenanigans, I back into the slot he has created for me, that of tired executive in need of a few days out of the office.

What of it? We're on the road, with Conor in the back, so pleased to be on board that he keeps coming up with overly responsible statements, reminders to my father and me that he is worthy of his place with us. Some of these statements have the ring of instruction.

'Aren't you not to say you don't like something . . .'

Anticipating there is more to follow I do not reply.

'Aren't you not to say you don't like something,' he says again, this time adding, 'just leave it on your plate.'

'It depends,' I reply. 'If someone asks you if you like cabbage and you don't then obviously you must say so.'

In the rear mirror I see the whole of his round, freckled face bunch with revulsion at the mention of cabbage. This in turn seems to trigger off some anxiety or other. His eyes blank out and his face slackens until he appears witless. Maybe he is worried that he won't be able to deliver, that he will blow the whole opportunity.

I smile when I hear him talking to himself a minute or so later. 'No thanks,' he is saying, 'I don't want cabbage.' Then after a spate of deep thought he adds the word 'actually', slightly surprising himself. Pleased to find he has the skill to get out of eating cabbage at Frank and Aideen's, he moves on to his next concern.

'How long until we're there?'

'About two hours,' I say lazily, keen to discourage this line of questioning.

'For God's sake, we aren't even out of Dublin yet,' my father snaps impatiently, then straight away rearranges himself in his seat, as though discomfort, rather than Conor's question, had prompted his irritation.

'We are out, there's fields,' Conor says earnestly, leaning forward, poking my father's shoulder in a bid to make him look out the side window.

'Those fields don't necessarily mean we're out of the city,' I say, aware that I am not so much responding to Conor as offering my father guidance on how he ought to respond.

He rearranges himself again, clears his throat, then takes a brief, reluctant glance out the side window. It is clear that if he had his own way he would tell Conor to 'whist up'.

His unease with the way Claire and I relate to Conor and Aoife goes unvoiced for the most part. It is perceptible only in minor shifts of mood, in tetchy irritations, in the occasional throw-away observation. If it ever were to emerge it would most likely take the form of advice. He would probably tell us that we have made the mistake of trading authority for intimacy, that all our tedious reasoning with the children

256

will end badly, that we are indulging ourselves at the cost of teaching them to know their place. The difficulty with this is that we are trying to teach them to know their place but it's not a place my father recognizes. When he thinks of *place* he thinks largely in terms of the place he occupies, that expertly camouflaged bunker from which he makes forays into the world at large. Much of my own energy, down through the years, has gone into leaving that bunker. Staying out and keeping Conor and Aoife out is not a whim.

Until two or three years ago I used to call the road we are on 'the road home'. Now a multi-lane motorway, it was the route we took both to Templeard and to Derryveigh. I smile to myself when I think of the conversation Claire and I had about it, the one that prompted me to call it by its correct name, the M7. She said that calling it the road home was 'sort of nice', a description too close to 'sort of pathetic' for my liking.

'I can't get used to calling it the M7. It's just a number. Says nothing about where we are going.'

'Why should it say anything about where we are going?' Claire laughs. We are heading out of town for a weekend without Conor and Aoife.

'I don't know. I just suppose there is something impersonal about calling it the M7.'

'Impersonal? If you want to make it personal then maybe we should call it the sex trail.' She laughs loudly, pokes me in the ribs. 'What with everyone going to Hidden Ireland guest houses to bonk for the weekend.'

Claire is more or less unstoppable when she gets on to a jag like this, which is why I'm not a bit surprised when she takes out the Hidden Ireland Guide and starts reading out the names of the houses, following each with a description of how suited they are to meet the needs of 'weekend bonkers'. She gives each a special recommendation, 'equipped to meet the requirements of the ageing bonker', 'the discerning bonker' and so on.

I laugh at these descriptions, laugh at her laughter, at her determination to be outrageous, then just at her because she is unable to continue without splurting the words in every direction.

'The worst part is the dining-room in the morning,' I pitch in, 'the post-coital purr, the quiet complicity.'

'Five different ways to have your eggs done,' she gulps, 'and the waitresses going around asking everyone how was it.'

'It's like –'

Claire cuts in. 'How was it for you, Madame? And for you, Sir?'

'It's like as if there had been group sex going on and they arrive in to mop up and feed people.'

And on we continue, dancing our way through a ritual of laughter, a prelude to two or three days alone, a riotous twirl in the present for which I begin to yearn.

'What has you so pleased with yourself.' My father's voice is curious in a warm sort of way. I lift my hand to my face, absent-mindedly searching for evidence that I look pleased. For a thin sliver of a moment I imagine that the scene I am conjuring up with Claire has somehow become apparent, that we are there for all to see.

'Oh, nothing. I was just thinking that it's difficult to get used to calling the road home the M7.'

He throws his head back a little, no intention whatsoever of trying to get used to calling this or any other road by a number.

'I never saw a milder autumn,' he says. 'Hardly a turn in the leaves at all.'

I look at the trees, then up at the sky where a lone crow is diving into the enormous October sky. Conor is asleep, a pearl of saliva on the cusp of his lower lip. My father is in a state of high alert. His face pains when he sees a field of sodden, greyish hay bales. His eagerness to identify with the farmer who failed to get them in on time is almost unbearable. He understands these tragedies much better than those on his own doorstep, the discarded syringes, the mounds of ragged blankets in the shop doorway.

I have absorbed his belief that this, our so-called *road home*, is the road away from all that squalid waste of life. And maybe it is, but it is also the road to Templeard, to a despotic world of quiet savagery, wholly capable of destroying lives. In some ways Templeard is more dangerous. There are no discarded syringes, no mounds of ragged blankets alerting the world to its cruelty.

All Saints' Day is a Holy Day of Obligation in Derryveigh. Everywhere else too, but here obligation is taken more seriously. The village has a Sunday air about it. Outside Mooney's the newsagents, people gather, their subdued chat and groomed looks belying the fact that it is a Monday. By lunch-time the last of the pious strollers has gone indoors. Forks, shovels and buckets appear outside Mulvannys, the hardware shop. From the window of Frank and Aideen's first-floor sitting-room I watch a delivery van draw up. The delivery man, full of perk, greets the retired schoolteacher, Mrs Shaw. Frank and my father talk to the Garda sergeant while they watch the council men lift red and white bollards off a truck. And the church, gaunt in the background, casts a dancing shadow over the whole scene. It is tempting to believe that hearts beat in a more kindly way here.

Aideen has brought Conor for a walk which is turning into something of a grand tour. He is being escorted around like a boy prince, gratefully receiving gifts of sweets and money from the townspeople. I wave at him, an exaggerated wave full of reassurance, which I imagine he will welcome. But he just folds up. Then he fobs me off with a tight, rapid wave, implying that I am making a fool of myself and, furthermore, putting his rewarding tour at risk.

For no apparent reason my thoughts turn to the boarding school my mother and her sisters went to in the 1930s. No more than half an hour's drive; the idea to go there suddenly takes hold.

17

I'm well aware that this may turn out to be nothing more than an uneventful trip to the outskirts of Limerick and back. It has not been functioning as a school for well over a decade. But I have this idea that if I see where it happened I will understand it better.

But then, what building, what room can explain how a child could be born in such a clandestine way? A child which could not be spoken about, snapped away so fast that its mother did not see it, did not even know its gender. My hands clamp on the steering wheel as my mother's unhappy part in the whole charade takes shape again.

The school, Our Lady of the Psalms, has been converted into a conference location called The Sylvan Downs Centre. A golf course, fastidiously preened, slopes away to the west, merging into the distant blur of housing estates. One wing of the building serves as a clubhouse. There is a gym, a sauna and some kind of indoor jogging facility.

My grip on Nora's story begins to loosen, slips away altogether as I walk across the spacious lobby to the reception desk, my footsteps crunching quietly in the snowy floss of the foyer carpet. Everything, the dark chocolatey wood panelling, the great octopus of a candelabra, the anaesthetizing piano music, even the face of the receptionist, seems to be conspiring to tell me that my quest is absurd.

'How can I help, Sir?'

'I'd just like to look around, if that's OK.'

'Certainly. The conference rooms are through to the left.' She points to a set of glass, double doors, 'The clubhouse to your right. Application forms.' She smiles, flicks back her hair as she points to a sheaf of glossy folders.

I want to leave straight away. I want to reclaim the sense of expectancy which brought me to this suffocating place. I can scarcely remember what my mother looked like, let alone imagine her being here. As for a baby being born in some sick room, nothing seems more implausible. If all this sumptuousness is some kind of collective bid to forget the primitive sacrifices of the past, then it is working very well.

I don't want to draw attention to my disorientation, so I saunter into the conference wing and peer through the small, glass panel of the first door on my left, a room which might have been a classroom in the days of The Psalms. It's some kind of a studio now, with complex-looking cameras, white, luminous screens, large globular light fittings. I try to envisage Nora and Flossie sitting at desks there.

Then suddenly, as if springing from a wholly separate line of thought, comes the notion that this elaborate conversion from school to conference centre is entirely cosmetic. The same impulses, good and bad, which made Our Lady of the Psalms the kind of place it was, are still at play here. Just channelled in a different direction, that's all. Deployed to create a feel-good atmosphere. Here people do not have to look at whatever it is they do not wish to see. For a moment or two I wonder what the current no-go areas might be, what cruelties and injustices will become the subjects of tomorrow's TV documentaries.

Outside, the fallen leaves gust along, furling into whorls which a groundsman is trying to sweep into a pile with an outsize yard brush. The Sylvan Downs logo, a yellow golf ball emitting sun rays, is displayed on the back of his blue overalls. He turns as I drive toward him, but remains directly in my path, staring at what I assume is the car registration. He gestures to me to stop, then stoops down and picks what turns out to be a dead bird snarled up in the grill. He raises it up into the air and examines it as though he had not fully made up his mind what it was.

'For God's sake,' I say as the car window rolls down. 'I didn't even know I had hit it. Thanks.'

I get out, check the grill for damage, then stand beside him trying to think of something to say, both of us staring at the cluster of downy feathers stuck to the perforated chrome.

'A lot of changes around here.'

'Yep.'

'Are you here, I mean working here, long?' I ask, unexpectedly pleased to talk to someone.

'Long enough,' he answers, turning to throw the dead bird into the wheelbarrow behind him. 'I worked under the nuns before this.' He flings his right hand carelessly towards the golf course.

'Different then, I suppose?'

'The nuns. I'll tell you, they knew a thing or two about putting a decent dinner on the table. More than can be said for this crowd.'

'Is there anyone else here who worked under the nuns?'

'No. The last one to go was Sal Cummins. God rest her soul.' He points the length of the avenue, down to a row of estate cottages opposite the entrance gate. 'Here well over fifty years and there wasn't as much as a nod and she going. That's the sort you have here now. She just walked down that avenue of a Saturday. And she never walked up it again. That'll tell you.'

He looks at me, his face full of curiosity.

Explaining my interest was not an option. But even if it had been I would hardly have known where to begin. What had happened to Nora there was even more difficult to imagine then than it had been when I set out.

18

On the journey back to Dublin my father tells me he is considering selling up and moving to Derryveigh. It is not the first time he has floated this idea, but he has never gone into the pros and cons so thoroughly. He is fidgeting with his seat belt, periodically glancing in my direction as he tells me about violent assaults on old people, armed robberies and the like.

He recounts details of one particularly gruesome assault, a man he knows who was attacked by a teenager wielding a meat cleaver. It occurs to me that this time he has made up his mind. But when I say so, he assures me he hasn't. Then a little while later as we speed through the darkness he reveals that he has asked Frank to look out for a suitable place in the village – or the town as he calls it.

'We went to take a look at a place out on the Culnacoille Road,' he announces, raising his hand to block the glare of oncoming headlights. 'Too big for what I want. Far too big.'

I toss in a casual 'Oh'.

'It'll probably go too dear, with the size of it.'

'Are you telling me you put a bid on it?'

'Frank is looking into that, waiting for a week or two, otherwise it would be known that it was me that was after it. He'll let it be understood that he wants it for himself and Aideen. That should keep the price steady.' I smile into the tinselly lights of the oncoming cars, wonder how I would react if he had told me this at the outset. 'Pat, I have put a bid on a house in Derryveigh. All going well, I'll be moving down in the new year.'

A light gauze of rain blurs the flitting hedgerows, merges all the night shapes into a single moving crystal, swept away every few seconds by the quick swish of the wipers. I enjoy my father's subterfuge. I like the pace at which he divulges his plans, the half telling, the recanting, the reluctant admissions. It's him as he is, playful, elusive, calculating and always keen to make things work in a world he generally considers hostile.

After I drop him off I sit and look at the house, catching something of its anonymity in the liquidy yellow light of the street lamps. I keep imagining that the indifference I feel at the prospect of its being sold is about to give way to a sense of loss, but not so. It never had a chance in the first place, I think, as I start up – bullied as it always was into insignificance not only by Templeard but by Derryveigh as well.

Before I have opened the car door Claire is out, ready to manoeuvre Conor from his seat to his bed without waking him. Staggering upstairs, his feet rhythmically striking the banisters, she leans over and whispers, 'Nora has been on.' Then disappears into the darkness.

Her stealthful retreat from the children loosens as she comes into the kitchen. 'Nora's daughter,' she announces, turning to close the door. 'She's coming.'

I laugh.

'I'm telling you. She's on her way as we speak.' She picks up the spiral pad beside the phone. 'Flight due in tomorrow. Shannon. 11.55.'

'How did this come to light?'

'The Health Board people rang Nora. They were trying to contact her all day yesterday but she and Malcolm were in London at a charity thing. They didn't get back until lunchtime today. She's coming here via Montreal, something to do with not being able to get a flight from Chicago.' Claire considers this for a moment. 'Yes, it was Montreal. Imagine what it must be like for her?' She winces, bunches her shoulders, shuddering the thought away.

The consequences for Nora are suddenly tangible. I feel vaguely hostile to this woman, find myself moving to my father's position, becoming part of the collective resolve to exclude her.

My thoughts turn to the Nora I knew in Templeard, her quiet patience with Flossie, her willingness to listen to Ber, to mediate between my mother and Flossie, to laugh with Girlie. I wonder if she played those parts because she felt she had to earn her keep among her sisters? Repair the damage she believed she had caused? I am standing at the fridge, trying to remember what I came for, at the same time idling in the kitchen in Templeard. My grandfather is sitting by the window, his newspaper held out to catch a shaft of light, his walking stick hooked over the frayed arm of his chair.

'Has anyone said why this happened so fast?' I ask.

'I think she was away since the end of the summer,' Claire uses her hands to sort the details as she goes along. 'She came back yesterday morning, back to her apartment in Chicago, to find the letter from Sister what-you-may-call-her, you know who I mean, Sister Mairead, waiting for her.'

There is a loud clang from the street, a truck speeding over the ramps, followed by the long shriek of breaks. Claire angles her head to listen for the children waking.

'Was Nora upset?'

'Not at all. The opposite,' she says. 'She's going to get a flight across in the morning. Be there when she arrives. They told her to wait, said it was too rushed. So did I, more or less. But she had made up her mind. No question about it.'

The gaps begin to widen. I rush back in search of facts to bridge those gaps.

'She's obviously Nora's daughter,' Claire says. 'Why else would she drop everything and come like this?'

'It's a mistake, a big mistake. I don't understand it.'

'It's a mistake all right, but you can understand it.'

Straight away I decide to phone Nora. Persuade her to wait. To arrange a meeting through the social worker and the nun. I'm only half listening to Claire as I tap out the digits, planning the approach I will take.

Malcolm answers, labouring over every syllable of their number. He thanks me for ringing, his gratitude suffused with exasperation.

I ask to speak to Nora, but she is already on her way to London to catch an early flight to Shannon. Malcolm describes her decision as 'very, very unfortunate'. He's apologetic, sees his failure to dissuade her as shameful. I ask him where she is staying, tell him I will talk to her. 'Very kind of you, Patrick,' he replies, 'but I doubt if she will change plans at this stage.' Hesitating, 'I'm afraid another attempt to stop her might just increase her burden.'

'Why don't I go to Shannon? In the morning.' Claire is nodding approval, mouthing words I cannot make out. 'Nora may well be glad to have someone with her at that stage.'

I think he is about to voice a reservation, which I try to anticipate.

'If you thought you could, I mean, if you would,' he stammers. 'I can't think of anyone she'd –'

'I'm on leave this week,' I interrupt.

'That was inspired,' Claire announces as soon as I hang up, then in the same sweep asks why Nora did not want Malcolm to travel with her.

I wander off as she moves from one possibility to another. I try to imagine Nora insisting on going to Shannon, find it impossible to see her as resolute, or even determined. Her decision becomes reckless, the response of someone unable to see a way out.

'She wants him there when she gets back,' Claire muses. 'In the flat, you know, mooching around or working at that big desk, politely enquiring how she got on.'

'Probably,' I say, already following thoughts which in the wakeful hours to follow, force me to question Nora's reaction to the emergence of her child. I wonder if all along she had been hoping that efforts to bring her together with that child would come to nothing. Flossie, intuitively attuned to this hope, stomps through these thoughts, becoming the mouthpiece of all that Nora is containing.

I wake early, my father's stern grin fading back into the dreamworld, but his voice clear as a bell. 'It's like I said with Nora and that child. She doesn't want it turning up. Why would she?'

[19]

A light, powdery frost bleaches the outside world, drawing hedgerows, pavements, cars into a single shape. I drive slowly.

Apart from a brief stopover en route to the US a few years ago, I have not been in Shannon since I was about six or seven. We used to drive down sometimes when we were staying in Derryveigh. The airport and the hydro-electrical station up at Ardnacrusha were icons of progress which never failed to rouse a feeling of national pride in my father and his brothers. I remember the three of them on the balcony overlooking the airport runway one wintery Sunday, their fascination with a Russian jet inuring them to the sub-zero temperatures which had me hopping from one foot to the other. The whole thing was living proof that independence was working, that the long struggle had not been in vain. The great events of the past, the 1916 Rebellion, the War of Independence, came into view from that wind-swept balcony, inspiring a kind of garrulous excitement, my father and his brothers talking ten to the dozen of other projects, all cause for celebration afterwards in the airport bar.

Questions about Nora, where she is, what she is thinking, keep emerging. Some, particularly those gathering around my mother's place in her story, will not go away. My mother is dead and nothing is going to change the course her life took.

But there is a growing satisfaction in knowing that her defiance, her often inexplicable mood changes had a definite source.

A different person is emerging from behind that defiance now, a light-hearted person around whom stray memories of long-ago laughter are beginning to cluster.

I catch a glimpse of her recounting Flossie's reception of Rooney when he arrived back drunk from his brother's funeral.

We'd all travelled down for that funeral. I'm not sure why but I think it had something to do with accompanying Flossie, who didn't want to go with Rooney. There was some long rigmarole of an explanation about showing up as a couple, giving Rooney's nephews the impression that they stood to benefit from her in some way.

After the funeral my father and I drove on down to Derryveigh to visit Frank and Aideen, leaving my mother with Flossie. Some time during the afternoon, Flossie, sitting at her drawing-room window with my mother, saw what she first thought was a refuse sack slung over the garden gate. Her indignation burst into outrage when it began to move.

'I declare to God . . .' She swung around, 'clearly,' my mother said, 'in search of an implement.' The poker which she grabbed was heavily caked with soot. This, my mother laughingly explained, was her main concern as she watched Flossie wedge it under Rooney's collar in an attempt to lift him off the gate. With all the heaving and pulling he came to, but fell to the ground, revealing a large wet stain spreading from his midriff to his knees. Flossie immediately turned on her heels, stormed up to the house, reaching the doorsteps before she even acknowledged that he was calling after her.

'It was the soup, Flossie, the soup that spilled on me above in the hotel. I'm telling you, I'm half scalded.'

She paused to consider this, turned hesitantly, and trailing the poker behind her, approached him with a mixture of curiosity and suspicion. He tried to get up off the ground but failed and had to lie there like a patient undergoing an examination while Flossie inspected his sodden trousers. Suddenly she was brandishing the poker, shouting abuse, swiping wildly at him over the gate. Using his elbow and his forearm to drag himself out of range, he scuttled to the garden wall, where he managed to climb to an unsteady stance. By sticking close to the wall, 'like a snail', as my mother put it, he made his way back up the town.

'It was the smell. No mistaking it,' Flossie said afterwards. 'A whiff like in a nursing home with all the bed pans being emptied. He must think I'm a right onseach telling me it was soup.'

We laughed a lot, my mother's laughter spiralling out of control as she mimicked Flossie's bursts of outrage that afternoon. 'Soup. I ask you. Soup, my eye.'

My mother never tired of telling Rooney stories. Flossie's cruelty to him was as consoling as it was comic. The fear that he was a calculating sleeveen receded when he became that pathetic figure scuttling out of range of a swiping poker or scratching his head at the greyhound track in Limerick. Maybe Flossie felt obliged to demean him to her sisters, felt she had to offer them constant proof that she ruled the roost, that he would never get his hands on the Templeard money. That money may have been diminishing, but there was a sense in which its value remained unchanged, because in my mother's eyes, and in Ber's eyes too, its value lay firmly in its provenance. Had it been a few thousand, a few hundred pounds, it probably would have been every bit as contentious. Anyway, my mother's laughter, whatever its nature, invested that journey back from Rooney's brother's funeral with a giddy happiness which springs to life now as I drive through the same dreary midland towns. And she, as though buoyed up by the prospect of a happier destiny in my memory, wanders off, opening the way for Nora who stays for the remainder of my journey to Shannon.

Long before I spot her, sitting at the end of a row of black vinyl seats in the arrivals lounge, I have a sense of her presence. In anticipation of what I would do when I got there, I had already approached her in a number of different ways. I had walked up quietly, a stock of well-rehearsed greetings prepared. Strode up, confidently, all set to persuade her to come back to Dublin with me, line up a meeting between her and her daughter some time over the next few days.

That all collapsed the instant I saw her. I stood still, tried to realign my thoughts, plagued by a wish that I had the power to save her not merely from the fear which had her poised at the edge of her seat but from her whole story.

She appears old. I search for the person she has been for as long as I can remember, but find only advancing age. I recognize the tilt of her chin, her upright posture, hands neatly clasped on her lap, maybe some ancient, internal voice still promising that decorum will be rewarded. A remnant of that Templeard conceit, part of the archaic language which told the world that the Mackens were a cut above the rest. Either way it is conspicuously redundant here among careless gum-chewing youths and breezy, affluent girls, dolled to the nines for a weekend home from busy jobs in New York or wherever.

Nora draws her chin in to examine the brooch she is wearing. It sits on the collar of her grey coat, turquoise and gold, a small burst of colour. She unpins it carefully, repositioning it as I call her name from a few feet away. The brooch falls, landing on her lap.

'Patrick,' I say. 'Came to see how you were doing.' But that jovial greeting remains awkwardly suspended between us.

'Patrick?' She looks at me. 'For a minute I thought you were Daddo. Your voice.' She goes to stand up, a bit dazed, gathering herself to shake hands.

'I rang Malcolm last night,' I offer by way of explanation. It's as if I had begun to speak about someone she did not know. 'Malcolm,' she says with a sense of discovery, lips trickling to a smile.

'Yes. That's why I came.'

I wish I could have said something more courageous, something like *I came because I wanted to, because I wanted to do something, because I want to know how in Christ's name it could all have come to this, you waiting here like someone about to go on trial.*

She asks how Claire and the children are, drifting off as I reply, remaining there until I have finished. It occurs to me that I may have no part to play here, no useful part at least. My arrival has just presented her with a new set of problems.

'We should ring Malcolm, let him know all is well.' I run my hand across my coat pocket, checking for my phone.

'I don't know what to do,' she half whispers. The tears which follow flow without any crumpling of her features, they stream down her face evenly, as if from a source so deep as to cause little or no surface change.

'We could go. I mean, leave now. She's not expecting to be met. Nobody will be any the wiser.' I move closer, the minty scent of her cologne instantly transporting me back to Templeard, to a page in a storybook, children building a tree house, Nora's hand guiding me up the steps of a make-shift ladder until I am hopping up and down with those children, raising a ragged flag to alert a passing liner to our desperate plight. There was never anything, not a whisper, not a glance, to suggest that Nora's lot was other than it seemed. Home from London for Christmas, nothing mysterious about her, except perhaps her patience with Flossie.

274

For a second or two her story un-happens, spins into reverse, uncoiling frantically like the innards of an over wound clock. But there is, in the wake of that jolt back, a sickening sense of having been deceived. I place my arm around her shoulder, tight with anger.

'I want it to be over,' she says, swallowing. Her breathing grows less fitful, eases to occasional, deep, tremulous intakes.

'We won't ring Malcolm yet.' Her voice is hoarse but no longer fraught. She is finding her own way out of her distress. 'I'll ring him later. When it's over,' she adds.

'You were right to come,' I say, though I'm not sure what I think.

'Right or wrong, I didn't have a choice.' She straightens her shoulders, touches her brooch as though it was a charm. 'From the minute I spoke to Sister Mairead yesterday my thoughts have not been my own. I've lost everything. Everything is gone.'

I wait for a fuller explanation, but none follows. I examine the pieces, *my thoughts have not been my own, everything lost, everything gone.* I string these fragments together, see Nora in the crippling grip of mistrust, trying but failing to hold on to whatever belief and self-possession she had won back over the years.

'This morning when I woke up I thought I was in Templeard. It was as clear as anything.' She shakes her head.

'Templeard?' I smile, unsure if she was pleased or upset by this.

'Maybe it's because I've been thinking about the place so much, about when we were growing up. Long before there was anything, anything else.' She looks directly at me. 'Do you remember Ammie?'

'Just about,' I reply, never altogether certain if the recollections I have of her are my own or my mother's.

'Something I hadn't thought about for years, for decades,

came back to me. Here, just a while ago. Ammie teaching us to dance in the kitchen. Dancing, not the kind we learned at school. Waltzing to proper music, to the gramophone.' She pauses to consider the scene she has conjured up, nodding a little as she recalls the steps in a light, melodic voice. 'One, two, three, one two, three.'

A woman approaches, holding a polystyrene cup at a dramatic distance. Until a few minutes ago she was sitting nearby, sorting the contents of her handbag, glancing occasionally in our direction.

'I thought you'd like a cup of tea,' she announces, stalling a few steps away, indicating that I should give the tea to Nora. She smiles eagerly. I take the cup, unprepared for the quick rush of words. 'She was there for hours before you came. Talking to herself. And crying.'

'Very kind of you,' Nora says formally, an English crispness to her gratitude which alienates the woman. I nod, say, 'Thanks,' then 'Thanks,' again, hoping she will go.

'You were saying about the dancing.'

A smile crosses Nora's face, depleting to abandonment as she closes her eyes and returns to the kitchen in Templeard. 'You know Daddo never joined in, but he enjoyed it all the same. He would tease Ammie whenever she spoke of beaux and dance cards, say she was trying to turn us into Protestants.' Nora laughs, self-mockery coursing mildly through her laughter, prelude to a return to the here and now. 'I often ask myself what it was all about, the preparation, the getting ready, the looking forward. All those things that never came to pass.' She sinks into thought, there for no more than a few seconds when she bolts right out. 'Daddo was a good man, Patrick. You know that don't you?'

I nod, but she pays no heed.

'His world was his world, that's all. He didn't have any need to look beyond it, no more than any of the others did.

None of them. The Campions. The Quinns over in Friar's Island, Crottys of the Glebe, Laceys of Derinalty Cross. That was it, land and farming, that was the sum of Daddo's world.'

Those names go on ringing in my head, closing in on Templeard, a circle tightening until it becomes a stranglehold. Something of the cloistered security of that world begins to take shape, an outline for a tapestry, growing densely textured as Nora skips from one memory to another, gathering them up like a child gathering sea-shells, each a treasure Girlie, five years old, making perfume under the limes; Ber launching into a decade of the Rosary when they pass a motor-cycle accident; my mother crying when the car got stuck in the sand on Kilkea beach. Recollections which trail into insignificance the second she arrives at the Eucharistic Congress. Breath drawn, she pauses at the precipice of that day of days, as if to view it from afar, raising her hand to pick out her sisters and herself, Daddo, Ammie, Aunt Cassie, there among the hundreds of thousands of people gathered in the centre of Dublin to celebrate fifteen hundred years of Christianity. 'I was eight or nine at the time, never seen anything like it, so many people in the same place. We left Templeard at four in the morning,' she says, 'to be sure to get a good place. And we did, we got the best of places. O'Duffy passed this close.' She gestures to the space between us. 'Aunt Cassie nearly lost her reason.' She smiles, self-consciously reining herself in. 'You remember Cassie? I'm sure you must.'

'Only when she was senile, sitting beside the cooker. I was terrified of her, the way her eyes popped out of her head.'

'The poor old soul. For years afterwards she talked non-stop of O'Duffy. I think he was in charge of it all, the whole Congress.'

I shrug my shoulders. All I know about O'Duffy is his subsequent drift towards fascism.

'There was an atmosphere, a feeling that it was the beginning of some great, I don't know what – some great beginning – but it wasn't. Things got worse after that, a lot worse, with the Economic War.'

Nora overstates whatever restorative qualities the tea might have. Each sip is followed by a bracing movement, a step forward in regaining her poise. She takes a handkerchief from her handbag, dabs her lips with it. 'No one will ever know the hardship that Economic War caused,' she says authoritatively. 'Of course that couldn't be said. You took your life in your hands if you said that.'

I am slow to remind her that Daddo spoke out against it, reluctant to leave the Eucharistic Congress, with its thousands of prelates and curates, an enormous millefeuille of surplices and albs, righteousness in every face. I trace that righteousness back to an era when it fuelled the drive to get the land back, to win independence. Worthy quests no doubt, but here it is at the Eucharistic Congress, that same righteousness, nothing to fuel except itself. And I see it turning inwards, spawning a tight-lipped, mutant piety, cornerstone of a world which could not admit Nora's story.

'Didn't Daddo speak out against it? Against the Economic War'?

'He did and to his cost. He was threatened, openly told that if he didn't . . . Oh, I don't know,' she sighs, relinquishing her recollections, slipping towards what I think is resignation when her hands suddenly clench. 'How am I to tell her? Yesterday I thought I could, but I can't.' Nora's face flinches with agitation. 'You see, Patrick, he was a priest,' she blurts out, watches the fact settle, then hurries on, 'which made me, still makes me think I'm the one to blame.'

I fix on the word *blame*, repeat it, unable to register anything except incredulity.

'Oh I know it's foolish. I know that,' she says, eyes

downcast. 'But the truth is I've never fully got away from thinking it was my own doing. If I had sung when he told me to, or said something to stop him . . .'

'Sung?'

'He wanted me to sing the song I sang for him and the others in the Bishop's Palace, sing it in the car when he was driving me back to school.'

She looks up, searches my face for understanding, which I provide as wholesomely as I can, nodding rapidly as she continues. 'I know it's hard to credit, but you can believe something for so long that even after you see that you are wrong, you still believe it. The way it was, I didn't have the strength or whatever it is, the courage to look at what happened until years after, until I was on my own, after Templeard was sold, Daddo, Ammie, Cassie dead. Maybe if I had looked sooner things would have been different, I might have come to see it differently.'

I'm about to point out that she was in her fifties by the time Templeard was sold, when it occurs to me that she does not need, or want, to be reminded of how long she spent in the grip of that guilt.

'He came to the school a few weeks afterwards, had me called to the parlour to give me a song-book. A present. Then when Sister Alphonse went to get him tea,' she shuts her eyes, tightly as though she were rushing in to retrieve something from a raging furnace, 'he said he'd hear my confession. Forgive me.'

'And what did you do?'

'I did what he said, I confessed. That's the way it was. You did what they said. But I didn't feel forgiven.'

'But what did you have to confess? I mean it was, surely, it was rape. What else could it have been?'

'But who was there to say that?'

I move swiftly through Nora's childhood world, searching

for someone who might say that word. Return to the Eucharistic Congress, to where every single person in her world was assembled. Wander around the crowd, looking for a voice which might speak out. A call for silence comes over the public address system. All eyes shut tightly in prayer. It is as though a spell has been cast. The whole nation is there, lips sealed, eyes shut.

'It was more than that.' She hesitates. 'More than . . .' hesitates again, creating a gap into which she clearly wants me to place the word, which I do. After all these years she is still a stranger to this language, still part of that world where it went unspoken.

'What I'm saying is that it's more, more because it doesn't say anything about what went before.'

'Went before?' I ask, racing ahead in a bid to understand what she means.

'Everything I was told in school, at home, in the church, everything everywhere went to make sure I would not say a word against him. And I didn't. I didn't say a single word, not one word did I say from beginning to end.'

Nora's lips tighten as she tries to swallow the swell of anguish already coursing down her cheeks. 'He just did what he wanted, and I didn't say a word, tore at me until I thought I was going to die.'

Everything I think of saying seems wildly inadequate. But then unexpectedly, there is a gap, a moment when she seems to be taking stock. In that moment we find ourselves distanced from the scene, as though separated from it by the pool of words used to depict it.

A little while later she takes out a small silver compact from her bag, opens it, and seems to arrive at a conclusion. The lipstick which she puts on – glancing to make sure no one other than myself is observing her – is a bright, fiery red. It occurs to me that she has made a truce with memory. Maybe promised her ghosts free rein later if they stay at bay until this is all over. She smooths her hair with the palm of her hand, taking me by surprise when she says, 'I'm glad you're here, Patrick.'

20

The growing ease with which we settle into waiting, less than half an hour to go, is broken by the piping sound of my phone.

'Claire,' I announce loudly, hoping to take the frightened look off Nora's face.

'Flossie has been on, just now, looking for you,' she says hurriedly. 'Sister Mairead rang her. Told her the state of play. You can imagine.' Claire pauses.

'Go on.'

'Suggested that Nora could do with her support.'

'Did you say where I was?'

'I had to. She had already decided to go down to the airport herself. She's hoping to get to Nora before the flight arrives.'

'She's on her way here?' I ask, knowing the answer can only be yes. I check my watch, register that there is a chance, a very slim chance, that Flossie – or Flossie and Rooney as it's bound to be – could get here before the flight gets in.

I rush the call to a close.

Nora is alarmed by the news, but not for long. Some impulse, a sudden rush of affection for Flossie quickly replaces that alarm. 'Flossie, poor old Flossie,' she says, sliding into thought, only emerging when I point out that time is running out and we must get a contact announcement made.

'Maria Ericson. Mrs Maria Ericson,' Nora says, extending the name as if for scrutiny, repeating it at the information desk. The attendant takes the flight details, smiles the name, passing it back lightly inflected to Nora. 'She'll be paged once the passengers are inside the terminal building.'

We stand within view of a bank of arrival monitors. Nora's anxiety is tightly contained, one hand clamping her bag, the other checking, then rechecking the buttons of her coat, her collar, her brooch.

'Did Claire say when Flossie had left?' she asks, but leaves no space for a reply. 'How long will it take her?'

'She ought to be here in half an hour, maybe less,' I answer.

'*Would Mrs Maria Ericson, passenger on Air 2000, Flight No 331, please pick up a courtesy telephone.*' The announcement reverberates around the arrivals hall, chorus like, drawing the whole world in. '*Mrs Maria Ericson, passenger on Air 2000, Flight No 331, please pick up a courtesy telephone.*'

Each time a middle- or late middle-aged woman walks out from the baggage collection area Nora's grip on my arm tightens. All seem likely candidates for a few seconds. Some for longer. A tall, olive-skinned woman, sun-glasses resting in her hair, picks up an airport telephone not very far from where we are standing. Taking instructions, she rapidly surveys the various waiting groups, her brow rippling like a fan as she homes in on us.

Within seconds she is approaching. Nora is quicker, much quicker than I am, maybe because she had all along clung to the hope that there was no daughter out there trying to make contact. Or maybe she had some immediate, overpowering intuition that this person could not be her child. Either way, her grip on my arm loosens. All apprehension drains away. She steps forward hand outstretched, introduces herself, then me.

The spectre of Sister Mairead moves busily around the encounter, the social worker too, their contention that Maria is disguising her true identity suddenly the stuff of teen magazines.

So much got said in the first, overreaching moments of the encounter that I have lost sight of the precise sequence in which we came to understand who Maria was. Among the many obstacles was the initial confusion about where she was from. Maybe we were pleased to stumble on that point, pleased to slow down the pace, to move backwards and forwards as we worked out that she was born in Italy and had not emigrated to America until she was in her twenties.

I suggested we move from where we were. Pointed to a row of empty seats nearby. Maria sat down but Nora did not move, prompting Maria to stand up again.

21

Sifting through the opening moments now, I find Maria taking a first, definite step into her story by telling us she had unearthed the name Macken in the archive of Casa degli Angeli, an orphanage in Rome. This discovery, she went on to explain, came at the end of several years of intermittent searching prompted by the death in 1957 of what I understood was her foster brother, Angelo.

There was no single moment of revelation. The disparate pieces of her story fell into place one by one, the order of nuns involved, the date on which the child arrived in the orphanage, all confirming the fact that the child she talked about was Nora's son.

Nora listened. She asked no questions and offered only thin, barely discernible, wisps of affirmation. I was thrown by this, wondered if what she was hearing was suddenly going to hit her, trigger the grief she felt for that child. But no, nothing.

Nora's silence unsettled Maria. She tried to engage her directly, cutting short her account of the difficulties involved in getting access to the Casa degli Angeli archive.

'So many questions. All this time,' she said, but all Nora did was nod, a single speculative nod, prompting her to try again. I smiled by way of encouragement but mine was not the affirmation she was looking for.

'All this time, you are the mother. It seems so strange now.'

Her voice was suffused with sympathy. After a long pause, Nora said, 'Yes,' then glanced over towards the entrance, her eyes momentarily fired with the hope that Flossie would come.

By that stage I too was hoping Flossie would come, more or less reconciled to the fact that she would always be there offering Nora a return to a world where her story remained untold. Flossie, embattled standard-bearer for the Mackens, had kept the home fires burning. And Nora, worn out by it all, now had her heart set on biding her time beside those home fires before returning to Malcolm.

I felt an overwhelming urge to offer some sort of explanation. But whenever I got close it seemed to shoot down through the decades, disappear into the austere, enclosed world of Templeard and The Psalms.

Flossie may as well have come in a chariot, a great, rolling Roman chariot, such was the palaver with which she entered the airport building. She stormed towards us, lips drawn so tightly together that they had all but disappeared. Nora rushed to her.

'Flossie. Nora's sister,' I said. We walked over to them, edging to a standstill when we heard Flossie's voice rise in anger. 'I don't care who she is. You had no business coming near this airport.' Nora went to say something but was cut dead by Flossie. 'You'll come with me now. Jim is waiting outside.' She nodded firmly in the direction of the entrance, to Rooney who was leaning rakishly against a pillar.

Nora looked at us, every muscle in her face strained in a plea for understanding.

'If you want to go, that's fine,' I said, looking to Maria for agreement, adding, 'We'll be fine,' when I see how bewildered she is.

Flossie led Nora away by the arm, quickening the pace almost to a trot as they approached the exit. There was one backward glance from Flossie, a look of outright defiance, accompanied by a hardy nod, making sure I knew she had won the day.

22

Whatever impression I had formed of Maria up until then was almost wholly eclipsed by the person she became in the light of the story she told. Whenever I think of her now, I see her only in that light. I listened carefully, thinking that one day Nora might want to hear it. But as the story unfolded I let go of that notion.

After Flossie and Nora had left, we headed for the restaurant. On the way there I began to explain how Nora and I came to be at the airport. Before long I was stumbling around Nora's story, dogged from the outset by a feeling of disloyalty to her. I glossed over large tracts, tried to wrap it up at every turn. Maria was anxious to make her own position clear, to impress on me that had she known the difficulties her arrival was going to create she would have gone about things very differently.

She explained that she had spent the past few months with her daughters, and on returning to Chicago she got Sister Mairead's letter. Straight away she decided to make contact.

'The sister was sympathetic, very, very sympathetic,' Maria said, 'but the truth is she didn't want to answer my questions. Maybe I asked too many, too quickly. I don't know. Every time she just says we need to know each other better. To talk more about it, to meet. In the end I say I'm coming, tell her I'll call back soon as I get a flight.' She shrugged, as though describing what she had done had prompted her to see how impulsive it was.

'What did she say when you rang back?'

'It was someone else. I just left the message. Then when I heard my name announced here, I think it must be the Sister. Even when I am meeting you I think it. Think Nora is her.' She smiles, ageless for an instant, then suddenly ancient as the parched skin around her eyes puckers into a matrix of hundreds of tiny, thin, criss-crossing lines.

'I have wanted to know about Angelo for so long. Find out about him, try to understand. This was the only way back after what he did. And it's the same now. He killed so much then. Not just himself. Almost everything.'

'Suicide?' I said. She nodded, eyes stark, looking beyond the middle distance, wading into his bleak story as though he was there, an apparition beckoning her forward.

She explained that he had been brought as an infant to Rome, part of a pilgrimage from Ireland organized annually by an Irish-based nursing order whose mother house is located on the outskirts of Rome. Arrangements had been made in advance to have him placed there. She thought I might be able to confirm this.

'I think there was probably an urgency about placing him,' I said, realizing only as I spoke that I would not be able to leave it at that. 'His father was a priest.'

She drew a deep breath. 'A child of the church,' she said quietly to herself.

The opportunity to tell her what I knew about the conception was there. But so too was Nora's anguish, her deep distress that morning, prompting me to hold back.

Like Nora's own story, Maria's childhood seemed rooted in a distant, historic past, an age when God and Satan battled for souls on open ground, a world where children born into circumstances like Angelo's were doomed.

I followed her into that dimly lit world. Rushed to catch up as she scampered with Angelo through the Casa di Riposa, through its vast, echoing halls and up the great stairs to the bat-infested loft. She had such a definite sense of this place that she assumed a familiarity on my part, leading me to guess that it must have been some sort of church-run institution, a home for the destitute, a place at any rate where her mother and her grandmother were employed as housekeepers.

There were few opportunities for questions. Maria rushed forward, drawing episodes from Angelo's short life into a saga so well hewn, so rhythmic in the telling that I could almost visualize it coursing through her mind over the years, mingling with far flung speculations, shaping and reshaping itself until it became a fable where the disturbing facts of his life, and indeed her own, could be safely stored.

As I listened I tried to imagine what he looked like. But he remained imprisoned in that fable. Whatever glimpses of him I did catch were distant and fleeting. A small boy quickening his step to catch up with a dark figure, a priest, hurrying across the town square to a church. A painfully shy boy, secure in a world of play until the concerns lurking beyond childhood began to encroach. Then an obsessive youth, posing as a guide to the town, maniacally burying himself in the story of that town, because as Maria put it, 'he had no story of his own'.

A former administrator of the Casa di Riposa, Padre Ramon, was Maria's main source of information about Angelo's early life. He was the first person she tracked down once she had begun to recover from the shock of his suicide. She explained that the orphanage, Casa degli Angeli, is now administered by the state. That's where she found the entry recording his arrival. 'Macken. La nascista non è certificata,' it read. Macken. No certification of birth. The name he was given in the orphanage was Marco.

Keen to find a foothold, I pointed out that there were thousands of unwanted Irish children sent abroad, many of them to the US, but some further afield, Mexico, Australia, New Zealand. Assured her that there was nothing extraordinary about such a child being sent to Rome.

From Padre Ramon, she also learned that some time towards the end of the war, or shortly after it ended, Marco was fostered to an elderly couple who lived some two hundred kilometres north-east of Rome. There is no record of his departure from the orphanage but she had worked out that he must have been five years old at the time of this move.

And there I caught another glimpse of him. On a train. A frightened child seated between a sour old man and a defeated woman travelling north. Already they sense that he is going to make no difference, perhaps they are even beginning to wonder what they will do when they have to admit that the son they are attempting to replace is irreplaceable. The boy's presence will aggravate their sense of loss until, wholly deranged by it, they will come to see him as a pretender and ultimately begin to hold him responsible for the death of that son.

Maria believes that there must have been a question mark over this couple from the outset, because Padre Ramon, newly appointed director of the Casa di Riposa, no more than fifteen kilometres from where the couple lived, was contacted by the orphanage authorities and requested to check on the boy. The first time he travelled to the remote farmstead, he was unable to climb the flight of stone steps leading to the entrance because of 'a vicious, frothing dog', which Maria described as 'leaping the length of the chain tying it to the wall every time he came near'. After some time, a woman's voice from an upstairs window demanded to know what he wanted.

'I have come to visit the boy,' he announced, to which the

voice replied, 'You will not find him here. He is with my husband. They have gone to the market in Castel Rigone.'

Some weeks later he called again, only to be told, by the same faceless voice, that his journey was in vain. 'He is not here,' she said. 'He is with my husband. They are far away, gathering wood.'

Determined that his next visit would not be fruitless, he set out at first light, reaching the farmstead before the day's work had got under way. However, he was again disappointed. No sooner did the dog begin to bark than the woman's voice sounded from above. 'He is not here,' she said. 'He is with my husband. They are helping with the slaughter of a pig at the other side of the valley.'

Reluctantly Padre Ramon turned and began his journey back to the Casa di Riposa. He had not gone very far when a short, unnaturally thick-set man with a lumpen face, a simpleton, accosted him. Startled at first, Padre Ramon soon realized that this man meant no harm and set himself the task of trying to make sense of his speech. Among the sounds he made, Padre Ramon thought he heard the name Marco. Consequently, he did not resist when the simpleton took him by the arm and led him off the dust track and across the olive grove below the farmhouse.

Before long they were at the back of the house, crouching behind the low coop in which an assortment of fowl, ducks, geese, chickens, were corralled. The simpleton made a loud sucking noise, a sound the fowl associated with the arrival of food. The geese, wings spread like shields, came hissing towards them, blocking the scurry of chickens which followed behind, all raising great clouds of dust, creating such uproar that Padre Ramon did not see the boy, heaving himself along the ground on his skinned elbows, his salivating mouth gobbling in anticipation of food, his sore-blotched face suddenly inches away from the chicken wire which divided them.

I felt the name Marco slip between my lips in a dry whisper. Cleared my throat, said it again, inflected to question what I already knew to be true.

'Marco? Angelo? what does it matter?' Maria shook her head, paused for a moment then began to recall his arrival at the Casa di Riposa later that same day. 'Carried up the many flights of stairs to the infirmary room by Padre Ramon, his limbs taut and his eyes fixed in an unchanging stare.'

She went on to explain how he came to be called Angelo, followed with other episodes, all in quick sequence. I kept thinking I was going to see some similarity between him and Nora, something which would draw their stories closer together. But no, nothing. By the time we left the restaurant, their stories seemed in some ways more separate than they had been at any point that day.

23

I asked Maria about her plans, vaguely thinking of suggesting that she come to Dublin, maybe stay with us for a day or two.

'I need to reassess,' she said. 'But what I need first is to sleep. I haven't slept for days.' She smiled, effort breaking through almost immediately.

We sauntered back to the arrivals hall where she booked a room in one of the airport hotels.

'I'll arrange to meet with the sister. Tomorrow maybe,' she said.

'Make sure you call, tell me how it went.'

I wrote my address and phone number in the brown velum book she took from her shoulder bag, wrestling with the sensation that I was in some way failing, that I had an obligation to her which I had not fulfilled.

Within seconds of parting, that sensation had became acute, a rallying point for thoughts about how I had handled things, not just that day but from the beginning. Thinking about the fragmented way I had related Nora's story to her, about how incomplete it was, a fuller more coherent version began to take shape in my mind, piecing itself together for some future telling.

Trawling through the gathering scenes in search of a beginning, I come to the sunny lawn in Kent where I find Nora surrounded by Flossie, Ber, my mother, Girlie. They are all vying to tell her how beautiful she looks, their voices rising above the lazy murmur of the other guests. A moment later their heads are thrown back in laughter, glasses carelessly held, swigging and gulping unceremoniously. Two women who have been talking quietly with Malcolm are making their way over, speaking as they approach.

'Malcolm tells us you have an exceptional singing voice, Nora.'

Girlie, already a bit sozzled, repeats, 'exceptional singing voice' under her breath. Makes it sound ludicrously stuffy.

'It's true,' Flossie volunteers, plumage ruffled to distinguish herself as head of the clan.

A waiter arrives, fills the glasses pompously.

My mother braces herself to speak, 'Nora Macken, you have the voice of a linnet,' she says very emphatically, 'the voice of a linnet.'

There is a moment when it seems as though Nora might burst into song, but she just smiles.

'Oh I could sing once,' she says blithely, 'sing like a bird.'